THE
Family
BUSINESS
Alex Kane

hera

MIX
Paper from
responsible sources
FSC FSC° C016972

First published in the United Kingdom in 2022 by

Hera Books
Unit 9 (Canelo), 5th Floor
Cargo Works, 1–2 Hatfields
London, SE1 9PG
United Kingdom

A CIP catalogue record for this book is available from the British Library.

Print ISBN 978 1 80032 848 8
Ebook ISBN 978 1 912973 89 7

This book is a work of fiction. Names, characters, businesses, organizations,
places and events are either the product of the author's imagination or are
used fictitiously. Any resemblance to actual persons, living or dead, events
or locales is entirely coincidental.

Look for more great books at www.herabooks.com

Printed and bound in Great Britain by Clays Ltd, Elcograf S.p.A.

I'm dedicating this book to every one of my readers. Without you I wouldn't be able to do what I love. Thank you.

Prologue

2019

Clutching the bag to her side, twenty-year-old Demi Simpson walked quickly towards the man waiting on her. As she approached him, he nodded, turned and that was her indication to follow him.

If she could do this, get the cash and get back home, then she'd be living the fairy tale. It was just within reach and she couldn't help but feel excited. Things had been going so well between her and her boyfriend. She'd only been seeing him for two months, but she was completely head over heels for the guy. She'd been nervous when she'd started to date him as she'd never had a boyfriend before. She was so inexperienced in all aspects of intimate relationships that she'd been sure he wouldn't stick around. He'd proven her wrong and, within such a short space of time, they'd fallen in love with each other. He was the one. Not that any of her family or friends knew about him. They'd never met him; she'd only mentioned him in passing because she was worried that telling people would put a curse on things. That and the fact that he was older than her, not to mention married, although he'd promised her that he was leaving his wife for her. Having a secret boyfriend had been the most exciting thing that had ever happened in her life. But in order to be with him, she'd had to get the cash for a ring he'd given her so that they'd be able to use it to start their new life together. She was almost giddy at the thought of living with him, somewhere entirely new, somewhere no one would have heard of them. She'd be able to walk around in public with him, hold his hand and not have to hide their relationship.

The man entered a small building and held the door open for her. Stepping through, she heard it close behind her and the loud bang made her jump. The place was dark, smelled of damp, old rags, and her skin prickled. The quicker this was done, the better.

'You have something for me?'

'Yes. And you have the cash?' she asked. Demi was under strict instruction: no cash, no jewellery.

The man nodded as he stood in front of her, and then a smile crept across his face slowly, a menacing expression she'd never seen in anyone before. It made her blood run cold.

'Not that I'm going to give it to you.'

Frowning, she swallowed and said, 'Why not?'

'You're all the same, aren't you? So. Fucking. Gullible. I'd rather have a fight on my hands if I'm honest. This job gets too fucking boring at times.'

Before she had a chance to comprehend what was happening, a hand slipped around the back of her neck and she was pulled to the floor. She wrestled, kicked and screamed but as quick as she started, she was silenced with a hard punch to the gut and then the side of the head.

'Shut the hell up, eh? I said I wanted a fight, not a screaming fit.'

The punch to the side of the head caused her to freeze from fear and pain. If she was silent then he'd just take what he wanted and leave her alone.

She couldn't have got it more wrong, she realised as he began to tie her up, binding her hands together.

'Say bye bye to all you know, sweetheart. You're going abroad to live an entirely different life.'

The man sniggered and lifted her over his shoulder before carrying her out of the room and into a garage.

'He will never let you get away with this. When he realises what you've done, he'll kill you,' she whimpered.

'Ha,' the man laughed as he threw her down onto a mattress in the back of a large Transit van. 'Like I said, gullible. Your boyfriend knows exactly what's going on here, and there isn't a thing he's going to do to stop me. He orchestrated the whole thing, sweetheart. I'm only following orders.'

Demi tried to process what her captor had said. Was he really trying to suggest that her boyfriend was involved in this? He was kind, beautiful and passionate? There was no way. This guy had it wrong.

'You're wrong. He'll find you and make sure you never walk again.'

Demi struggled. The man slapped her hard across the face, and the act silenced her.

Demi fought against the cable ties that cut into her skin. She couldn't let this happen. She had to fight, had to survive this. The horror of realising what, possibly, was about to happen to her seemed to paralyse her, as a second, more forceful slap struck her.

A dirty white rag fell over her face as the man pressed down hard on her jaw. Demi faded out, and even though she tried to fight, she succumbed to the invading, drug-induced sleep.

Part One

2002

Chapter One

The music thumped in Kev's chest as he wandered around the rave site at Barrhouse Farm Estate. The ecstasy tablet he'd taken earlier had well and truly kicked in and he felt like his chest was going to explode. He'd been plunged into darkness, having climbed through a hole in the surrounding fence to take a piss since all the portable toilets were either in use or had been already destroyed. The music the DJ was playing was the sound of the summer, Missy Elliot, 4 my people, the Basement Jaxx remix.

Kev could hear the boys laughing, giving it the usual Scottish rave chant, 'Here we, here we, here we fucking go.' It made him smile, even though his jaw was stiff as an iron bar from the E he'd taken earlier.

'Oi, Kev, what you doing out there?' A familiar yet distant voice floated on the beat of the music from the dance tent at the bottom of the field. Tucking himself back in, Kev turned around and headed back to the fence, hoping that he'd be able to find the hole he'd climbed through, and thankful that the day hadn't been a typical Scottish summer wash out, otherwise he'd have ended up covered in all sorts, cow shit, mud, the lot.

'Toilets are fucked, mate,' Kev shouted. He tried to focus on where the voice was coming from. He couldn't even be sure he'd heard it at all. He was too off his face to be sure of anything.

Kev was headed back in the direction of the dance tent when he heard a noise coming from the long reeds at the east side of the field. This rave wasn't your typical T in the Park festival. It was a much smaller, more local rave. Catered only for people of a certain age, from certain areas of the city of Glasgow. Kev knew almost everyone there. The Barrhouse estate had bought up most of the tickets, as had two more estates, Mainhill and the Southloan.

'Where the fuck are you?' Kev shouted. When he didn't get a response, he decided to go back to the tent and find the boys. But that's when he spotted him. One of his very best mates, ruining some girl's life.

'What the fuck are you doing?' Kev said, putting a jog on as he moved closer to the horror unfolding in front of him.

His mate looked up from him with a smile on his face and dark eyes. 'Shut it, Kev. You don't know what's going on here.'

Kev balled up his fist and took a swing, grazing Donnie's jaw before falling over. Donnie let go of the girl's throat, but instead of scrambling to get away, she simply lay there, staring up at the sky with wide eyes and a vacant expression and her skirt up around her waist. Next to her lay a two litre bottle of Coke, most of it empty and the lid still on. That's what most of the ravers were drinking at the rave. Half Coke, half vodka.

'What the fuck is your problem?' Donnie shouted, pushing Kev hard in the chest.

'I could ask you the same question. What the hell are you playing at?'

8

Donnie laughed wildly, and Kev could tell he too was off his face on drugs. Likely coke.

'It's called autoerotic asphyxia,' Donnie said. 'You should try it.'

Kev frowned and looked down at the girl, who still seemed to be on another planet, then back to Donnie. He felt his own drug beginning to wear off.

'You're lying,' Kev said.

'Am I? Prove it.'

Kev crouched down next to the bottle lying beside the girl and looked at it. He picked it up and took the lid off, inspected the rim of the bottle and the inside of the lid, before putting it back down.

'And no, I didn't drug her, if that's what you're thinking.'

Kev got back up and stood nose to nose with Donnie. 'I never said you did. Funny how you try to defend that before it's even out my mouth.'

Donnie was quiet for a moment, but over the music coming from the tent at the bottom of the field, Kev could hear his laboured breaths.

'Whatever you think is happening here, Kev, you're wrong.'

'And what exactly do I think is happening here? That you drugged that girl and were trying to, or were in the middle of, raping her?'

Donnie sighed. 'Come on, mate. You really think I'd be capable of something like that? I'm your pal, we've been pals since we were kids. You know I wouldn't do a thing like that.'

Kev shook his head and glanced down at the girl, who was now starting to come back around from whatever drug high she had been on.

'Oi, tell him he's wrong,' Donnie said, grabbing the girl's hand and pulling her into the sitting position as she tried to adjust her skirt.

'Eh?' She looked up at Donnie, confusion on her face. Then the giggling started and she lay back down.

'See,' Donnie said. 'We're just having a bit of fun out here in the field, Kev. You know that's all it is.'

Kev looked down at the girl. 'Is that true? Are you okay with him?'

Donnie poked Kev in the shoulder. 'Oi, I said so, didn't I?'

'And I want to hear it from her, otherwise I'll be bringing the rest of the boys up here to make sure you never fucking walk again.' Kev's voice was low, and Donnie narrowed his eyes.

'I'm fine,' the girl said sharply.

'You sure?' Kev asked. But before she responded, the girl was up on her feet and staggering away from them, back towards the tent.

'Cheers, you fucking cock-block!' Donnie hissed. 'Kev, since when did you become a fucking pussy?'

'I'm sure Layla won't be too happy to hear that you've been up here with that girl. Regardless of whether I'm wrong about what looked like you attempting to rape her, she'll kill you either way.'

'Fuck off, Kev. And as for your little threat, don't think for one second I couldn't get the boys to turn on you. So, unless you want to become the lad who was chucked out of the gang for thinking one of your own is a fucking rapist and up with your head caved in because of it, then you'd better keep that dirty little mouth of yours shut. Or do you want me to take that bottle to the police? I mean, it's got your prints all over it now, hasn't it? That would be highly interesting in court. A girl reports being raped at this rave, and your prints are all over the bottle she was drinking from?' Donnie sucked air in through his teeth. 'And I'm sure I don't have to remind you who my old man is, Kev. Donald senior wouldn't take too kindly to you accusing one of his boys of something like this. If you keep your mouth shut, then we should be fine.'

Kev gritted his teeth. He'd never trusted Donnie. But he never thought he'd ever be on the receiving end of his wrath.

'Do we have ourselves a deal?'

Kev tried to turn his back on Donnie, to walk back to the tent and tell Cammy everything. But Donnie pulled him back, his fist connecting with his jaw and then his eye. As Kev fell to the ground, Donnie was on top of him, his hand around Kev's throat.

'I said, do we have a *fucking* deal?'

His eyes were wide with the coke, and his strength was intense. Kev had no option but to agree. He nodded rapidly, and Donnie let go.

'Good,' he replied, getting to his feet.

Donnie walked back down to the tent, and Kev decided he wasn't going to keep this quiet. No way was he going to allow Donnie to think that the mere threat of his old man was going to stop him from telling the boys about what had happened. He'd wait until after the rave, though. There was no point telling the lads here. Too many of them would be off their faces to remember it.

-

Kev felt his calf muscle burn as he stretched, and the pain woke him instantly. He jumped out of bed and started hobbling around the room, his head pounding.

'Fuck!' he shouted, falling onto the bed and rubbing furiously on the back of his leg. The pain began to ease and, as it did, his mouth was crying out for water.

He headed out of the bedroom and along to the kitchen to get himself a glass of water to wash away the desert he had seemingly swallowed the night before. His head was fuzzy, heavy from the comedown.

Reaching the kitchen, he pulled a glass from the drainer and turned on the cold water tap. Before he had the chance to drink anything, he felt a sudden force push him into the sink, his chest crushed against the edge of the cold metal.

'What the fuck?' he shouted, trying to fight back.

'Ssshh. Don't fight, just listen.'

Kev's blood ran cold. It was Donald Black, Donnie's old man.

'I hear you had a bit of a to-do with my boy last night at that rave. Rumour has it that you threatened him?' His voice was calm, so calm it chilled Kev even further. 'I asked you a question.'

'He was trying to—' Kev started before his body was spun so quickly he missed it. His face was directly under the running water as Donald senior held him solidly under the stream.

'Unless you want to go sleeping with the wee fishes in the Clyde, young Kevin, I suggest you listen to me. What you think you saw, what you think you know, get it out of your head right now. If you don't, I'll fucking shoot it out of you, and your final resting place will be the bottom of that river. Do you fucking understand me, you little prick?'

Kev spluttered as Donald pulled him to the side, out of the stream of freezing water.

'Breathe, boy, and fucking answer me.'

'Yes, Donald. I understand.'

Kev felt Donald pull him up, and he blinked against the water in his eyes. He looked into the eyes of the monster who created Donnie and Steff Black and realised that there was no way he would survive telling someone about what he saw the night before. He had no choice but to keep his mouth shut.

Donald let go of Kev, reached around him and picked up the glass from the drainer and filled it with water. Turning off the tap, he held it out towards Kev and nodded. 'Here, I hear the rave was a rough night. You should drink something, get some fluids in you.'

Kev hesitated, took the glass and tried to hide the fact that he was trembling. Water dripped from the end of his nose as Donald regarded him.

'There's a good lad. Silence is golden, Kevin. Remember that and you'll go far.'

Donald dried his hands on a towel by the sink and turned around before leaving. Kev let out a breath and his heart thrummed in his chest.

'Oh, and one more thing,' Donald said, rushing forward. He caught Kev by surprise and he dropped the glass. It shattered at his feet, and it crunched under Donald's shoes. He pressed a handgun into the side of Kev's head and looked straight into his eyes, his own wide and unblinking. 'You so much as think about what happened last night with my boy, I'll make sure to blow that thought out with one bullet. It'll only take one to silence you. Remember, I have eyes and ears on you. So, I'll know.'

He lowered the gun, slid it into his suit jacket, straightened his tie and left.

Part Two

2009

Part Two

Chapter Two

Donnie and Steff Black, along with Cammy McNab, stood side by side as they handed out mugs of tea and coffee at the old folks' home. The residents loved them for it, and the elderly ladies would often joke about how if they were fifty and sixty years younger, they'd be the type they'd introduce to their parents.

'If only they knew,' Mel Black laughed quietly. 'My brothers are most definitely not the type you'd take home to meet your parents.'

Layla laughed with her. 'You shouldn't talk about them like that. They're good people.'

'Ha, you're only saying that coz you're shagging Donnie.'

Layla felt herself blush, and nudged Mel in the ribs, glad that most of the residents were close to being completely deaf.

'Let's face it, Donnie might be a good laugh, but do you really see yourself being with him for the rest of your life?' Mel asked.

Layla struggled to understand why she would be speaking about her eldest brother in such a way.

'Look, I love my brothers in equal measures, but you know the score. They're going to turn out just like our old man. Dangerous, violent. Do you really want to become the woman married to a gangster?'

Layla picked up the knife next to the lemon drizzle loaf and started to slice into it slowly, considering her future sister-in-law's words. Was that what she was going to become? A gangster's moll?

'Your mum doesn't seem too bothered by it.'

'Aye, well, she's cut from the same cloth as my dad. She'd happily slice off the finger of an enemy if my dad held him down. It's a sick kind of love they have for each other.'

Layla couldn't hide her shocked expression. Jesus, was that the kind of life she was going to marry into?

'You're exaggerating.' Layla set the knife down on the table and glanced down at the sliced lemon drizzle, imagining it to be the fingers of the enemies Donald Black senior had acquired over the years.

'Layla, you're delusional. Trust me when I say, if he ever asks you, don't marry my brother. You'll regret it.'

With that, Mel Black gave Layla a serious look before lifting the plate of lemon drizzle slices and handing them out to the residents.

'Hey,' Steff said, appearing next to Layla. 'You okay? You've turned a funny colour.'

Layla smiled widely. 'Yeah, we were just chatting about the wedding actually.' The lie seemed to roll off her tongue so easily. 'I hope you've got the best man's speech all prepared?'

Steff nodded. 'Course I do. I'm not an amateur. He's my brother, and you're my sister-in-law to be. I wouldn't do anything to let you down.'

She smiled, but Layla wasn't listening. She was too busy watching Donnie as he played the part of kind and gentle local lad helping his community. She knew there was a side to him that was still to come out. Mel had told her about it often enough. In all honesty, she was too scared to call things off, because at the end of it all, she loved Donnie more than anything or anyone else in the world. And no matter what anyone said, if Donnie ever did ask her to marry him, she would say yes. He might turn out like Donald, but he would never hurt Layla.

–

'Christ, look at her just drooling over you. It's a good thing Mel took that cake off her, otherwise it would be lemon fucking dribble,' Cammy said.

'You're just jealous that the only birds interested in you are the old birds in here.' Donnie laughed as he placed the teapot down on the table after serving the last resident.

'What can I say? I'm a charmer,' Cammy replied as he took a step back from the table.

'My old man was saying that we should organise a bingo night for the old biddies in here,' Donnie said. 'Personally, I can't be fucked with it. Serving them tea and coffee is bad enough.'

Cammy looked out at the residents of the old folks' home and sighed. 'Why exactly are we doing this? It's not my idea of a good Saturday morning. I'd rather be lying in bed with a bird on my arm, hungover, up to my eyeballs and on a comedown.'

Donnie leaned in close and lowered his tone. 'Being a pillar of the community gets you places, doesn't it? Gives us that clean-cut look. Everyone will have good things to say about us the more we do this. Keeps the gossip merchants off our case, and then when shit goes down folk will be quick to defend us.'

Cammy raised a brow. 'So, we're not doing this out of the kindness of our hearts then?' His sarcastic tone rung out.

Donnie laughed. 'The Blacks only do things that make us money, Cammy. If you want to work for the Black empire, then you'll have to get rid of that good heart of yours.'

Donnie Black had a heart of stone; Cammy had always known that about his mate. It didn't matter who you were, if he wanted to get ahead in life, he'd always throw people out the way. As much as he told people he loved Layla and that was why he was marrying her, Cammy knew that Donnie loved having Layla on his arm. She made him look good. She was a good, clean-cut girl who would improve his image. Cammy wondered if, on some level, Layla knew that herself.

'Having a conscience isn't a requirement of the job, Cammy,' Donnie continued. 'My old man is moving into new realms of business that mean there's no room for that shit. But you have to pretend you're a good guy.'

'I am a good guy,' Cammy said, readjusting his position. He caught Mel Black's eye as she served the lemon drizzle and smiled at her. She smiled back. Thankfully, Donnie never saw it.

'Exactly.'

Part Three

December 2018

Chapter Three

Donnie Black stood above his old man's place of rest in silence at Barrhouse Cemetery and closed his eyes against the reality that his father was dead. The gathering of mourners had long gone, even his brother Steff had gone back to the house to be with their mother, Maggie, and Donnie had told his wife to go home. He wanted to be alone, to gather his thoughts about what lay ahead of him without the head of the family to influence the future.

Not only would things change for the Black family, but Glasgow would be a very different place without him. Some people would rest easy knowing that the old, hardened gangster was dead in the ground, no longer able to put drugs on the streets. Others would be grieving the loss of a great man. And Donald Black was a great man to the people who worked for him who weren't blood. There was always a pressure on young Donnie to act a certain way. He was the son of a king after all. That pressure had weighed heavy on the relationship he had with his old man and, in the end, it was as though Donnie was an employee rather than a son. An employee who would one day take the reins.

The purple night had crept in above the city and, as Donnie looked up, Barrhouse in Glasgow was glowing. It looked beautiful, but Donnie Black knew that under those twinkling lights were streets in despair, riddled with drugs and prostitution. The dark underbelly of the Glasgow streets would continue to stir because Donnie would carry on the work of his old man.

'Donnie?'

He was surprised to hear the European accent, but as he turned, Goran was standing at the pathway leading between the rows of headstones, his expression solemn.

'What you doing here, Goran? Thought you'd be back to business by now?' Donnie replied.

'That's why I've come to see you. Now that the funeral has passed, we need to sit down to discuss what it was that your father wanted us to do next.'

Donnie frowned. 'What are you on about?'

'Before Donald died, he and I had a meeting. He set out a strategy that he wanted you and Steff to take on as your own after I ran a business proposition by him. He said that you would be the man for the job on this side of the water.'

Donnie shook his head. It was typical for him to be the last to find out something like this. 'Steff know about it?'

Goran shook his head. 'No. You're the head of the Black empire now. Everything goes through you first.'

Donnie glanced back down at the grave and took a steadying breath before turning his back on it and stepping down onto the pathway where Goran was standing.

'Okay then, let's head back to my place and you can lay everything on the table. I'll get Steff to meet us there.'

Goran nodded, said nothing and climbed into his Range Rover. Donnie watched him go and wondered what kind of business proposition Goran had put to his old man. What else could they do to run the city? They were already in charge of most of the drug distribution and prostitution in the area.

Donnie began walking along the top of the cemetery to where he'd parked his car. He enjoyed the stillness and silence of the night. This was a place he never came to, but he thought about making his visits to his old man a regular thing if this was the calming effect it had on him.

Reaching his Audi Q8, Donnie climbed in and headed for his house. He knew his wife, Layla, would be there, but likely she'd be lying in a drunken, unconscious state either in the bathroom or in bed. Regardless of which, he wanted her to be out of sight for the meeting between himself, Steff and Goran. Just a few hours ago he'd buried his father and Donnie hadn't even had time to process that fact before he had to get his business head back on. As annoying as it was, he accepted that it came with the territory of stepping up to be head of the Black empire.

He decided to call Steff from the car. 'A'right, mate. Any chance you could swing by the house? Goran wants to talk to us about a business proposition Dad already agreed to before he died.'

'Already here, bud. Layla got herself into a bit of a state so I took her home.'

'Fuck sake,' Donnie hissed. 'Is she awake?'

'Naw, she's out cold. I put her to bed myself.'

Donnie shook his head. 'Stupid bitch.'

'Come on, that's a bit harsh, is it no? She's your wife.'

'She's a pain in the fucking arse, Steff. Ever since Kerry died all she does is fucking drink.' Donnie paused. 'Anyway, I'll not be long. Goran might get there before I do. Pour us all a jar, and we'll see what he has to say for himself.'

Donnie ended the call and headed out of the cemetery gates and onto the back roads towards home. He had a lot to think about on that journey. The future of the business now that Donald was gone, how he was going to step up to be the head of the empire, but mostly, he wondered if it was time to stand on his own. Layla was a liability nowadays, turning to the bottle any excuse she got.

ZZ Top's 'La Grange' started to pump out the speaker system in the car, and Donnie turned the volume up and put the windows down. For now, all he wanted was to drive in the dark and for the music to drown out the thoughts in his head.

Chapter Four

Mel Black dabbed the corners of her eyes with a tissue and tossed it into the bin next to the bathroom sink. She'd always known that going to her dad's funeral was going to be rough, but she hadn't expected to feel so raw. The day they'd gone fishing together was supposed to be a day of bonding between the two. He'd chosen the activity, of course. She hated fishing. But if it meant that they could hash things out, if Mel could make her dad see that she was her own person instead of comparing her to her brothers all the time, then they might have stood a chance of salvaging their father-daughter relationship. No one knew that they'd argued that day, right before his heart gave out. She'd promised herself that she would keep that secret close to her, until the day she died herself. It was bad enough that her mother blamed her for his death purely because she was present when it happened.

Looking in the mirror, she saw him looking back at her, willing her to help the family business succeed. She'd never agreed with the criminal underworld lifestyle. It wasn't something Mel had ever wanted to be a part of. But she'd always been outnumbered. Even her boyfriend was involved, had been from the minute he'd become friends with Donnie and Steff.

'I'm sorry, Dad,' Mel whispered, wiping her thumb under her eye, smudging the mascara tears that continued to fall.

A knock on the bathroom door sent a surge of adrenaline through her. She grabbed another tissue from the box at the side of the sink and dabbed at more tears. It was no use, they continued to fall.

'Two minutes,' she called out, hoping that whoever was on the other side of the door would take the hint and go to one of the other bathrooms in the house.

'It's me. Let me in, Mel.'

The sound of Cammy's voice melted her, and she turned to unlock the door. Seeing the sympathy in his eyes made the waves of emotion come quicker and, as Cammy shut the door behind him, Mel fell into his arms and began to sob.

'Hey,' he whispered. 'It's okay.' He ran his hand up and down her back, attempting to comfort her. It didn't matter what anyone said or did at that particular moment, she couldn't stop sobbing.

'I'm sorry,' she said.

'Don't apologise for grieving, Mel. Your dad has just died.'

Being in Cammy's arms was a welcome comfort. She knew she could be herself around him and he wouldn't judge.

'I just feel like we wasted so much time when he was here, Cammy. He was always giving me a hard time about not being up to running the business with Donnie and Steff. And Mum was always judging me alongside him. I wish I could have changed for him.'

Cammy pulled away, held her face in his hands and sighed. 'You didn't have to change. I'm sorry to say it,

Mel but if you weren't good enough for him, that was his problem and above all else his loss. You know what he was like. He was always spouting about family coming first, but he always put business before family. Even Donnie and Steff know that.'

Mel took a deep breath. She didn't want to speak ill of the dead, especially when the dead was her own dad. But Cammy was more than right; she just couldn't stop the feeling of guilt when she thought about things that had happened in the past.

'You know, I always kept my mouth shut when they talked business. I still do. But I don't want to live this life, Cammy. Why don't me and you just go away together, start somewhere new?'

Cammy's eyes dropped away from her gaze and he let go of her. She knew what that meant.

'I can't just up and leave, Mel. You know we're trying to make a go of the boxing firm, here.'

'And you think Donnie and Steff are going to allow you to make that a priority? If it's something that is going to directly affect the trading of Black Enterprises, then you know what he'll say.'

Cammy sniggered. 'He doesn't have a choice, Mel. Just because he's my mate doesn't mean he can rule me.'

Mel shook her head. 'But he's not just your mate now, Cammy. He's your boss. Now that Dad's gone, he automatically steps into that role.'

Cammy raised a brow then softened his expression. 'Look, I didn't come in here to talk business. I came in here to check if you're okay. Let's go out there and get a drink, or some food? You've not eaten anything all day.'

He held out his hand, and she took it. Mel was happy to stop the conversation there. It wasn't going in either of their desired directions. It would only lead to the same one they'd been having for months now.

'I'm not hungry,' she replied.

'You don't have to eat. We could go for a drive somewhere, get away from the funeral, the grief.'

'Yeah, okay.'

They slipped out of her parents' house and from the funeral wake unseen and got into Cammy's car. She wanted Cammy to stop working with Black Enterprises. She wanted them to have a normal relationship, a normal life. But the mayhem of the criminal underworld in Glasgow was embedded in Cammy and in her family.

Chapter Five

Pulling into the driveway of his million-pound home, Donnie clocked Goran's Range and his brother's Merc. Everyone was here, waiting for him to arrive so they could start the meeting. He went into the house and straight through to the bar, where Goran and Steff were waiting.

'Boys,' Donnie greeted them.

Steff held out a glass of Jack and handed it to Donnie. He slid behind the bar and took it from Steff, before knocking it back in one go. Both Goran and Steff raised a brow.

'It's been a tough fucking day, I'm entitled,' Donnie said, wincing as the liquid burned in his throat. He lifted the glass to the optic and poured himself a double this time.

'Right,' Goran said, 'let's not make small talk. I want to tell you about the business opportunity your father agreed to just before he died. He set it up specifically for you two to run, and I will be in charge of the merch when it reaches European waters.'

Donnie looked at Steff, who was staring at Goran. 'Fuck me, Goran, you don't hang about. Didn't even get to take a sip of my Jack there.'

'No point hanging about. The quicker we get started, the quicker we all make some serious fucking cash.'

Donnie frowned and placed his glass on the bar top. 'Hang on. The Black empire is already distributing drugs across the city and is in charge of the city's sex workers. So what is it that we'd be working with that would be shipped across the water? More drugs?'

Goran shook his head.

'What then?' Steff asked, his expression showing how Goran's words had piqued his interest.

'Girls.' Goran licked his lips.

Donnie and Steff glanced at one another and then back at Goran.

'You mean, sex workers overseas?'

Goran nodded, a smile creeping across his face. 'British girls bring a certain something to the industry that no one else can. There's a gap in the market here, boys. And you' – he looked directly at Donnie – 'you, my friend, are going to help to fill that gap. You'll be in charge of bringing in the girls that will be shipped overseas.'

'Human trafficking?' Steff said, sounding aghast. 'Really?'

'There's no difference between UK prostitution and European prostitution. And the Blacks are at the top of their game in the Glasgow sex worker industry. I've seen the figures. Donald showed them to me himself. Think of the money involved in the overseas sex industry.'

'And our old man was up for this?' Steff asked, his hand poised on the glass of whisky.

'He was. Very enthusiastic about it.'

'So why didn't he come to me about it then?' Donnie asked sharply. 'I was next in line to run the business, so why didn't he talk to me directly instead of going through you?'

'He was going to, but he died before he got the chance. It wasn't as though he asked to die in that fishing boat.'

Donnie tried to compose himself. Punching Goran in the face for his blunt words was not the way to go. Dying of a heart attack on a fishing boat wasn't the way he'd expected his old man to go, but it was. Mel said she had tried to save him, but he was gone before he'd even hit the deck of the boat.

'Goran, you're going to have to explain to us how this is going to work. We need every single detail before we can agree on this,' Steff said.

'Agree?' Goran laughed. 'The agreement was already made with Donald senior. You boys are signed up and ready to go. You just have to follow my instructions; well, they're his instructions really, I just have to deliver them. Like I said, Donald was going to sit you both down and go through it all. But since I'm the only other person who knew about this, then it had to come from me.'

Donnie swallowed back the double he'd poured for himself, along with the truth that Goran spoke. If their old man had already agreed, signed and sealed the deal with Goran, then there was no way Donnie or Steff could refuse. If Donald had agreed, then their mother, Maggie, would be in on this. And there was no way in hell that she would allow her boys to go against their father's wishes. Even if Goran was lying, and using Donald's death as an opportunity and using Donnie and Steff to make money, they wouldn't be able to go against him anyway. Goran was a very violent man and very persuasive. They didn't have the control Donald had. Not yet, anyway.

'A'right then,' Donnie said, filling his glass with another double, 'let's hear it.'

Chapter Six

Mel Black looked at her brothers with suspicion. She didn't believe a word that came out of their mouths when it came to business. She understood where she came from: a father who ran the city, infiltrating the clubs and the pubs with drugs, the streets with prostitutes, who was now dead, leaving behind a legacy and reputation for his eldest son to pick up and carry on. Mel knew her city well enough to know that when one gangland boss puts down his whisky glass for the last time, another picks it up, serving himself much bigger measures than the last would ever pour for himself.

'You're trying to tell me that you two are going into a new venture with Goran, a venture that will have you liaising with Goran's men over in Amsterdam and further afield and it's legit?'

Mel raised a brow as both brothers failed to meet her eye.

'Of course it's not fucking legit. Do you think I'm stupid? You think I'm blind to what this family business is all about? I'm the one who does the fucking books. I see how much money is coming in and where it's coming from. So what is so special about Amsterdam? Is it drugs?'

Steff glanced at Donnie, as if asking silently if they should tell her. Donnie's brow furrowed as he shook his head.

'If you're expecting me to do the books for this new business deal with Goran, then I need to know where the money is coming from so I can make it look legit, Donnie,' Mel said as she reached for her pack of cigarettes. 'It's not as if I've been wrapped in cotton wool all my life. I know what we do here.'

Donnie's expression lightened a little. 'I know that, Mel. But the less you know, the better. It's not your average deal.'

Steff swung gently on the chair and laughed. 'What the fuck is average in our line of work? Look, sis, it's simple. We're branching out to Amsterdam's sex industry. We're working with Goran and his firm abroad to bring together the sex workers from Scotland and Amsterdam. That's it.'

Mel felt her skin tingle. 'Bring together? As in what?'

'Girls from here to there. It's all legit. Passports, flight tickets, you name it and we'll have it covered. We interview the girls who apply for the jobs and then we pass them on to Goran. His firm will set up accommodation for them, make sure they have a regular place of work. We get a finder's fee.'

Mel took a deep and steadying breath. She knew it was bullshit. The biggest amount of bullshit she'd ever heard in her life.

'Human trafficking. That's what it is. Fucking hell, Donnie. Are you seriously going to go through with this?'

Donnie stood up quickly and adjusted his suit jacket. 'Mel, it's nothing more than the prostitution rings that we run here. And you don't seem to have a problem with that, do you? Just do your job so we can do ours, eh?'

Mel felt the anger building in her stomach and she shot off her chair. 'Don't talk to me like I'm a fucking child, Donnie. You know fine well the prostitution ring in Glasgow is different to what you're proposing. For a start the women involved here are there through choice. You're telling me that it was Dad who organised this?'

Donnie headed towards the door, and Steff was smiling. It was as though he enjoyed family dramas.

'And another thing: do Cammy and the rest of the boys know about this? I can't say Cammy would be best impressed.'

'I don't give a shit if your precious boyfriend approves or not. He works for me now, Mel.' Donnie gritted his teeth before relaxing his jaw. 'Look, if you don't want to be part of this empire anymore, then you know where the door is. But if you walk out on the business, you walk out on this fucking family. Do you really want to put our mother through that after she just lost her husband? She still fucking blames you for not being able to bring him round. Do you really want to make things worse between the two of you?'

Her big brother's words were like a dagger piercing right through her chest cavity. He could be a right bastard at times.

'I can't believe you just fucking said that. You sure it's not you who holds that grudge?'

Steff got to his feet and stood between the two. 'Right, enough. We've got a fucking business to take over here.' He looked down at Mel, who was trying her best to fight back the tears.

'All you have to do is your job, Mel. You're an accountant for the Black empire. You don't need to know the ins and outs of what we do. You just need to make sure the money is in all the right places. You don't have to have morals to do that, do you? Bankers do it every fucking day and they were the reason for the 2005 collapse. Bet they've still got cash in their back bins, with no guilt.'

Mel felt numb. As much as she hated to admit it, Steff was right. She was the accountant. Nothing more, nothing less. But the new venture just didn't sit right with her. And how would Cammy and the rest of them feel about that?

'Can you do your job?' Donnie asked, his hand poised on the handle of the office door, his back to her.

'Out of sight, out of mind,' Mel replied through gritted teeth. She didn't want to be ousted by the family. It was bad enough that she'd always been compared to her brothers, by both her parents. As much as her dad had said he was proud of her, she knew on some level he'd always wished she'd been a boy, another brother to take over the business when he was gone.

'Good,' Donnie said. 'Now, if you don't mind, I have a family business to run. Steff, you coming?'

Donnie opened the door and left the office. Mel looked at the empty space where her big brother had been standing, feeling like she wanted to pick up the chair he'd been sitting on and throw it at him.

'He's not angry at you,' Steff said, seemingly noticing the tears in her eyes. 'He just wants to get on with things now that Dad's gone. And no one blames you for Dad's death, Mel. The doctors told us the heart attack killed him immediately. A lifetime of booze and fags along with high stress in his line of work, is it any wonder he died earlier than he should have? You didn't cause that, Mel. Don't let Donnie or Ma tell you different.'

Mel felt her mood soften a little as Steff wrapped his arms around her and gave her a reassuring hug. He always was the softer of the two.

'I need to go, Mel,' he said, pulling away and heading for the door.

'Tell him from his loving wee sister that he's the world's biggest prick, eh?' Mel wiped a tear from her cheek.

'Let's not pretend that he wouldn't love that title.' Steff smiled.

He left, closing the door behind him. Mel sat down at her desk and gave herself a shake.

It didn't matter that she didn't like their way of business. It was like Steff had said, she had a job to do.

Chapter Seven

Mel Black opened the door and stepped into Cammy's flat, heart thumping in her chest as she imagined what would happen as soon as the words were out of her mouth. As much as she loved her brothers unconditionally, that didn't mean that she agreed with everything they were doing.

'Hiya,' she heard him shout from the living room. As he came into sight, she felt sick. This wasn't going to go well, she knew that. But Mel had to tell him.

'What's wrong?' Cammy stood up. 'You've got that worried look on your face.'

'I have to tell you something. It's about Donnie and Steff.'

Cammy held out his hand and she went to him. They sat down on the black leather sofa, and Mel took a breath.

'What's happened? Have you had a fight with them?'

Mel shook her head. 'No, well not like that.' She sighed. 'They've told me something about the business that you should know. You're not going to like it.'

'Fuck sake, Mel,' he laughed. 'Spit it out.'

'They're going into business with a guy called Goran, who worked with my dad before he died. He's a nasty piece of work, Cammy.'

Cammy raised a brow. 'Aye, I remember hearing his name here and there. So what's the venture?'

'It's trafficking,'

'What do you mean, trafficking? What kind?' The look of horror which spread across his face didn't surprise her. The same feeling was wedged between her stomach and chest.

'All I know is that it will involve young girls here, going abroad to work for Goran and his men over there. Donnie told me that if I don't like it, I know where the door is.'

Cammy's eyes widened. 'What the fuck is he playing at getting into that shit?'

'Apparently it was all organised before Dad died. A deal was struck between him and Goran just weeks before the heart attack.'

Cammy got to his feet and started pacing the floor. 'I mean, the prostitution rings are one thing, those women choose to work in that industry.'

'That's what I said.'

'You think his hand is forced?'

Mel shook her head. 'No, he sounded like he was up for it. Like I said, he told me to go if I didn't like it.'

Cammy pulled out his mobile and started tapping the screen, before lifting it to his ear and waiting. 'Aye, it's me. We need to talk, can you get Kev, Frazer, Mackie and Chud over here?'

Mel's stomach flipped. This was going to be the beginning of the breakdown in Black Enterprises. With Cammy summoning his cousins, she knew there was going to be problems. None of the boys were going to like this.

–

Cammy had finished telling the boys about Donnie's business plan with Goran, and Mel couldn't help but notice the look on Kev's face. Abject horror and fear.

'Are you okay?' she whispered to Kev as the rest of them chatted amongst themselves about the situation.

'Eh? Aye, fine. Just shocked like the rest of us.'

Mel took in the words, but they didn't match his expression. Something else was bothering Kev but she chose not to press him on it.

'So, what we going to do about this?' Mackie asked. 'We can't just let him go ahead with it. I don't want to be linked to a human trafficking ring. It's fucking disgusting, sending lassies abroad against their will.'

'According to Donnie it'll be a legit recruitment process,' Mel said. 'Although I think we all know that's not going to be the case.'

Kev got up from the sofa and headed out of the room, reappearing a few moments later with a glass of whisky in his hand. He was silent as he listened to Cammy talking about what was going to happen. No one else seemed to notice how quiet Kev was.

'I say we tell him straight,' Frazer said. 'We're having nothing to do with it. I mean, we're looking to raise the stakes with the boxing firm anyway. This could be the perfect reason to step away from Black Enterprises.'

Mel felt a sudden pang of awkwardness and wondered if she shouldn't be in the middle of the situation between her family and her boyfriend. If Donnie knew she was part of this, he'd lose his shit. As would Steff.

'He'll lose it,' Kev finally said. 'You know what he's like. He's a dangerous guy, always has been.'

'Aye, but he always had the backing of Donald. Now he's gone, he's not got that shield,' Dunny replied.

Cammy glanced at Chud, who'd said nothing since arriving at the flat. 'What do you think?'

'I dunno,' Chud replied. 'I didn't think Donnie would do anything like this.'

'Well, he has, unfortunately,' Cammy said. 'And I think it's up to us to either stop him, or step away.'

Everyone fell silent. Mel knew that attempting to stop Donnie and Steff in their quest with Goran would cause a war. It wasn't worth that. They were Mel's brothers. She didn't want things to come to that, because if she took Cammy's side on this, they wouldn't hesitate to punish her either.

'We go ahead with the boxing firm,' Cammy said. 'We pull away from Black Enterprises. We can't be associated with that shit. It's as simple as that.'

Everyone nodded in agreement, except Chud. No one noticed except for Mel.

Part Four

2019

Chapter Eight

Why on Earth had she chosen to wear such a fancy outfit with stupidly high heels, when all she would be doing was standing in a warehouse, acting as though it was some sort of main arena? Already, Louise's feet were hurting, but she didn't want to act as though she wasn't happy for Tam. All he'd ever wanted was to box and now he was beginning to close in on that dream. Or at least, he thought so. Bare-knuckle wasn't exactly what she'd thought of when he'd said he wanted to become a boxer. It was far more brutal than gloved boxing and at a quicker pace too. She'd seen Tam come home in some states, but no matter what, Louise had always supported him. He wasn't just her brother, he was her best friend. Growing up in a household where alcohol was the main focus of their father, and their mother was meek and too scared to stand up for herself, Louise and Tam always promised to give each other what their parents hadn't. Strength and support.

'I can't believe tonight is finally here,' Louise said, reaching up and hugging her brother tightly. 'Are you bothered that Mum's not here?'

'She doesn't give a shit about us, Lou. Never has done. It was always about keeping the old man happy. Fuck what we needed or wanted in life.'

Louise frowned. 'That's not fair, Tam. She was a battered wife.'

'Aye, and she never, ever put us first. Fuck her. People only stay the victim if they want to be the victim,' he replied, his sharp words making Louise wince. As much as it pained her to admit it, she knew her brother was right. Their mum always fell for their dad's bullshit excuses. The apologies, the promises that the beatings would stop, that he would try to stop drinking if she gave him another chance. On some level, Louise understood that her mum loved him. But surely there must be a line where you say enough is enough?

She saw the look on Tam's face. Talking about their parents wasn't something that Tam revelled in, so she decided to change the subject.

'My feet are *fucking* killing me already,' Louise hissed before taking a drink from her flask of vodka and Coke. Glancing around the Portacabin acting as a dressing room, she caught Tam's eye in the mirror.

'Stop complaining,' Tam said as he stood up. 'You're not the one who could get their face broken tonight.'

Louise laughed, glad that the subject change seemed to have swayed his mood. 'That doesn't sound like the confident boxer you so claim to be.'

'Aye, well you have to be realistic.' Tam rubbed his hands together, as if warming them up for the fight. 'I might come away with a broken jaw, but I know I'll win.'

Before Louise could respond, the door behind her opened and Kev Barclay walked into the Portacabin.

'That's the fucking spirit, Tam,' Kev said, gripping Tam's shoulders before guiding him towards the exit.

'Darcie not here tonight, Kev?'

'Nah. Boxing isn't really her thing.'

Feeling a little disappointed that her cousin wasn't here to have a drink with her, Louise plastered on a smile.

'Louise, get out there and start cheering with the rest of Tam's fans. He's the main event tonight, so I need to get him fired up. Go, get a drink or something. He'll be out soon.'

Louise laughed again. She couldn't imagine her brother having fans, but she was proud of him all the same. 'Aye, I'll go and get pissed, that'll make it easier to watch the fight.'

Before Kev snatched Tam away, she wrapped her arms around him and held him tightly, just for a moment. In those short seconds, Tam wasn't a boxer and Louise wasn't about to go and watch him get seven shades of shit knocked out of him. They were merely brother and sister, best friends. Tam was the only close relationship she had in her life, and she didn't want anything to come between them. Not boxing, not shitty childhoods. Nothing.

She left the Portacabin and took the few steps before going into the warehouse. The place was already packed out with people there to watch the fight. Not just Tam's, there were others too. She was there to support her brother, since no one else in the family wanted to.

Draining the rest of her vodka and Coke, she walked across the concrete floor towards the bar, weaving in and out the crowd. People were already hammered and she struggled to balance properly on her heels. She wished she'd just worn trainers and jeans. It would've been much more comfortable.

Just as she was about to order a drink, someone to her right knocked into her and she wobbled on her heels before toppling to the side. Luckily, there was a tall, rather stocky man next to her. He clutched the crook of her elbow and steadied her.

'Watch what you're fucking doing. Idiot!' Louise shouted at the drunk lad who'd nearly sent her tumbling to the concrete floor. He glared at her, ready to retaliate. But then his eyes moved above her head and his expression fell before turning away.

'Are you okay?'

Louise glanced up, realising that the man who'd caught her was still holding on to her arm. He let go when their eyes met, and he smiled widely at her.

'Aye, fine. Thanks. Just a drunken arsehole.' Louise tucked a lock of her blonde hair behind her ear and readjusted her stance.

'You sure? I thought you were going to take that guy's face off.'

'Ha,' Louise laughed. 'I would have. But he seemed to be more scared of you than me.'

Louise took in his features. Day-old stubble, dark eyes and a chiselled jawline made her stomach flutter. He was gorgeous. Much too old for her; she could see that from the faint lines at the corners of his eyes.

'I'm Donnie.' He held out a hand. Very formal, Louise thought, but also very gentlemanly.

'Louise,' she replied, allowing him to take her hand. He didn't shake it though; he raised her hand to his lips and kissed it. Feeling his lips on the back of her hand sent a wave of electricity through her, and she felt her cheeks blush.

'So, forgive me but I'd have thought a girl like you wouldn't be into this. Bare-knuckle boxing?'

Louise raised a brow. 'Just goes to show you shouldn't judge a book by its cover then.'

Donnie's mouth raised at the corner a little. 'Fair enough. Can I buy you a drink?'

Louise ordered another vodka and Coke, and as she waited she wondered why a man like Donnie would be interested in her. He was older, had to be in his forties at least. And she noticed the wedding ring dent on the fourth finger of his left hand. Divorced, or planning to cheat?

'Here,' Donnie said, his voice pulling her from her thoughts.

Thanking him, Louise turned her back to the bar and began watching the crowds as they cheered and partied while waiting for the first fight to commence.

'So, you here to see anyone specific?' Donnie said as he leaned down to her ear to speak. He didn't touch her, but she felt his breath in her hair and against her skin, and her spine tingled.

'No,' she lied, unsure why. 'You?'

'Nah, just like the sport.'

Louise knew she should end the conversation there, but for some unknown reason all she wanted to do was stand there, right next to Donnie, and talk, drink and have fun. She was drawn to him, more than she'd been drawn to anyone, and she'd only known he'd existed for the last few minutes.

The lights dimmed in the warehouse, and the crowd's chants became louder. They were chanting for Tam and it made Louise smile.

'You don't sing along then?' Donnie asked.

She shook her head and sipped her vodka. She was going to need a few more to calm her nerves.

'You staying here all night then?'

'Yes, want to catch all the fights.'

'I've got some people I need to catch up with. Will you be here when I get back? Maybe we could have another drink?' Donnie asked.

Louise glanced up at Donnie, his body turned in towards her. He was definitely flirting with her, and even with the ring on his finger, she was enjoying the attention.

'Yes, I'll be here.'

He smiled down at her, leaned in as though he was going to kiss her and then pulled away before disappearing into the crowd.

'Jesus,' Louise whispered to herself as she watched him go. Her heart thumped excitedly in her chest before she turned her attention back to the ring.

Tam would always want Louise to be happy, but she knew that he wouldn't be best pleased if he found out she was talking to someone old enough to be her dad. Though Louise only half worried about Tam and what he would think as she watched Donnie move away, and all she could think about was when she'd next be standing by Donnie's side.

Chapter Nine

Cammy McNab stood at the back of the warehouse in the outskirts of the city and took it all in. The old warehouse grounds which were situated on the perimeter of the Barrhouse estate, just a few miles before hitting the main roads, were the perfect place to host the event. The surroundings were quiet, enveloped by the undiluted sky, far enough from the city lights and pollution.

Tonight was just the beginning for the BBF. The Barrhouse Boxing Firm was something that Cammy was proud of. He had built this firm up from nothing. Just a couple of the boys getting together, training out in the fields at the back of the Barrhouse estate. Bare-knuckle boxing had been a part of their lives since they were young, and they'd decided to use it to build a family business. Bringing the family in on things was just good business sense. Kev, and Duncan 'Dunny' McNab were not only cousins with Cammy and the others, they were also the boys who organised and recruited the boxers, and they were bloody good at it.

'Cammy?'

He'd recognise that voice anywhere. A voice he'd heard almost every day since his school days.

Cammy turned in response to his name and watched as Donnie Black walked towards him, Steff Black by his side. It was the first time he'd seen Donnie since he'd told him that he would no longer be working for him or Steff, that none of the boys would be working for them anymore because he'd heard that Donnie and Steff were venturing into a line of work that Cammy didn't want to be a part of. Donnie hadn't taken the news well, had denied all knowledge of the claim.

'Donnie, good to see you.' Cammy nodded. Both men looked at each other, knowing that Cammy's words weren't sincere. 'You got yourself a drink.'

Donnie held up a beer and smiled, and Cammy couldn't help but wonder who the hell Donnie thought he was, turning up to a boxing match in a full suit. Under that well-dressed, well-turned-out man in a designer suit was nothing but a top-of-the-charts scumbag who earned money off other people's misery. The Barrhouse firm's involvement with Donnie and Steff had been through historic friendship and loyalty. Drug runs, deliveries and pick-ups, and security set-ups for local pubs and clubs. But aside from their new, not so clean venture with that guy from Amsterdam, Cammy didn't want to be anyone's lapdog.

'This is' – Donnie hesitated as he took in his surroundings, as if looking for the right word – 'impressive.'

Cammy held in the sarcastic laugh ready to burst out of him. He'd keep his eye on Donnie, and Steff. If he didn't know any better, Donnie would be thinking about ways to make the evening fail. It would be his revenge for Cammy and the rest of the boys' departures from Black Enterprises. But there was no way Cammy and the rest of them could've stayed and continued working for Donnie and Steff. There were some things even Cammy wouldn't be part of. Their departure just six months earlier had put a strain on his relationship with Mel, though. She'd been stuck in the middle for the last few months while she still grieved the loss of her dad.

'No Mel tonight?' Donnie asked.

Cammy shook his head. Donnie would've known Mel wasn't in attendance at the event. She was doing her job for Black Enterprises, working on the accounts side of things. One of the reasons she and Cammy had been arguing a lot. He'd tried to persuade her to quit her job with her family. But she had a loyalty to her bloodline, even if she didn't agree with it. It was part of the reason she was still grieving for Donald, even though he'd made her feel inadequate; deep down she was a good person.

Mackie and Thomson stood either side of Cammy and stared out at the crowd. Cammy noted how Donnie took it all in and could tell by the look on his face that he hadn't expected such a big crowd. It would be killing Donnie Black that he wasn't the kingpin in this scenario. As far as Cammy was concerned, Donnie would never be viewed as a king in his eyes, not now.

'You'd better head off to find a decent spot to catch the fights. They're going to be fucking brilliant, you won't want to miss a single blow,' Cammy said. He wanted Donnie to know that things were going well. If his former best mate and colleague was going to stay for the show, Cammy wanted him to see that he had no regrets leaving.

Donnie smiled, eyed Steff and they both slipped into the crowd.

'Keep an eye on them,' Cammy said to Thomson and Mackie. 'The first sign of anything dodgy on their part, I want them out. They're scum, boys. Don't forget that.'

'Understatement of the fucking century,' Mackie said.

As the crowd grew louder as they sang, chanted for their favourite boxers, Cammy moved through the throngs of people and followed Donnie and Steff from a distance. Donnie was speaking to Steff, his expression agitated. Steff, as always, kept his own expression neutral. That man never seemed to crack under any sort of pressure. Cammy wondered if he was a bit of a sociopath in that respect. It would make sense, being the brother of Donnie Black. They were like the Krays; except they weren't twins. One was outwardly nuts, the other calm and collected. It would take a lot to make that one snap.

The first fight was about to start, and Tam Bellshaw's music started. Cammy turned in the direction of the entrance aisle, and Tam bounced down towards the ring, Kev and Dunny at his back. Cammy's ears buzzed from the noise, and he couldn't help but smile. Tam would be buzzing. He'd fought many a fight, now, and won all of them in the field matches. Now, his first indoor, ticketed event and the place was completely packed out.

Tam climbed into the ring, and Kev and Dunny stayed down on the ground as Tam's opponent entered. Cammy returned his focus to Donnie, who was standing back, mouthing something to Steff but with his eye on Tam. His words looked like they were coming through gritted teeth. It was clear Donnie was angry. But then his eyes fell from Tam to Kev before he smiled. Whatever he found amusing didn't sit well with Cammy. Donnie turned his back to the ring and headed for the bar.

There was something going on with Donnie Black. He had something planned, and Cammy and the rest of the boys wouldn't know what until it was too late.

Chapter Ten

Right hook, left jab and then the uppercut was what sent his opponent down to the canvas. Tam stood above him, sweat dripping from his chin, and Louise screeched loudly for her brother. Proud wasn't the word. Ecstatic, elated and bloody bursting with excitement. There was no way that his opponent was coming back after that shot. She stood with bated breath as the crowd noise almost deafened her. As the guy fell to his knees, the noise seemed to die down, like everyone was waiting for the ref's verdict.

'He's fucking out cold,' Louise heard the ref say as he dropped to his knees and tried to raise the guy's hand. When it fell dead to the floor of the ring, the place went into an uproar.

The crowd screamed as Tam's song blared from the speakers: 'Bonkers', Dizzee Rascal. As soon as it came on, Louise watched as Tam glanced down at his trainer, Kev, as he stood on the sideline, awaiting the ref to confirm that the fight was over and Tam had won.

As if on cue with the beat drop, the ref stood up and waved his arms, before gripping Tam's wrist and lifting his arm in victory.

The ring was invaded by Kev, Dunny and the rest of the Firm boys. Tam was up in the air, and Louise felt the sudden surge of tears take over. She watched her brother celebrate and felt hands on her. She turned, saw Cammy smiling down at her as he guided her through the crowd towards the ring.

'You should be up there with him, hen. You two deserve to celebrate this together.'

They reached the edge of the ring, and Cammy stood at her back. She managed to catch Tam's eye, and he moved towards her, pulling her over the rope and grabbing her face with his hands.

'You did it!' she said, her eyes blurry from the tears.

'I can't believe it, Lou. I fucking won.' His voice cracked and this caused another stir of emotion in Louise's chest.

'I knew you'd do it. I've always had faith even if none of the rest of our family did.' And she meant it. Tam wasn't just her brother. He was everything she'd never had in life. A mum and dad, a best friend too. Their bond was utterly unbreakable and standing there in that ring with him solidified that even more.

Louise knew that Tam would be wanted by the crowd. He'd have to talk to people who came to watch him fight. So she hugged him one last time and headed out of the ring and decided to go back to the bar to get herself a drink to gather herself. Reaching the bar, Louise ordered a drink and took a deep breath. As she exhaled, she felt a gentle brush of fingers on her shoulder.

'That was some victory.' It was Donnie.

Louise couldn't stop herself from smiling. 'Aye, it sure was. Bloody proud of him. He deserved that win.'

Donnie smiled down at her, and Louise felt her stomach flutter. He was definitely flirting with her, there was no doubt. The brush of fingers on her shoulder was enough to tell her that, even if he hadn't said anything at all.

'Let me get this one,' Donnie said, bringing his wallet out of his back pocket and pulling a twenty out. 'Call it a congratulations drink.'

Louise felt her cheeks flush, but she embraced the moment as she smiled widely at him. This guy really knew how to turn on the charm. And she was happy to allow herself to be the object of that charm.

Chapter Eleven

He kissed Louise on the cheek, close enough to the mouth that it would leave her wanting more. Those types of kisses always worked, even on his wife, Layla, after all this time. Although it wasn't as though he needed to do that. Donnie could tell she was attracted to his appearance all on its own. Why wouldn't she be? Smart suit, carried himself well, of course she'd want more of him.

'I'll see you soon then? I'll take you out, just the two of us?' Donnie smiled.

Louise nodded, and he watched her throat move as she swallowed. He made her nervous in a good way. That's what he wanted.

He watched as she walked away and didn't move until she was in the taxi and out of sight. He didn't want her to see what was about to happen, and he certainly didn't want her to think he was a bad person and put her off. He needed Louise to view him in a certain light. Charming, successful and an all-round good guy. He'd managed it before with the others, so his experience would go in his favour.

'You ready?' Steff asked, appearing from the crowd as they filtered out of the warehouse.

'Aye. I can't fucking wait to see the look on their faces.'

Steff led them round to the back, where the Barrhouse Firm vans were parked. Donnie eyed Kev's van and glanced at Steff.

'It's definitely set to go?'

'Aye, all done during the fights.'

Donnie nodded. The Barrhouse Firm were already outside, waiting for the crowds to disperse so they could go home. One of them wouldn't be going anywhere. Donnie had always planned to take Kev Barclay down, ever since the days when they were at high school together. That night at the rave on the outskirts of the city at Barrhouse Farm Estate, the year they all celebrated turning eighteen, Kev had thought himself the big guy, even tried to lamp one on Donnie. Not that he'd managed it, although that had angered Kev even more.

'I'll make sure everyone fucking knows what you are, Donnie Black,' he'd said. But Donnie knew he'd be able to talk him down, get him back on side. It wasn't that difficult; Kev was always a soft touch back then. Now that he was working fully against Donnie and Steff with Cammy and the rest of them, Donnie had to make sure that things wouldn't come back to bite him. As petty as some might think it, Donnie wasn't going to take any chances.

Cammy acknowledged Donnie with a nod but continued talking to the rest of them. Donnie listened as the sirens in the distance grew in volume. Cammy and the others didn't seem to pay any attention to them until they were close enough to suggest that something might be wrong.

The police vans pulled in. There were three of them. Officers spilled out of them and chaos ensued. Cammy tried to calm the situation, but the officers weren't listening.

'What's this about?' Kev Barclay asked, trying to stay calm.

Donnie's stomach lurched with the thrill of the scene unfolding in front of him.

'We've reason to believe that one of these vans has a high volume of cocaine inside, and we've a warrant to search them,' one of the officers said.

Cammy and the rest of them laughed, and Cammy glared in Donnie's direction. 'This is you, isn't it?'

'I've no idea what you're on about, Cammy.'

Kev turned, gave Donnie a death stare before the police opened his van.

Donnie felt exhilarated when he saw the packages. The back of the van was almost full to the top with drugs packages. That was a lot of jail time. Now that Donald senior was gone, Donnie had to make sure that Kev honoured his agreement with his dad. As little a problem as it was now, it would still put a strain on Donnie's reputation. All the years he'd spent making sure people thought well of the Black family could be ruined if Kev opened his mouth.

'Jesus, Kev,' Donnie said. 'You could have stashed it somewhere a little less conspicuous.'

'This is because of what I know, isn't it?' Kev sneered. 'You're worried now that the old man can't keep me quiet, that I'll speak out against you, so you've decided to warn me off yourself.'

Donnie watched as Cammy took everything in. He could tell by the look on Cammy's face that there was no way Kev had said a word to anyone about what he knew. And that was good for Donnie, but he had to make sure that it stayed that way.

'What are you talking about, Kev?' Cammy asked, stepping forward. 'What do you know?'

Everything and everyone stilled for a moment. Donnie wondered if Kev was about to reveal all.

'Go on, Kev,' Donnie said, testing him. 'Tell them what you think you know.'

Kev scowled at Donnie and then eyed Cammy. 'Nothing.'

'Is this because we left Black Enterprises?' Mackie said, stepping closer and standing next to Donnie.

Donnie shrugged his shoulders. 'I can't say I know what you're talking about, Mackie.'

Donnie watched as Cammy balled his fist. This was the reaction he'd wanted.

'I'll fucking have you, Black,' Cammy shouted, but before he could launch himself across the car park at Donnie, the officers were on all of them.

'I can help,' Donnie said. 'I'm not your enemy, Cammy.'

The Barrhouse Firm were huckled into the back of the police vans and driven away, while a cordon was placed around Kev's van.

'And you think this isn't going to start a war?' Steff said, his hands in his pockets. 'You're fucking mental, bro.'

'I don't want a war. I just need that bunch that call themselves a firm to know that there's only room for one fucking boss in this city, and that's me.'

'You mean us?' Steff said.

Donnie shot his younger brother a look.

'No, I mean me. Dad didn't leave the family business to you, did he?'

Steff shook his head. 'You've just declared a war on those lads. It takes away focus from business, Donnie.'

Donnie frowned. 'No, it doesn't. It takes away the possibility that we'd have competition. Dad didn't hire lads for them to up and start their own shit, Steff. If you work for Black Enterprises, you don't leave. This will teach them a fucking lesson.'

Of course, there were only two people who knew fine well the real reason behind the set-up. Kev and Donnie. If this didn't warn Kev to continue to keep his mouth shut, then Donnie would have to resort to the next option. Now that the threat of Donald senior was no longer effective, he needed new ways to keep him quiet.

'And I take it Mel has no idea that you just had her man arrested?' Steff asked.

Donnie glared at him. 'Oi, whose fucking side are you on here?'

'I'm a Black, Donnie. You shouldn't have to ask that question.'

'Aye, well maybe Mel needs to have a think about that herself. I question where her loyalty lies.'

Chapter Twelve

Layla picked up the second bottle of 2009 Château la Mission Haut-Brion Blanc, almost losing her grip. Although for Layla, she could open a bottle of paint stripper and knock it back in one go, just so long as it numbed her from the pain and grief she was suffering.

Tomorrow. She always told herself that tomorrow would be the day she would stop drinking. Get sober. It was something she always said out loud, so that she would hear the words herself. It never made a difference. Each morning, she'd wake up with a stinker of a hangover, and by ten o'clock she'd be feeling a lot better because she'd had that one to take the edge off. By the end of the day, she was two bottles down at least.

Tonight was no different, yet the wine she'd chosen from the bar she and Donnie had built at the other end of the house had been one she didn't often drink. At six hundred and fifty pounds a bottle, she always told herself that she would keep that stock for a special occasion. But what special occasion would she have to celebrate? As Layla stared at the bottle in her hand, it took her a few seconds to register that it was empty, mostly because she was seeing two of that bottle. 'Ha,' she said. 'Six hundred quid gone, just like that.'

The bottle slipped from her hand and bounced onto the thick cream carpet. 'Shit!'

Good thing it was empty, otherwise Donnie would have complained about the stain. Layla bent down to pick it up but lost her already compromised balance and fell flat on her face.

'For *fuck's* sake.' She heard from behind. The voice of her husband. 'Can you not go one night without getting on it? Jesus, Layla, you're acting like the fucking drunks who live on the street. Except you're not, you live in a luxurious house and drink expensive fucking wine which I pay for.' The angry words didn't match his tone. The way he spoke made him sound like he couldn't be bothered to deal with her, but he was her husband and had no choice.

'Aye, you pay for it with dirty money, don't you?' she slurred. 'Businessman. It's so fucking blasé. I've been married to you for years and been a good little wife, kept my mouth shut and never once asked any questions.' She paused as she hiccupped. 'I mean, this whole place is built on dirty money. What is it? Drugs? Security rackets?'

Layla left the words hanging in the air as she attempted to get to her feet but stumbled once more. Donnie forced his arms under her, and she allowed him to grip her. She didn't have much of a choice, she could barely make herself move. His grasp was rough as he pulled her up from the carpet. She wanted to be sober. She didn't want to be this drunk. It was embarrassing. She had no control of the words that left her mouth. She had no shame until she woke up in the cold light of day. But it was also the only way she could numb the pain of having lost Kerry. Even after all this time, it still hurt as though it only happened yesterday.

'Shut the fuck up, Layla. You're a pain in the fucking arse when you're in this mood.' He dug his fingers into the skin of her upper arm, and she almost let out a yelp. 'Don't

64

go saying stuff you'll regret later. You've been warned before: you keep your mouth shut and the money keeps coming. That little salon of yours isn't enough to sustain your lifestyle or your expensive drink problem all on its own.'

'Sorry,' she slurred, wishing she hadn't said a word. 'I didn't mean it.'

As drunk as she was, Layla remembered how, when they were younger, she had asked Donnie what it was he did for a living, being in the family business with Steff and their dad, Donald. He'd always been so vague; said they were into a little bit of everything. That was the most she ever got, and the more Layla asked, the more he avoided the subject. Until he gave her money to start up the tanning shop. No strings attached, it wouldn't be in his name, nothing to do with him. Layla had always known that him doing that was a way to take her focus off the work he did.

'Just get to bed, eh? It's the only place that's good for you right now.'

'Donnie, do you love me?' she asked.

She was hammered, there was no doubting that. But she could tell by the silence that hung in the air after the question what the answer was.

He pulled her out of the living room by the elbow and guided her up to their bedroom.

'I still love you,' she said, hoping that he would eventually answer her with the words she needed to hear.

'You make it hard for me to love you, Layla. Alcohol, or Kerry, is always in the way.'

Hearing him speak of her like that was like an ice-cold blade through her chest.

'Well, excuse me for grieving,' she slurred, pulling away from Donnie's grip and shoving him hard in the chest. 'You're the fucking one—'

'Fuck off, Layla,' he said, his tone low with anger now. 'Don't start your shit. Kerry hated me for reasons we'll never know. Doesn't mean it's my fault she fucking died. The fucking car... You know what? I'm not doing this again. It's the same shit every single night. I'm going to bed. Sleep in another room. Sleep right here at the bottom of the stairs if you want. Just do it quietly, otherwise you can leave.'

But how could she leave? He said it himself. She had no way of surviving by herself, emotionally or financially. She was trapped in a marriage to a man she barely recognised now, but still loved. But most of all, she was trapped inside herself, full of grief and demons.

Donnie climbed the stairs, and Layla picked up the empty bottle and attempted to throw it at her husband. But her limbs seemed to turn to jelly and she slumped to the floor, the expensive bottle rolling away from her.

As Layla's head hit the thick, plush carpet of the expensive house that didn't feel like home anymore, she closed her eyes and saw Kerry's face at the exact moment her life ended.

Chapter Thirteen

Mel lay in bed, staring up at the ceiling in the darkness as she wondered where the hell Cammy had got to. He was supposed to have been back hours ago and she hadn't heard a thing from him, having tried to call him several times when his phone kept ringing out.

'Where the fuck are you?' Mel said aloud, sitting up and throwing the covers off. She reached for her phone and reluctantly called Donnie. She knew that he'd been planning to go to the Barrhouse Firm event, something she'd tried to dissuade him from doing. But she'd received a mouthful from him, calling her a traitor for continuing to stick with Cammy after he and the rest of them had abandoned Black Enterprises.

'Why are you phoning me at this hour?' Donnie said as the line connected.

'Did you go to the event tonight?' she asked, ignoring his question.

'Aye, seems the Barrhouse Firm have a short temper. Your man got lifted.'

'What?'

'Aye, Kev got caught with thousands of pounds of drugs in the back of his van, and the polis lifted him. Cammy tried to blame me and lost his cool, went for me. It was fucking traumatic, man.'

She could hear the humour in his voice, and the fact that he was doing it to get a rise out of her made her feel sick.

'And you didn't think to let me know this?'

'It's not my responsibility, Mel. If I'd been the one to get lifted then fair enough. Now if you don't mind, it's three in the morning and I have a pain in the arse drunk for a wife to deal with.'

Frustration began to build and Mel couldn't stop herself. 'Why are you being such a dick? I'm your sister, you're supposed to help me if I need you.'

'You're right, you are my sister. And that means I'm you're family. And family are supposed to stick together. You'd do well to remember that, Mel.'

The line went dead and Mel had to stop herself from launching her phone across the room. So, Cammy and the rest of the boys were in for a weekender at best. There would be nothing she could do about that until Monday morning. That was over twenty-four hours away. She'd just have to wait.

–

Sitting in her car outside the police station, she watched the door, waiting for Cammy to appear with the rest of them. The last day had been like a slow torture, but she knew it would have been worse for him.

As Cammy emerged from the station, Mel got out of the car and leaned against the bonnet.

'Good weekend then?' he asked when he saw her.

'Would've been fine if you'd actually called me to tell me what had happened,' she replied.

They climbed into the car, and Mel started the engine. Sitting back, she glanced over at Cammy. He was angry.

'Bastard polis wouldn't let us have our phone call.'

Mel shook her head. 'But by law you're allowed to call one person.'

'Aye, but you've forgotten that your brother has lined the pockets of some of these fucking officers.'

'Cammy, that's ridiculous.'

Cammy shot Mel a look and her stomach flipped. 'What kind of accountant are you? You're the one who does the books, surely you must see the payments going between Black Enterprises and the polis? Fucking hell, I thought you were smarter than that, Mel.'

Stunned, not just by his tone but by the insult, Mel sat back in the seat and tried to compose herself.

'Wow, you've been spending too much time with my brother. His behaviour towards Layla is rubbing off on you, if you think you can get away with speaking to me like that.'

'I'm sorry, I didn't mean that. All I'm saying is that Black Enterprises is taking over everywhere. You must know the ins and outs. Either that or you're just playing blind.'

'I don't like where this conversation is going, Cammy. You're acting like a dick right now and I don't deserve it.'

He hesitated, took a steadying breath and then placed his hand on the handle before opening the car door.

'What are you doing?'

'I'm going home. I can't get into this with you right now. He's getting what he wants, Mel. He's coming between us already. It's a good thing we don't live together, it'll make things easier.' As he moved away from the car, he stopped and turned towards her. 'In fact, it's probably better we end this now. It's not like we've been getting on lately anyway. This was always going to happen.'

Mel stared at him from inside the car in shock. 'Are you being fucking serious?'

'Deadly serious. Sorry Mel, but we're done. I can't be with you when your brothers were responsible for putting us away last night. If they can do that, fuck knows what else they'll do.'

'Cammy...' Mel said, but there were no words to follow. 'I'm sorry.'

'Aye, me too.'

He closed the door and moved away from the car, and all Mel could do was watch.

Chapter Fourteen

Donnie Black stood with his back to Cammy, and Cammy noticed how still his enemy was. His shoulders didn't seem to rise or fall; his fingers didn't twitch. It was as though he was a waxwork model of himself. Cammy remembered this of Donnie from back in their school days. He was always trying to show himself as the cool, calm and collected guy, but everyone knew when there was shit going down in his head; you didn't have to see his face to know that. He'd be hating the fact that he was being confronted by the firm. But he'd started a turf war and had picked on Kev for a reason neither of them could fathom.

Cammy turned, eyed each of the Barrhouse Firm. Mackie and Thomson stood either side of him with the baseball bats in their hands. Dunny was standing in front of Steff Black, who was sitting behind his desk in the far corner. Dunny didn't don the same weapon as the others. Instead, a knuckleduster glinted in the light from each hand. Chud stood behind Steff like some kind of bodyguard. He couldn't even look Cammy in the eye. Fucking turncoat.

'I'd go as far as to say this was an ambush. And by old friends, too. Shame,' Donnie said, lifting the whisky decanter from the filing cabinet and pouring himself a large measure, before turning and glaring at Cammy.

'Most definitely an ambush, by old friends not so much,' Cammy said.

Donnie drank back a large mouthful but kept his eyes on Cammy. The tension in the Portacabin was thick, and even Steff looked a little uncomfortable.

'You're not happy with what happened with Kev. I get that, I would feel the same if someone in my firm was sent to the jail. But he was found guilty, boys. You can't possibly think that had anything to do with me. There was a witness to say he saw Kev load that van up with cocaine packages. There was CCTV.'

Mackie stepped forward, the bat gripped by one hand and resting in the other. 'You're damn fucking right we think you had something to do with it. It doesn't take a fucking genius to work out that you set him up, including doctoring that footage. Get someone to dress up like Kev, fill the van and fuck off? You could see the Firm was going places, and you thought that taking Kev out of the equation would put a halt to things. Take out the trainer, none of the lads can box and the Firm will fold? It's written all over your fucking face.'

Donnie's eyes fell to the bat, and he raised a brow before taking another drink. He didn't say anything. What could he say? Deny that he set Kev up to go to prison? Of course, he wasn't going to say that out loud. Donnie never was good at owning his shit, always had someone else do his dirty work for him.

'You're good at making shit up, I'll give you that,' Steff said, getting to his feet but remaining behind his desk. By the look on Steff's face, it was as though even he didn't believe that.

Cammy, who kept his weapon tucked away in his pocket as a surprise if he needed to use it, licked his lips before he said, 'We're out, were a long time ago.' He eyed Chud again, but still he couldn't bring himself to look at Cammy. 'You just couldn't handle the fact that we left you. Without your old man, you're nothing. That's why you've had to resort to the filthy business you're into now with that scumbag from Amsterdam.'

Donnie pulled his mouth into a sly grin. 'Is that right?'

'Aye, that's fucking right. We don't work with or for scumbags, Donnie. We won't be associated with that shit.'

Donnie shook his head slowly but Cammy didn't stop.

'You thought we were just going to continue to follow your lead, like we did when we were at school? And we weren't going to retaliate? Well, fuck you, Donnie. We're far from the wee guys in trackies we used to be back in those days. You set our Kev up, and we ain't going to let you get away with this. You hear me?'

Mackie slammed his bat against the table, and a surge of electrical energy rushed through Cammy then. It was almost as though that bat had smashed what little remained of their pasts together, when they were all on the same side. But now that Donnie thought he was something because his old man was gone, and he was involved in a disgusting side to their criminal careers, there was no way any of them could go along with it. Donnie didn't jump at the sudden crashing against the desk, but Cammy could see that Donnie wasn't quite as still as he was before.

Steff reached into his pocket, and Cammy anticipated the move. Both men pointed their guns at one another as Mackie and now Thomson swung their bats, bringing them down hard on the desk.

'Four against three, Donnie. Fancy your chances, big man?' Dunny laughed before Steff turned the gun on him.

73

Donnie glared at them all before raising a hand and silently instructing Steff to put the gun down.

Cammy's heart thundered in his chest.

'Aye, there's a good boy. Listen to your big brother and put your fucking gun away. We both know you've not got the fucking bollocks to use it.'

Steff glared at Cammy, his eyes so narrow they were almost shut.

'If you're going, then get the fuck out,' Steff said. 'Go on, fuck off. You think I won't use this? Fucking try me. I'll shoot every last one of you in the head.'

Mackie's and Thomson's bats fell still, the desk a splintered mess. Cammy looked up at Chud and motioned for him to join the rest of the boys.

'Nah,' Donnie said. 'Chud's with us now.'

Cammy let out a laugh, but he knew that Chud had made his decision. Whatever the reason, it didn't matter now. Chud had jumped ship, and Cammy felt a betrayal he hadn't thought possible.

'If you stay here with these fuckers, don't expect to be able to ever be let back in. Once you're out, that's it. You know what they're into, don't you?'

Chud stared past Cammy, glaring at the door. Dunny took a few steps back and stood by the rest of them, Cammy still pointing the gun at Steff.

The Barrhouse Firm lads backed out of the Portacabin into the yard, and Cammy was the last one to leave. He kept his eyes locked on Donnie, who still had a sarcastic grin on his face.

'We'll be running things our way now,' Cammy said. 'We learned from the best, didn't we? You know, security, drugs, alongside the boxing club. You wanted our firm to fail so you could have us do your work for you, so you could step into the old man's shoes? Well that plan smashed you right in the face, didn't it? There's far more of us than you. You wanted a fucking war, you've got one. And don't expect us to be quiet, Donnie. If you come for us, we'll be loud about you and your filthy fucking business. When the city finds out about it, your fucking empire will crumble. And we'll be standing in the front row to watch.'

It amazed Cammy how calm Donnie Black could appear on the outside. But he knew that he'd be losing his shit on the inside because he *was* the boss, the main man, and Cammy had just made him look like an amateur in front of everyone. That's the least he deserved after sending Kev down for something he didn't do.

'Like the folk in this city are going to listen to the likes of you,' Donnie said. 'I mean, look at you all. In your thirties, still dressing like neds from the scheme you all come from. You think people will take your crap about us? I mean, we're pillars of the community, have invested in care homes, have volunteered in them. We're well turned out, with nice cars and good homes. You lot still live on the estate, dress like eighteen-year-old neds and conduct yourselves like them too, running that fucking boxing club. I'd like to see where you think this will go.' Donnie said it with a glint in his eye and a hint of a smile.

'Watch this space, Donnie. The Barrhouse Firm is going to fucking destroy you. And there will be fuck all you can do about it.'

Cammy backed out of the Portacabin and didn't bother to steal one last look at Chud in the hope that he'd follow them. Whatever Donnie had on him, it was enough to make him turn his back on the boys.

'Chud?' Mackie asked.

Cammy shook his head.

'Fuck him, man, he's a fucking traitor.'

Cammy shook his head again but walked towards the car. It was time to get business moving.

Part Five

Eighteen Months Later

Chapter Fifteen

'Jesus, that fucking hurts.' Louise laughed as the tattoo artist began working the needle across the transfer on her wrist.

'It's not that bad, surely?' he said without looking up.

'Let's just say I'm glad we went with the small one.'

Louise had been dating Donnie since she'd first met him at her brother's boxing event. They'd been together a long time. She'd been impressed by how much effort he'd put in with her. He'd sent her designer handbags, shoes, jewellery. They'd dined in five-star restaurants, all paid for by Donnie, of course. It hadn't taken him long before he was whisking her off to five-star hotels for overnight stays. She really felt lucky to have met him, and he was certainly the type of guy who set the bar high for other men who might want to date her. Not that she wanted to date anyone else. Donnie was perfect.

'We?'

'Yeah, my boyfriend picked it. Well, we were talking about tattoos and I said I'd always wanted one but never had the guts to do it, and I wouldn't even know what to get. For a joke I told him to pick one for me and this is what he picked. Found it on Google apparently.'

The tattoo artist nodded but didn't say much. He was too busy concentrating. The sensation was more like a burn than actual pain. Like a hot needle being dragged across her skin.

Underneath all of Donnie's expensive suits and flash dates, she knew there was a sensitive man there. She'd experienced a little of him now and then, when he held her hand or when he kissed her as she was falling asleep next to him. It was that part of him that wooed her, not the money or the flash and lavish lifestyle. She'd really fallen for him.

Louise thought about surprising Donnie with the tattoo. She hadn't actually told him she was going to go through with it. Even if she had, he probably wouldn't have believed her. She still couldn't wrap her head around the fact that she was seeing a married man. He was incredible. So handsome, passionate and full of life. She couldn't have picked a better guy. Although when she thought about it, she knew that eventually things would become complicated. These types of situations always did. Being the other woman wasn't easy, because at some point he always had to go back to his wife. Louise wasn't proud of what she was doing. Essentially, she was a homewrecker. But she wasn't the married one. He was. If he didn't want to be with Louise then he wouldn't have gone to so much effort.

'That's you done,' the artist said, sitting back and allowing Louise to admire the work.

'It's stunning. I love it. He'll love it.'

The artist smiled and began cleaning her skin and telling her how to look after it. As Louise stared down at the tattoo, she was glad that even if things didn't end well in her relationship with Donnie, at least she'd be able to look back and remember how happy she was at this very moment.

'A tattoo is a bigger commitment than a wedding ring these days,' the artist laughed. 'Hope you like it because you're going to have it forever.'

Louise smiled. At twenty years old, she'd never imagined finding the person she wanted to spend the rest of her life with. But she had. She was over the top in love with Donnie Black, and she would do whatever she could to make sure that he felt the same way.

'Ah, well, I can't marry him yet. He's not divorced from his wife.'

The tattoo artist gave her a look that told Louise she was being silently judged, but she didn't care. It wasn't easy being the other woman, but it was also really fun.

Chapter Sixteen

Louise rolled off him and reached over to the bedside table, grabbed the cigarette from the pack and lit it. Inhaling deeply, she exhaled thick smoke rings, her jaw clicking with each one. The hand she held the cigarette in revealed the new tattoo she'd just had done a few days previously. He smiled at the sight.

'I still can't believe you got that tattoo. I was only joking when I suggested it.'

Louise smiled as she took another draw of the cigarette. 'It's only a tattoo. And the idea of having one that you picked was kind of cool. Shows we love each other, doesn't it?'

'Sure does, babe.'

Donnie rubbed at his chest, trying to ease the sensation of the thud from his heart. She'd gone to town on him. Unlike Layla had in a long time. Layla didn't have it in her to put a shift in when it came to sex. She was too busy planning lavish holidays or getting her nails done. Yes, she looked good on his arm, but compared to the little beauty who he'd just been inside, she was nothing. Too many years on her, one too many ripples on her skin from age and booze. Donnie liked them young. Not young enough that the police would come sniffing round. Louise was twenty, the perfect age for people's judgement not to have any weight behind it. At twenty, they were adults, old enough to make their own decisions. They were also easy to manipulate. All he had to do was flash his car, his wallet or buy them something pretty and they'd come running. Layla was always too preoccupied with the drink nowadays to notice.

Layla had once matched the beauty Louise had in her now. She was once a trophy wife that Donnie could show off to people. But as the years went on, Layla had become a drunk, someone who relied on the bottle to numb the pain of her grief. At first, he'd felt sorry for her. Not now. She was a pain in the arse and only he knew the state she was in. Layla was still able to put her face on in public when she needed to, but Donnie saw her at night, her body slumped over the toilet pan as she retched from another night of alcohol abuse. He'd often leave her there to sleep, too disgusted by her to attempt to put her to bed.

Since her sister Kerry had been killed, Donnie had watched her slowly become a shell of who she used to be. Layla was the type of person who'd had like-minded friends, looks obsessed, who wanted to holiday in places like Marbella, Ibiza, Tenerife. But the more she began to drink, the less and less she'd seen of her friends until, one day, they'd all dropped off the radar. The only person who really showed any kind of interest in Layla nowadays was Mel.

Layla was a lonely drunk, and Donnie was sick of it but, on some level, he still felt obliged to care for her. Maybe that was the old him, the one who still loved the old Layla from back in their early days. On another level, Donnie needed to have a wife on his arm that looked good, as it was good for his business image. Having a long-standing wife, who kept herself pristine for public appearances with him, meant that the public would perceive him as a loyal, happy and caring man when it came to the community. Moving in high society circles with councillors and businessmen was all fine, but doing it with Layla on his arm made him look better than not.

The young, pretty blonde to his right offered the cigarette to him, and he took it from her before taking a long, deep draw.

'So, what do you want to do today?' she asked.

'Louise,' he drew out her name and exhaled loudly. 'I'm busy for the rest of the day. Got stuff on.'

He heard the tutting sound escape her lips. 'You're always busy after we have sex. I'm beginning to think that's all I'm good for.'

'Come on, Lou. You know that's not true. I love you. But I have to work. If I don't work, I don't earn and if I don't earn, I can't afford fancy hotel rooms like this for us, can I?'

Donnie flipped onto his side and propped himself up with his arm. He smiled his usual charming grin down at her, and she folded, as they all did.

'Fine,' she said with a wide smile that made her eyes sparkle.

'Good girl. Now, why don't you go and get a shower and I'll give you a call later?'

Louise smiled again and got up before prancing her way through to the bathroom. He watched her go and laughed as she gave a wiggle before closing the door.

When Donnie heard Louise switch on the shower, he picked up his mobile from the side of the bed and tapped out a text.

He quickly got dressed and slipped out of the hotel room
before heading down to his car. It was important that he
left as early in the morning as possible. The earlier he left,
the less chance there was of anyone seeing him.

Louise was something entirely different to the other
girls he'd recruited. This was personal, and the Barrhouse
Firm would rue the day they fucked with him.

Chapter Seventeen

Louise walked along the footpath which led to the canal, sat down on the nearest bench and lit a cigarette. She pressed her back into the wood and let out a long breath as smoke billowed into the air above her.

Donnie ran through her head at a million miles per hour, his face flashing in her mind over and over. She'd never felt like this about anyone before. It was exhilarating to know she was having an affair with an attractive, older man. A man who was not free for the taking.

The only thing that Louise didn't enjoy about her relationship with Donnie was that she couldn't tell anyone about it. Even though she was well within legal age and able to make her own decisions, Donnie had told her to keep quiet about it. He didn't want people to judge them, or for his wife to find out from someone other than him. At first it hadn't bothered Louise. But they'd been together for eighteen months now. She was in love with him and he was in love with her. He'd been very open about his feelings, telling her that he'd never met anyone like her. It felt incredible to be loved by him. The envy and jealousy Louise felt at the thought of Donnie going home to his wife was overwhelming. Louise knew who she was. Layla Black. A stunning, leggy woman with class, sophistication, but above all else she had Donnie. Louise envied Layla, wanted to be just like her. In Donnie's bed, by his side in life.

Louise supposed that was why she'd become so obsessed with telling Layla, but the thought was making her ill. She'd imagined going up to Donnie's front door and telling Layla everything. As much as her heart loved Donnie, she couldn't hurt someone else like that. It would be humiliating and could result in Louise getting a slap. She'd decided to give Donnie an ultimatum instead. Tell Layla himself, or she would do it. She'd planned to talk to him about it last night, but she'd been swept up in the moment with Donnie. He'd showered her with compliments, champagne and strawberries in the jacuzzi, and a new pair of shoes to go with the dress he'd bought the week before. Louise hadn't wanted to start an argument.

Taking another deep draw on the cigarette, Louise stared out at the canal and sighed. It would have to be over the phone or in the form of a text. That way, she'd avoid an immediate argument. Donnie would have time to think about it, come to terms with what he wanted to do. If he wanted Louise, then he could have her, but she was not willing to share him with someone else. Layla would likely have the same attitude. But new, exciting and passionate love was surely more appealing than what he had with his wife.

Pulling out her phone from her bag, Louise smiled down at the image on the screen. He didn't know she'd taken it, but she'd snapped a selfie of them together in the hotel while he'd fallen asleep. Donnie was snuggled in, his head resting on her chest. They looked good together. It would be the image she would use if she did have to tell Layla about them. There would be no denying the affair from it. Although, hopefully, it wouldn't come to that.

Donnie… She began to type out her ultimatum. *Tell her or I will.* No, that sounded too forceful. Deleting, she typed again. *I want to be with you, but I don't want to share you. I want you to tell Layla about us. Leave her for me. I can make you happier than you ever thought you could be.*

She shook her head. Deleted his name. That sounded too needy. She had to play this cool. She would have to think of a better way of putting it. Maybe she could send him a naughty selfie. She could wear that black lace set he bought her a few weeks ago, send it to him, telling him that if he left Layla, then he'd get to have her like that all of the time.

Smiling at the thought, Louise made a mental note to take that picture when she got home after college. She tucked her phone back into her bag, finished her cigarette and got to her feet. She began the short walk along the canal path towards the college building. But the more she looked at it, the less she wanted to go inside. All she could think about, all she could focus on, was Donnie. If she had him, she didn't need anything else.

'Oi, Lou?' A voice called. It was Tam, her brother. Older by two years. He was standing at the end of the path with one of his mates, who had a Rottweiler on a leash. 'Maw and Da are looking for you.'

Louise panicked. 'I told them I was staying at Ashley's house.'

'Aye, well Ashley phoned the house looking for you, to ask if you had one of her books for college and dropped you right in it. If you're going to lie, you might want to prewarn the mate who's supposed to cover for you.' Tam laughed.

Shit. What the fuck was she going to tell them now?

'I'm twenty, for god's sake. I don't have to tell them everything about my life,' she said, the attitude in her tone forced.

'I don't give a shit what you get up to, Louise. Just letting you know they're on to you.'

She reached Tam and shrugged. 'Right, I'll sort it.'

'So, where were you then?'

Her stomach flipped. Should she tell Tam? She was closer to her brother than any of her friends, but would he understand her affair with a married man who was old enough to be her dad?

'I was out.'

'Specific.' Tam nodded, a sarcastic undertone in his voice. 'Just don't drag me into your shit, Lou. I've got enough going on. I don't need the hassle.'

Louise rolled her eyes, smiled sarcastically and continued walking. The friend with the dog kept his head down, didn't say anything. She didn't recognise him, had never seen him before, but as she passed him he gave her a look from the side of his eye that made her shudder.

Tam didn't seem to notice.

Chapter Eighteen

Tam Bellshaw said goodbye to his friend, patted the dog on the head and headed out to the main road to where he'd parked his car. Today was his first day at his new cash-in-hand job. His job title was handyman, but he knew that working for someone like Steff Black would mean more than the odd manual labour job. People knew Steff Black as a bit of a dodgy character, dangerous if you got on the wrong side of him. But he paid good money and Tam needed cash to save for a flat for him and Louise to move into, so they could get away from their poor excuses for parents. Growing up with a drunk thug for an old man and a mother who enabled his behaviour had made Tam sure that he didn't want to be around them any longer than necessary. He'd promised Louise years ago that he'd get them out of their shitty situation, that he'd look after them both.

He hadn't stuck in at school. Hadn't really cared enough about it to try what with everything going on at home. All he'd really cared about was his love for boxing. He'd taken up the sport as a way to get rid of his pent-up anger against his dad. Meeting Kev through his cousin Darcie, and then being introduced to the Barrhouse Firm, had been followed by Kev and Cammy saying they'd be able to give Tam future success with boxing. But the Barrhouse Firm had put a halt to training due to Kev's stint in prison, though Tam had never found out what he'd done. Kev had promised that as soon as he got out he'd be in touch and the Firm would get his boxing matches back on the go. But until then, he'd be skint. Now he was on the dole, signing on every Tuesday, and it wasn't easy getting by on less than a hundred quid a fortnight. He'd met Steff in the pub a week ago, had overheard him talking to some other young lad about odd jobs needing done and heard the phrase *cash-in-hand*, so had offered up his services.

Now, he climbed into his old 'S' reg Clio, started the engine and headed to the place where Steff had asked to meet him, to go over the itinerary for his first day. The scrapyard was only a twenty-minute drive from the town where he lived, and he had enough fuel to get there. Once Steff paid him for completing the jobs, he'd be able to afford to fill the car up full and put the rest of the cash away towards a flat for him and his sister.

Pulling up at the scrapyard, he noticed that the entry gates were closed. No one was around, aside from a broad-shouldered, bald man with a crater for a face who stood at the side of the gate, arms folded across his black bomber jacket as though he was manning the door to some dodgy Glasgow strip club.

Tam rolled down the window and looked at the man, who unfolded his arms and stepped forward. Before Tam could say anything, Crater face said, 'Tam?'

Tam nodded, a little confused as to why there would be a man standing guard at the entrance to a dump. Instead of asking, he said nothing as the man turned and opened the gates, allowing Tam to drive in.

Once through the gates, he looked in the mirror and saw them close behind him. Something sat heavy on his chest then and just as he was about to change his mind and turn the car around, Steff knocked on the window.

Tam glanced up at him and saw the smoke from the cigarette hanging out of his mouth swirl around in front of his face. He rolled down the window and nodded.

'Park your car over there and meet me at the office. You need an induction before you can start,' Steff said before turning and heading in the direction of a Portacabin.

Tam did as he was told and parked his car over by a large heap of scrap metal before getting out and walking towards where Steff was waiting on him. There was a coppery scent in the air, and the heaviness on his chest intensified as he reached the slightly open door of the cabin. He tapped on it gently, and Steff called him in.

'Have a seat, Tam,' Steff said.

Tam noted the cigarette still present between his parted lips. Steff smoked it and exhaled a cloud of smoke without removing it. Tam sat down on the seat on the opposite side of the untidy desk, and Steff stared through him. Not at him, but through him, as though he were trying to read Tam's thoughts.

'So, fancy yourself as a bit of a handyman, do you? A bit of this and that, aye?'

Tam didn't know what to say, how to respond? It sounded like a challenge, rather than a question.

'You deaf, Tam?'

'Aye, I suppose I could turn my hand to most things if I gave it a go. Don't mind getting my hands dirty.' Tam cursed himself for the nausea and the beads of sweat forming on his brow.

'Well,' Steff said, 'being a handyman for the likes of me means you'll have your hands in some right sticky shit, Tam. I have two conditions for you, if you want to work for me. I need to know that the jobs you do for me will be treated with the utmost confidence. You say nothing to no one. And you do not question a job. If I call on you to do something, it's because I think you can handle it. Once you're in, you're in. There's no such thing as temporary work with me. You're in it until you die. That's the downside. The upside is that the money is good. Really good.'

Tam watched as Steff's expression remained neutral. He hadn't so much as blinked since Tam had sat down. That wasn't the kind of statement you made to a new employee of a scrapyard. The place was clearly a front for something else.

'Does that all sound like something you can handle, Tam?'

Tam considered the question. Maybe Steff was being a little overdramatic. You're in it until you die? He almost laughed but thought better of it. Steff Black wasn't the type to say something like that in humour. He knew the reputation the Black brothers held. They were dangerous men. But Tam really needed the money.

'Aye, I can handle it.'

They were both quiet for a moment, before Steff gave him the once-over. 'I hear you're into the boxing? You any good?'

Tam nodded. 'So I'm told.' He didn't want this guy thinking he was cocky, even though Tam cherished the fact that he was a fantastic boxer. He had a skill that came naturally, from a young age. And the fact that the Barrhouse Firm had taken a chance on him and it had paid off before Kev went away meant a lot to him. But they hadn't been able to look after him, and there'd certainly been no money coming from them to help Tam fund his plan. Working with Steff was his only option.

'Well, let's just say that your boxing skills might come in useful for this job,' Steff said. The way he stared into Tam's eyes, intensely, made him realise that there would be more to this job than he first thought. But Tam needed the cash, so he couldn't exactly knock back the opportunity of work.

'Right,' Steff started, before pulling his lips into a thin line. 'You start now. We've got a disposal job. The van is ready to go. Your job is to drive it to this location.'

Steff held up his phone and showed Tam an image and address. Westlands Agricultural and Waste Management. Tam was familiar with it. The site lay on the outskirts of town, just a few miles out from the disused airport.

'What do I do when I get there?' Tam asked.

'All you have to worry about is getting the van there and driving it back. No unscheduled stops. No communications with anyone, not even on your mobile. If you complete the job and there are no issues, you'll be paid. How does a grand sound to you?'

Tam glared at Steff. Had he heard him right? A grand for driving just a few miles, no questions asked?

'Sounds good,' Tam replied, turning his attention to the van and wondering what was inside. A dead body most likely if he was being made to drive to the incineration factory. Get rid without trace – that's what gangsters did, wasn't it? Tam wasn't stupid, he knew the likes of Steff.

'Right, get in then,' Steff said, throwing a set of keys in his direction.

Catching them, Tam headed for the van, got in and started the engine. The window was already down, and Steff peered through. 'Wait here while we load up.'

Tam watched as Steff disappeared from sight and sat there in silence for a few minutes, staring out of the front windscreen, wondering what exactly was going to be loaded into the van. Then something inside of him chilled. A shuffling of feet on gravel from behind the van, a muffled cry. He glanced in the driver-side mirror and watched in horror as a person was dragged towards the back of the van, a black, canvas-like bag over their head and tied at the neck. Steff was at one side, holding him up by the arm, while another pushed him from behind. The van rocked and the screams intensified as he was put into the back.

He gripped the steering wheel and exhaled loudly. Could he back out? Steff had said that once you're in, you're in for life.

'Right,' Steff called and knocked loudly from the back. 'Time to get moving.'

The van continued to rock but stopped suddenly. He heard a voice, not Steff's. 'You'll shut the fuck up if you know what's good for you.'

Shit, Tam thought. There really was no backing out now. Putting the van into gear, he moved slowly towards the exit where the bald man was standing.

He nodded and opened the gates, allowing Tam to drive out.

What the fuck had he got himself involved in?

-

Tam pulled up to the site that housed Westlands Agricultural and Waste Management, and Steff banged on the side of the van. Tam knew instantly that meant he was to stop, and he did not hesitate. He already had visions of

95

becoming the victim if he didn't do exactly what he was told.

Tam killed the engine and for a moment he thought his heart was going to burst out of his chest it was beating so hard. He didn't know what to do next. Wait for Steff to give him an instruction to go? Or was he supposed to wait?

There was a long pause before the van began rocking once more, but with it came the muffled screams again. Tam focused on the watch on his wrist, watched the third hand as it moved around the face, each second feeling like an hour as the screams intensified. Whoever was under that canvas bag was resisting whatever was about to happen to him.

'Tam,' Steff said, suddenly appearing at the driver-side window. 'Out. You're needed.'

Turning, Steff moved away and Tam forced himself to get out of the van and follow him. The other two were nowhere to be seen.

He reached the entrance to the building, and Steff stood at the door, watching Tam with intent. Tam stopped and looked at the door before turning his attention to Steff. He had so many questions, but he remembered that he wasn't supposed to ask.

'Do you know what this place is, Tam?' Steff asked.

'Animal crematorium?'

'Aye, that's right,' Steff replied before opening the door and gesturing for Tam to move inside first.

Tam stepped inside and looked around the vast space, before clocking the second man who'd taken the journey in the back of the van with Steff. He was standing next to a green cylindrical machine which resembled the front of an old steam train. To the right side of the large tube there was a unit which housed various buttons, and above that were various pipes surrounded by what Tam thought looked like insulation materials.

Tam turned at the sound of movement behind the machine, and he watched as another man appeared, guiding the man with the canvas bag over his head.

'Tam?'

Tam nodded in response.

'I'm Donnie Black. Your new boss.'

Tam frowned, turned to look at Steff, who was pulling the door to the cylinder open.

'I expect the highest standard of confidentiality from my staff. Is that something you think you can do?'

Before Tam could answer, Steff chipped in. 'I asked Tam this before we left the scrapyard. Tam assured me that this would be the case.'

Donnie Black pulled his lips into a thin line and nodded. 'Good. And you know that once you're in, that you're in for life?'

Tam took a breath. Maybe now was the time to say that he wanted out? By the look on Donnie's face, saying such a thing would cause Tam nothing but trouble.

'See that machine there?' Donnie gestured towards the machine. 'It's an incinerator. You know what it's for?'

There was a moment, a second, where everything stopped. Westlands Agricultural and Waste Management.

'Shit!' Tam whispered.

Turning towards the machine again, he watched as Steff moved, pulled the man with the canvas bag over his head towards it and shoved him inside. The man resisted but it was no use, Steff was too strong for him.

'This is what happens to men who don't abide by our policies, Tam,' Donnie said. 'By way of initiation, you get to do the honours.'

Tam felt sick as Steff pulled the bag off the guy's head. He locked eyes with Tam, tears pouring down his face, pleading silently with him to help.

'What the fuck do you mean, *I get to do the honours*?'

'See that button over there? You get to be the one to start the cremation process.'

Tam felt his eyes widen as he took a step back. 'No way. I can't do this. I'm sorry but I thought I was just going to be... well I didn't think I'd be involved in shit like this.'

Steff grinned as he shoved the man inside and slammed the door closed before locking it tightly.

Tam couldn't switch off from the screams coming from inside.

'Tam, you said yourself when you met with Steff, you have no job prospects, no qualifications. I hear the Barrhouse Firm let you down after Kev's arrest? They've left you hanging with no income? The only thing you have to call your own is your driving licence. We need a man like you to help us out with delivery and disposal jobs. You're a perfect fit. This is just something that everyone has to do. It's not like you've no experience with violence before, is it?' Donnie said.

'How do you know about the Firm?' Tam asked.

Donnie smiled, glared at Tam through narrowed eyes.

'I know everything about my employees, past, present and future. You think you stumbled across this job by accident? You were headhunted, pal, by yours truly. I was at your last match, looking for someone just like you. And here you are. The violence and aggression, it's in your blood. You crave it.'

Tam shook his head. 'No, I crave the match; I want to box. I don't want to cremate some stranger who's still alive.'

Donnie's victim hammered against the inside of the incinerator, and Tam tried to block it out.

'You could give a fatal blow in under thirty seconds. What if the man in there' – he gestured towards the van – 'was to be found dead with a fatal blow to the head? What if the polis were to be tipped off about that? You'd go straight to the jail, eh? Think you could handle that?'

Tam's stomach flipped. This man was threatening him, and with no witnesses on his side Tam really had no choice. Donnie Black could murder the guy in the van, and Tam's DNA would be all over the steering wheel. He'd have no chance.

'That doesn't have to happen, Tam. If you just do what I say here today, then you'll be a free man for the rest of your days.'

Tam looked at his feet. He had no choice.

Steff appeared by his side and put his arm around him. 'C'mon. I'll show you how to start her up, eh?'

Tam allowed Steff to lead him to the unit next to the cylinder, all the while listening to the man inside as he pleaded not to be turned to ash.

He watched as Steff showed him how to switch the machine on, before standing back and leaving Tam to do what he was expected to do: kill another to save his freedom or spend the rest of his life in prison.

Tam did what he had to do, to protect his freedom. But he knew he'd never be able to forget the sounds of the man screaming from inside before he was incinerated.

All he'd wanted was to make enough cash to be able to get a flat for himself and Louise to live in, away from the people who'd failed in their jobs as parents. Now he had blood on his hands and a grand cash coming his way. And that was the moment Tam knew his life would never be the same again.

Chapter Nineteen

'Babe?' Kev called out as he closed the front door. 'Babe, you in?'

Before Kev Barclay got the chance to drop his bag, the living room door flew open and Darcie Wright jumped into his arms, wrapped her legs around his waist and gripped him so tightly that he thought he was going to suffocate. But he didn't care. He'd take it so long as he was no longer in that hellhole cell that he'd had to share for months with quite possibly the smelliest bastard in Glasgow.

'You smell incredible,' he remarked as her hair hung around his face, thankful that he no longer had to put up with the stench of his old cellmate.

'It's so good to have you home, Kev. I've missed you so fucking much,' Darcie said, finally loosening her grip.

'I've missed you too.'

Kev couldn't stop staring at his girlfriend, who he had decided while he was in prison he was going to make his wife. But not before he sorted out the reason that he'd gone to prison in the first place. Being set up wasn't something he'd expected to happen, but it had. Working in the yard had earned him a few quid, but it was never worth going to prison for, for something he didn't do.

Darcie disappeared into the kitchen and returned holding a bottle of Kev's favourite beer. Taking that first sip was glorious. Not a drop had passed his lips when he was inside. He hadn't put a foot wrong while he was inside. He'd been offered the chance of a drink, a line here and there, a joint or two, all snuck in by inmates, visitors and even screws. But he'd declined all of it, taken on a job in the prison kitchen and kept his head down. His original three-year sentence had been cut to eighteen months due to his good behaviour and the fact that he'd never been in trouble with the police before. That wasn't to say he hadn't made some acquaintances, some friends on the inside. Not to mention knowing some of the boys from his younger days.

'I don't know how I'd have coped if you had been kept in that place for the full three years,' Darcie said.

'Well, it's a good thing I wasn't then.' Kev smiled. 'It helped that I knew a few guys in there from back in the day. It was good to catch up.'

'Bet they had so much to tell you.' Darcie gave a sarcastic laugh.

'Not for your ears.' He winked. And he meant it. The people he knew weren't the type he wanted Darcie involved with. They were dangerous, in for some brutal crimes.

And brutality was what he needed on his side if he was going to take revenge on the people who set him up. Kev Barclay was no mug, and he was going to prove it even if it killed him. It wouldn't kill him, though. It would send him and the rest of the Firm all the way to the fucking top.

Chapter Twenty

'Aw hen, that's bloody brilliant,' Susie said as she handed the tanning goggles back to Darcie across the counter. 'You were so worried he'd be away the full sentence.'

Darcie smiled as she took the goggles from her regular and placed them under the desk. 'It's the best feeling, honestly. He should never have gone away in the first place, but that's a story for another time.'

Susie nodded, placed a fiver on the counter and put on her denim jacket. 'Aye, well you make sure he stays out of trouble. I'll catch you later in the week. I'm not going to Tenerife looking like a milk bottle, so I'll be in here every couple days until I catch my flight.'

Darcie laughed and waved Susie off as she headed outside and onto the precinct. The woman was only in her early fifties but would easily pass for ten years older than that due to the number of sunbeds that she'd taken over the years. She was a nice enough woman, always chatting, and owned the pub across from the shop. She was hardly in the country nowadays. Who would be if they owned a holiday home in the Canaries? Certainly not Darcie.

Glancing down at the computer screen, Darcie noted that there were only ten minutes until closing time. Kev would be there to pick her up any minute, and she didn't want to keep him waiting. Just as she was about to turn out the lights and lock up the shop for the evening, the shop phone rang. Quickly debating with herself whether or not to leave the phone to ring, she thought better of it as it was likely to be her boss checking up on her.

'Hello, Sunshine Tanning?'

'Ah, glad I caught you,' the voice on the other end of the line said. It *was* her boss. 'Just wondered if you'd be able to do a few extra shifts this week. There's, erm...' Darcie waited, wondering if the line had disconnected. 'I've got a lot going on at home and I won't be around as much over the next few weeks. You know we've struggled for staff, and you're the only one I can really rely on, Darcie.'

Darcie rolled her eyes and held in the sigh that bubbled in her throat. The familiar slur to her boss's voice was present on the other end of the line. She'd been drinking. Again. Not that it was any of Darcie's business what her boss did in her own time, but when it affected Darcie's personal time it could become a problem. Kev had just been released; she really wanted to spend as much time with him as possible. But then, she did have rent to pay and with Kev out of work, the money would come in handy.

'Sure, Layla. No problem.' Releasing the sigh gently, Darcie asked, 'Everything okay?'

'Yep, just a lot on. I'll pop in over the next few days to check on things. But you'll have to do the banking if I'm not around. You know it's due in every second Friday?'

Ha, she thought. Pissed, yet still able to run a business. She didn't know whether to admire her boss or be annoyed at her. Keeping her thoughts from her lips, Darcie agreed to everything, not just because she didn't have much of a choice, but because she wanted to get out of the damn sunbed shop and home to Kev.

Chapter Twenty-One

Kev Barclay watched Donnie Black from behind the wheel of his car, gritting his teeth so hard he wondered if they might shatter from the pressure. That bastard was going about his daily business as if Kev had never existed, had been ever since he'd gone inside. Now Kev was free, released early on good behaviour. That wasn't easy, behaving in prison. There had been so many opportunities for him to make some decent cash while inside, but he'd refrained from getting involved in any of the schemes because he knew that if he kept his head down, his freedom would come much quicker. Cammy had visited him every week, made sure that Kev was left alone on the inside. He told Kev to bide his time, that the bastard, Black, would get what was coming to him. That was the kind of friend Cammy was and always had been, and he knew that Cammy and the rest of the Firm would help get Kev the revenge he deserved.

Donnie shook hands with his brother, Steff Black, and Kev watched as they began walking in opposite directions.

Who to follow first? Before he could decide, his phone rang. Glancing at it as it sat in the holder attached to the windscreen, his shoulders loosened a little. Swiping his finger across the screen, Kev answered.

'Hey, it's me,' the voice replied. 'Are you coming to pick me up? You said you'd be here by closing.'

'Aw shit, sorry, Darcie. I lost track of time. On my way.'

Kev started the engine, glared back at Donnie and then Steff as they climbed into their own cars far along the road. They wouldn't see him because they wouldn't expect him to be there, but he made a turn in the road and drove away from them.

It's not like they were going anywhere. Glasgow was their territory. Kev would just have to be patient. He'd get around to taking his revenge on them eventually.

–

Around twenty minutes later, Kev pulled up outside the sunbed shop where Darcie was working and saw her chatting to an older woman, who Kev suspected looked older than she was, perhaps a regular at the tanning beds.

He rolled down the window on the passenger side and smiled out at Darcie, whose eyes lit up when she saw him. He couldn't believe she'd stuck around and waited on him while he was inside. A good-looking girl like her should have had her pick of the decent guys, yet she'd promised to wait on Kev. He was thankful for that.

'Finally,' Darcie said sarcastically.

'Is this the famous Kev?' The woman Darcie was chatting to said.

Darcie smiled at her and nodded, and the woman stepped forward, bending down to look in the car at Kev.

'I'm Susie,' she said. 'I own the pub across from here.'

Kev nodded. 'Nice to meet you.'

'Susie's a regular,' Darcie said, moving towards the door before opening it. 'She's in a lot, using the beds before heading off to the real sunshine.'

Kev smiled.

'Yep. The holiday home in Tenerife is calling. Headed there in a couple days for a month.'

'Well, you enjoy, Susie. Bring back some sunshine, eh? The weather here is fucking miserable for summer. I had the heating on this morning,' Darcie said, closing the car door and pulling on her seatbelt.

'I'll drop the spare keys into you before I go. Okay?'

Darcie nodded, and Susie waved as Kev pulled away from the kerb.

'Spare keys?' Kev asked.

'Whenever she goes away, she leaves a set of keys for the pub and her house, just in case of emergencies. Not for me, but for my boss. They're really good friends, and I've become friendly with Susie since working here. She's lovely, always got time for a chat.'

'No family to leave them with?' Kev asked, pulling out of the precinct and heading onto the main road towards the motorway.

'Not that I know of. She lives alone. She has a daughter or something who lives in Tenerife, so I think that's why she's out there so much.'

Darcie sat back on the seat and opened the window, lit a cigarette and sighed. 'It's so good to not have to get the bloody bus, I tell you.'

Kev laughed. 'You didn't have to get the bus all the time. The boys picked you up to take you home when I was away, didn't they?'

'Well, yeah. But not all the time, Kev. They weren't always around. Sometimes they were busy.'

Kev nodded. He knew what busy meant. It meant they'd been going around, making sure they were connecting with punters and clients, building walls between them and the Blacks. Just like Cammy had warned Donnie would happen.

Donnie Black had always thought he was untouchable. Not anymore.

Chapter Twenty-Two

Donnie Black braced himself before putting the key in the front door. Did he really want to go home after the day he'd had with Louise? She was young, spritely and full of passion for life and fun, but most of all there was a shit ton of money to be made there. He couldn't let pleasure get in the way of business. He hadn't put eighteen months graft in for nothing. Then there was his wife. A drunk, argumentative and downright fucking infuriating woman. Hopefully, she'd be passed out on the sofa and he wouldn't even have to speak to her.

He pushed the door open in silence and stepped carefully into the house, closing the door quietly behind him. The house seemed still and Donnie breathed a sigh of relief.

Switching on the kitchen light, he saw three empty wine bottles on the counter and shook his head. Those bottles signalled that Layla would be lying in a pool of her own vomit somewhere in the house. He wanted to go to bed and leave her to it, to face the wrath of the hangover the next day, but he thought better of it and went through the house to find her, to make sure that she was at least still alive.

Kicking off his shoes at the door, Donnie began to climb the stairs. Their marriage hadn't always been like this, he remembered as he peered into their bedroom and saw that the bed was unoccupied.

'Layla? You here?'

Layla hadn't even been a drinker when they'd first met, twenty years previously. The alcohol had come much later, fifteen years later to be exact, when Layla's sister had died in a car accident. Now, it was all she did. Day drinking, night drinking, the odd line here and there. And with the alcohol had come the abuse. The constant nagging, telling him that it was his fault that her sister had died. Yes, they'd been arguing right before it had happened, but it wasn't Donnie's fault that she'd been hit by that car. In a way, Donnie understood why Layla had allowed the booze to take over. Grief did strange things to people and drinking herself numb was how she'd coped. Donnie had thought that as the grief process progressed, Layla would eventually stop using the bottle as a crutch for what had happened. Instead, it had just got worse. Five years down the line, Donnie was sick of the whole thing.

Pushing the bathroom door open, Donnie saw that Layla wasn't in her usual spot on the floor by the toilet. Then he heard a noise behind him and, as he turned, he managed to catch her wrist mid-air just before her hand came crashing down on his face.

'You fucking bastard,' Layla slurred, before falling to her knees in a drunken mess.

Donnie took a steadying breath and shook his head.

'Right, Layla. Bed.'

'You're a bastard. Who was it tonight? That bitch from the pub? I'll ask Susie, you know. She'll tell me.' Her words were slow and almost incomprehensible.

Donnie lifted her over his shoulder and carried her through to the bedroom. 'Layla, any man married to the likes of you would understand that one woman would be enough.'

He dropped her down onto the bed and, by then, she was already unconscious. Donnie glanced down at his wife and actually felt sorry for her. To be in her head was to be in hell. Along with the alcohol and grief, he often wondered if there was something else going on. On some days she could be absolutely fine, almost normal. On others, she was far from the Layla he used to love. If a psychiatrist was to take one look at her, she'd be advised to check in to some kind of clinic.

Backing out of the bedroom, he closed the door quietly. He was a different man nowadays. The only thing he was interested in was business, making as much money for his retirement as possible. He'd leave Layla, leave her with enough money to do whatever she wanted with it. She could drink herself to death for all he cared; although Donnie was sure that if she could blame him for that from death, then she would. The only thing Donnie could praise Layla for was the fact that she was able to hide her issues in public. To those who didn't know Layla well, or in fact at all, they would look at her and think she had all her shit together. That was exactly how Donnie wanted it. Layla had a part to play when they were seen together. Well-turned-out, doting wife. It was part of his appearance and how people saw him. Not that they were often seen out together these days. Donnie couldn't stand to be around her much at all.

Louise was his focus now. And once he was finished with her, he'd move on to the next. With each girl, there was so much more cash to be made, and Donnie wasn't going to let anything get in the way of that. The best part, though, was how the Firm would react when Louise finally disappeared. This wasn't all business. This was personal.

Chapter Twenty-Three

Louise sat down on the sofa and pulled her phone out of her pocket. It had been a long day and she knew she wasn't going to be able to see Donnie for another day at least. He was all she thought about, every second of every day. He was so handsome it made her stomach flutter when she thought about his face, how his lips felt on hers.

There were no messages from Donnie. He hadn't contacted her since she'd left him at the hotel. She knew he would be busy with work; he was always busy. Maybe she could go up to her bedroom and put on something enticing and send him a selfie?

Louise quickly tapped out a text to Donnie, saying that she missed him and that she couldn't wait to climb back into bed with him. Checking her phone was on silent, she slid it back into her pocket and got herself comfy on the sofa.

The local news sounded out on the television, and her mum turned the volume up a little. Louise sighed but couldn't be bothered to get up from the sofa and go to her bedroom to watch something else. She felt her phone vibrate in her pocket, and her stomach flipped with excitement. As she reached for her pocket, her attention was caught by the words spoken by the reporter on the screen.

'*The family of a young woman, who was reported missing in 2019, are distraught as they say they are no closer to finding out what happened to her. Demi Simpson, who is twenty, was last seen heading out for work on the morning of the eighth of May. No one has seen or heard from her since. There has been no activity on her mobile phone, bank account or social media pages.*'

'Bloody hell,' Louise's mum said, taking a sip of her tea. 'That poor family.'

Louise sat forward and focused on the screen, listening as the reporter continued.

'*Her family have said that it is completely out of character for her not to have contacted them and are extremely worried for her welfare. Police Scotland are asking for anyone who has information on Demi's whereabouts, to come forward ASAP.*'

Louise fixed her eyes on the screen when the image of the young girl, the same age as her, flashed up. She looked happy, carefree. And Louise recognised her.

'Oh my god, I know her.'

'Do you?' her mum replied, somewhat distantly as a crashing sound from above them made her look up. Louise knew it was her dad, drunk, and probably falling out of the bed.

'Yeah, we went to school together. We weren't friends or anything, I just remember her. Fuck, that's a bit close to home, is it not?'

'If that girl has disappeared off the face of the Earth, in my opinion she's long gone and probably dead by now,' Louise's mum replied.

'Mum!' Louise shot her a look. 'You can't say things like that. She could just have run away or something.'

Helen shook her head. 'You, my girl, are very naïve if you think that's the case. I'm a mother and if you'd been missing for all that time, I'd hold on to hope. Of course I would. But I'm not stupid. There are bad people all over the place and that young girl has come across one or more of them. Poor family.'

Louise felt entirely gobsmacked at the words leaving her mum's mouth. She'd never heard her speak so fondly of her like that before. She was always too busy worrying about keeping things quiet so as not to wake her dad from his drunken stupor. But she supposed she was right. If there had been no trace of Demi Simpson then she must be dead. Or maybe didn't want to be found?

'Fancy a cuppa?' Louise asked, getting to her feet and heading to the kitchen.

Standing against the counter as she waited for the kettle to boil, Louise stared down at her phone. A message had come through from Donnie. Just an icon. A black heart. It made her smile, but it quickly faded when a Google alert appeared at the top of her screen.

Family's appeal to find Demi Simpson.

Thank god she had someone like Donnie to protect her from the horrors of the world.

Chapter Twenty-Four

Tam stared out of the window of the van, yet what lay ahead of him wasn't what he could see or hear. The sound of the man he'd been forced to drive to his death sounded in his ears as though it was still happening. No matter how loudly he played the radio, the memory got louder and louder.

Who the hell were these people and how the fuck had he managed to get himself involved in their shit? Whatever the answer to that question, Tam knew that today would be the one and only time that he would ever do anything for Steff and Donnie Black.

A loud tap on the window jolted Tam from his nightmare. Turning, Steff stood by the driver-side window, a ghoulish smile on his face. Tam rolled the window down and waited for what Steff had to say.

'You did good today, boy, really good. You kept your mouth shut when you were told to, you drove straight to the destination and followed every instruction. You were built for this, eh?' Steff said.

Did good? Tam thought. He'd murdered a complete stranger out of fear that he'd be killed himself. And now he was going to be paid for doing so. These two psycho brothers had him by the balls.

'I dunno,' Tam replied quietly. 'No sure I'm cut out for this, you know?'

'Bollocks!' Steff laughed loudly. His voice echoed around the yard at such a pitch even Crater face jumped. He was standing just behind Steff, his arms folded across his huge chest. 'You're a natural. And if you're worried about the pay, you don't have to be.'

Tam watched as Steff pulled a bundle of notes out of his back pocket and handed them through the window. 'There's a little extra in there for you. Call it a bonus. That'll see you right, get that old banger of yours fixed up or something.'

Before Tam could protest, Steff had already turned his back and was walking back towards the Portacabin at the other end of the yard.

If Tam accepted the money, it meant he was accepting that this was what he did for a living. This wasn't exactly what he'd expected to do with his life.

'Oi,' Steff called. Tam glanced up at his new boss. 'Don't go far, eh? I'll be in touch. You're on call, twenty-four seven. Answer that phone no matter what.'

Crater face approached the van and handed Tam a small pay-as-you-go phone but said nothing. Tam wasn't about to argue with this guy.

'You can get off now,' he said.

Tam nodded, put the window up and stepped out of the van. He slid the bundle of cash Steff had just handed him into his back pocket, and the phone into his hoodie, before heading towards his own car. He glanced across at Steff, who was standing at the door of the Portacabin. He waved at Tam with an overly enthusiastic smile across his face.

The guy did seem like he was a bit of a loose cannon, and Tam knew he hadn't seen the worst of him yet. With Donnie and Steff Black as his bosses, the two were a deadly duo that Tam knew he couldn't step back from. He was in it for life, just like Steff said.

Tam climbed into his Renault Clio and started the engine. The car felt ice cold on the summer's night, but Tam knew it was nothing to do with the weather. It was him, and what he'd been involved in.

Pulling the cash out of his pocket, he began to count it. He held fifteen hundred quid in his hand. Fifteen hundred quid. They'd given him an extra five hundred and called it a bonus. Tam would never have imagined being able to possess that amount of cash at any point in the month, let alone after one job. He felt the corners of his mouth rise, but then suppressed the smile when he reminded himself how he'd earned that money. Tam knew it was blood money, he wasn't stupid.

He gave one last glance up at Steff, who was still standing at the Portacabin. He nodded at Tam, who in turn returned the gesture. He had no choice. Steff had watched him count the money. Steff had a phone in his hand, tapping out a message. Then the phone that Crater face had handed him vibrated in his pocket.

He read the message quickly.

> There's plenty more where that came from. Just turn up, drive and keep your head down and before the year is out, you'll be fucking minted. Delete this message. Now.

Tam did what the message instructed and put the phone in the door card before pulling out of the yard. Crater face was already at the front gates, waiting to close them as Tam left.

Keep your head down and before the year is out, you'll be fucking minted, went around his head. Yeah, he thought. Or dead.

Chapter Twenty-Five

It had been a few days since Layla's last drink, and she'd been having withdrawals from day one. But she was fighting the demons inside her because she could never remember what she'd done the night or the day before. The one thing she knew for sure was that whenever she woke up the next day, she had a stinker of a hangover and was never in bed next to Donnie. She was always in another room, usually the bathroom. An argument usually lurked in the back of her mind, one that Donnie always insisted that she started when she was drunk. Accusations, verbal abuse, sometimes even physical. No wonder their relationship was at breaking point if she was behaving like that. Layla knew that she couldn't help herself. As soon as she opened a bottle of wine, she just didn't know her limits. Then the memories of her sister would flood in, and that's when her mind would twist and she would turn on Donnie, apparently.

It was coming up to Kerry's anniversary. Five years to the day when Layla watched her sister die when that car hit her. It wasn't the car that killed her; it was how she'd landed, hitting her skull on the concrete. Her brain so badly injured, she had died instantly. Blinking away the nightmarish memory, Layla took a deep breath and tried to calm herself.

Heading down to the kitchen, Layla was surprised to see Donnie standing at the window, drinking a coffee and tapping away on his phone. The radio played in the background, and he didn't seem to notice her presence. Either that or he was ignoring her.

'Hi,' she said, trying to sound as casual as possible. 'Sleep well?'

He glanced up at her with a raised brow, then returned his attention to his phone. 'Fine.'

Layla's stomach flipped. He really didn't want to speak to her and as much as she couldn't take the tension, she chose not to push it.

Pouring herself a coffee, she decided that the best thing she could do was visit a few of her tanning salons, check on how things were going. She owned six. Well, Donnie owned them, a way of dodging the taxman if he ever needed to. But she was in charge. It gave her something to focus on when things like this happened.

Donnie drained the coffee mug he'd been holding, placed it into the dishwasher and headed for the door.

'What you got on today?' Layla called out.

'Not an affair with lots of women from the pub, if that's what you're wondering,' he replied, before the door slammed and Layla was left on her own in the house that Donnie had bought for them.

'Shit,' she hissed. Once again, he was referring to a comment she couldn't remember making. An affair with women from the pub? Who the hell had she meant? All of them? God knows what she was thinking when she threw that one at him.

Layla made a coffee for herself and sat down at the kitchen table to drink it. Her head felt full, like it was going to explode. Layla knew her alcohol intake always increased around the time of Kerry's anniversary, to help her to block out the pain and the guilt of what happened to her. She blamed herself.

Kerry had expressed her concerns about Donnie from the beginning, saying that he wasn't to be trusted, he wasn't good for Layla. But he was Layla's high school crush. They'd been friends since she was just thirteen years old. In fact, she'd been friends with Donnie and Steff, as well as a few others who'd fallen off the grid over the years. It didn't matter what people said to her about Donnie, she was just infatuated with him. Always had been. He and Kerry had never got on, and before Kerry died, Layla had accused her of being jealous that she was with him instead of Kerry. And for a while, she'd actually believed that. Why else would her sister say and do whatever she could to make Layla see the bad in everything Donnie said and did? It seemed that from the beginning of their relationship, people wanted to stop them from getting together. Even Mel had warned Layla off Donnie back in the day. But jealously wasn't the reason for Mel's warning. Not that anything anyone said would have changed Layla's mind. She loved Donnie.

When she'd confronted Kerry about it on the day that she'd died, Kerry had denied it. But Layla wasn't convinced she was telling the truth and had started to argue with her. That was when Donnie had turned up and all hell had broken loose. Kerry had started screaming at Donnie, saying that she knew all about him and his family, and what they did for a living. That he and his brother Steff were sick in the head, especially Steff. That's when it happened.

Taking a deep breath, Layla pushed the memory out of her head. She didn't want to remember what happened next, even though it lived in her head every moment of every single day.

Maybe that was why when she was drunk, she would say things to Donnie, accuse him of all sorts. She'd never got to the bottom of her sister's accusations, never found anything incriminating on Kerry's phone once her belongings were returned to the family. She'd never dug any deeper. She was too scared of what she might find. Instead, over the course of not only their marriage, but their entire relationship, Layla buried her head, drank enough alcohol to block out the possibility that her sister Kerry was right. Maybe Donnie wasn't what Layla thought.

Maybe the accusations had some sort of truth to them. Maybe, somewhere inside her head, hidden beneath the alcohol-fuelled blackouts, Layla already knew the truth about her husband. He was using the sunbed shops as a front to launder money. But where was that money coming from? It couldn't just be from drugs, or a security racket. Surely Kerry wouldn't have gone off her head for that kind of thing. There had to be more.

Picking up her mobile, she called the only person who would be able to answer her questions.

Chapter Twenty-Six

Louise got into the car and tried to contain her excitement. Donnie's call that morning had been unexpected, but instead of getting ready for college, she agreed to meet him.

'How you doing?' he asked, starting the engine and driving out of the car park not far from her house.

'All the better for seeing you. That and not having to go to college.' She smiled, pulling her cigarettes from her bag and lighting one. She handed it to Donnie and he took it, his fingers brushing against hers. 'I didn't think I was going to see you this soon.'

Donnie exhaled loudly and with the cigarette hanging from his lips, he put his hand over her knee. 'Had to see you, didn't I? You're like a drug to me, few days away from you and I start feeling like shit.'

Louise felt her heart flutter. She knew exactly what he meant because that was how she felt about him too. They'd only been seeing each other for a few weeks, but she just couldn't get him out of her head.

'Same,' she replied, trying to play it cool. 'So, where we off to?'

'Somewhere we can't be disturbed.'

'You mean somewhere your wife won't annoy you?' Louise said.

Donnie didn't reply, instead he removed his hand from her knee and focused on the road. They were heading out towards the Trossachs road, away from the hustle and bustle of the city, where no one would be able to find them. It would be just the two of them for hours. No traces of a hotel booking, no cameras on the road and more importantly, no phone signal.

Louise was so in love with Donnie Black that it ached in her chest, but she hadn't told him that yet. Even though he'd said she was like a drug, she couldn't be certain that it was the right kind of drug, the same as the one she was addicted to.

For now, she would have to enjoy their relationship for what it was.

Chapter Twenty-Seven

Kev watched as Darcie got out of bed, ready for her shift that day. He felt guilty not having a job so he could help to provide for their flat. He'd been earning money, good money, before he'd gone to prison, but it wasn't exactly legit. Working with the Firm, with Cammy and the rest of them, it felt like home. Those boys were his life. They were his family. And after everything they did for him while he was inside, how they made sure Darcie was okay, he couldn't turn his back on them. And Darcie didn't want him to either, but she did want him to go legit.

'What's up with you?' Darcie asked as she pulled on her dressing gown. 'You've got a right face on you.'

'Thanks.' Kev smiled.

'Seriously, I thought you'd be smiling ear to ear now that you're out of that shithole.'

Kev sighed, threw the duvet off and got out of bed. Pulling on a pair of shorts and a T-shirt, he picked up his mobile and moved out of the bedroom towards the kitchen.

'I just don't want you thinking that I'm taking the piss, living here rent free and unable to contribute to the bills.'

'Kev, it's not like you're just being lazy. You're just out of jail. You'll get a job as soon as you can, I know you will.' Darcie followed him to the kitchen, stood behind him and massaged his shoulders.

'Aye, but it'll be some shitty job that pays the bare minimum.'

He felt Darcie's grip loosen and he turned to see her face.

'Have you told Cammy and the boys that you're not going back?' Darcie asked, waiting for his response. When he didn't answer straight away, she sighed. 'Aw, Kev. You're not seriously considering going back to the Firm, are you? Kev, it's what got you into trouble in the first place.' Her face contorted as she spoke.

'No, of course not. Donnie Black set me up, Darcie. He's a dodgy bastard, the kind that would stab you in the back as quick as pay you a few quid. He fucking screwed me and the rest of the boys over because he wanted the Firm to fail before it even took off. We're not going to let that happen. We're going to end the bastard.' He laughed.

'That's not funny, Kev.'

'I know it's not funny. It's far from funny. Aside from the fact that I had to serve a jail sentence for a crime I didn't commit, I watched Donnie smile as the polis took me away, Darcie. He got away with setting me up.' Kev gritted his teeth so hard he could barely get the words out. 'Well, he thought he did.'

Darcie stepped back and filled the kettle. The atmosphere in the room was heavy and Kev instantly regretted pushing his bad mood onto her. It wasn't her fault that he was stupid enough to get involved with a gangster.

'Kev, it wasn't easy for me either. Everyone we know questioning me. Did Kev really do that? How can you stay with him? The shitty press constantly hanging around me when it happened. Did you think I wanted to work in a shitty fucking sunbed shop?'

Kev sighed loudly. 'I know. I'm sorry.'

He looked down at his hands, remembered the police cuffing him and being huckled into the back of the van while Donnie and Steff Black looked on with smiles on their faces.

'I don't think going back to the Firm is a good idea, Kev. What if Donnie sends more trouble your way? I mean, he started a war with you guys.'

Darcie made herself a coffee and stood with her back to the counter, staring at Kev.

'Of course I'm going back, Darcie. The Firm isn't a choice. I know you think me stepping away from that life would be the best thing for us, but it wouldn't. Cammy and that, they're family. And they looked after you when I was inside. We're not bad like the Blacks. They're dirty, venomous bastards.'

Darcie frowned, took a sip of coffee. 'There's no changing your mind, is there?'

Kev shook his head. 'I know you think it's mad, but just trust me. We'll be better off if I stick with the Firm.'

Darcie sighed loudly and shook her head. 'I can't believe I'm saying this, but you're probably right. Just, whatever you do, Kev, don't bring trouble to our door. I can't be bothered with it. Like you said, they're dirty bastards and I know for a fact that they'd do anything to hurt you lot.'

'You won't have to worry about him for long, Darcie. We'll sort it.'

Darcie shook her head and went into the bathroom. When Kev heard the shower running, he took out his phone and looked up Donnie Black. Images of him and his wife appeared, images of Donnie and his stupid brother, Steff Black came up too. Dressed in their best suits, shaking hands with politicians and bigwig business people, giving the Black empire the best reputation they could. They took after their old man all right. Donald Black, the man who had every finger in every fucking pie back in the day. The Black empire was untouchable because of him, as were his sons. Kev knew that first hand after what he'd witnessed at that rave back when they were just teenagers. As things stood, it looked as though Donnie and Steff Black had stepped right into his shoes.

As he continued to scroll, he discovered an image of himself. Of him going into court on the day he was sentenced. The last image was of the guy who'd testified against Kev, saying he saw Kev load the van. The whole situation had made him sick to his stomach. Shutting off the screen and shoving the phone into his pocket, Kev gritted his teeth. He couldn't look at the images, and the smug, powerful smiles on their faces.

Just an hour later, Kev was in the car, driving Darcie to the salon. He chose not to tell her that he was going to visit the guy that had stood up in court to testify against him. She'd only plead with him not to do it, to move on with his life for the sake of their relationship. But he'd only be able to move on when he'd dealt with what had happened.

Darcie got out of the car and crossed the road at the precinct before heading for the salon. Kev waited until she was inside before he pulled away, guilt already weighing heavy on his chest for lying to her about going to the job centre.

Kev's blood boiled as he headed to meet the guy who'd been forced to say that Kev was the one who attacked him. He'd had no choice. It was either lie in court, or the guy's family would suffer.

There was no way Kev could let Donnie Black get away with what he did to him or anyone else for that matter. Gangster or not.

Chapter Twenty-Eight

He'd been surprised to get a call from Layla. She only ever really spoke to him when Donnie was around. She had been short on the phone, saying that she'd wanted to speak to him and asked if she could meet him. Steff had offered to go to the house, but Layla had refused, instead asking to meet in a more neutral spot. The café at the other side of the bridge was perfect, she'd said. Steff was on his way there now, wondering what on Earth Layla could possibly want to ask him. He smiled at the thought of being alone with her. He wondered if, on some level, she knew about how he felt for her, and perhaps that was why she was asking to meet. Wishful thinking on his part, he knew that. But just for a moment, he allowed his mind to wander to that place where he'd tell her how he felt and she'd admit to him that she felt the same.

Steff pulled into the car park at the back of the café and saw Layla's car. She was already inside and, knowing her, she'd have ordered him a coffee for his arrival. Killing the engine, he glanced in the visor mirror, checking his hair and teeth. Stepping out of the car, he went into the café, and he saw Layla sitting at a table in the back corner. Like she didn't want to be seen.

'Hey,' he said, approaching the table.

'Hi Steff. I got you a coffee.'

He glanced down and smiled. He'd been right. He often thought that he knew Layla better than Donnie did. By the look on her face, Steff was beginning to piece together why she'd asked to see him. She wasn't there to declare that she loved him at all, like he did her. And this wasn't a social call either. This was serious.

'Cheers,' Steff replied, taking a seat opposite her, trying to hide his disappointment. Just like he had tried to hide his disappointment on the morning of her wedding to Donnie. He'd gone to the hotel room to see her, while Donnie waited down in the bar with the rest of the guests. She'd been quiet that day and confessed that she'd been thinking about Kerry, her sister, and wondered what she'd make of the wedding to Donnie since she'd made it perfectly clear that she'd hated him. That was four years ago. Been together twenty, married for four. Their whole adult lives together, and Steff had had to stand back and watch his brother live out the life that he should have been living.

Steff had hoped that Layla hadn't actually wanted to marry Donnie and that when it came to it, she wouldn't go through with it. He'd wanted her to turn and run, and for Steff to go after her and make her see that he was the one she should be with. But he'd kept his thoughts to himself. Maybe if he'd said something, actually told her how he felt, the wedding would never have gone ahead. He hadn't had the balls to speak out. Never had done when it came to going against his brother Donnie. To do so would be to go against the entire family. He couldn't do that.

They'd had a moment that day, he and Layla. Just the two of them in that hotel room, Layla standing in her wedding dress, looking more beautiful than he'd ever seen her, sadder than he'd ever seen her. She'd promised him she was sad about Kerry, not about marrying Donnie. She loved Donnie, always had. Hearing those words that day hurt, and they still did.

'So, what can I do for you?' Steff asked, pushing the memories out of his head and lifting the coffee mug.

'I want to ask you something in confidence, and I want an honest answer. No bullshitting me because he's your brother, Steff.'

Steff nodded, trying to look as though he had no idea what she was on about. But he knew fine well the question that was about to come out of her mouth, because he knew what Donnie was getting up to with that young thing, Louise.

'Is my husband having an affair?'

He detected a crack in her voice, and Steff wanted to get up and hug her. Instead, he said, 'Why are you asking me that?'

'It doesn't matter why. I just need an answer.'

'Have you seen him with someone or something?'

'No, but something isn't right. I know we've not been getting on recently but he's more distant than he's ever been. A married couple can go through hard times, of course. But he's changed. He's not the man I married. His behaviour, his mannerisms. It's like he doesn't care about me anymore.'

Steff knew all about it because Donnie had talked to him. Layla's drinking was getting worse, her behaviour when she was drunk was unbearable. Again, Steff kept his counsel.

'To my knowledge, he's not having an affair.'

Layla's eyes fixed on his, glazed and heavy. 'You're lying.'

Steff spat out a laugh. 'I swear, I don't know anything about Donnie having an affair. I promise. I wouldn't lie to you, Layla. We've been friends for too many years to do that. You're family.'

'Not blood, though. And your loyalties lie with my husband. I get it, I do. I don't know why I thought you'd tell me the truth.'

Steff sighed, put down his coffee mug. 'I promise, I'm not lying.'

And he wasn't. Donnie *wasn't* having an affair with Louise. He was getting her ready for business. Drawing her in so close that she would fall for every word, trust everything about him.

'I don't believe you, Steff. Of course you're going to lie for him. You've got more loyalty towards him than me, so I do get it. But I have to know the truth.'

Steff waited for a moment before responding. He didn't want to cause her any more upset or uncertainty. He said the only thing he could think of that wouldn't sound like denial or as though he was covering for his brother.

'If you don't believe me, then why don't you keep a closer eye on him? That way, you'll be able to see for yourself.'

Her expression softened then. 'You mean, follow him?'

Steff shrugged. 'Why not? If you say you think I'm lying, and you're convinced that Donnie is at it with someone else behind your back, then what other option do you have?'

Layla sat back, took a sip of coffee and seemed to ponder over Steff's suggestion. He held back a smile, knowing that he had Layla right where he wanted her.

Chapter Twenty-Nine

The sun shone through the windscreen, and Louise pulled the visor down as she tried to take in the view. The loch in front of her glistened under the light of the morning sunshine, and the water rippled against the shoreline.

'I didn't even know this place existed,' she said, sitting forward to take it all in.

'If you didn't have a car, you wouldn't know it was here. It's my little place of tranquillity,' Donnie replied.

The awkwardness from her earlier comment about his wife had quickly dispersed and things were peaceful between them now. That was how things were between them, mostly. Peaceful but electric. Louise had wanted to blurt out so many times that she loved him but had refrained from doing so in case he didn't say it back.

'You want to go for a wander down there, stick your toes in the sand?' Donnie asked, grinning widely at her.

Louise was almost giddy as she got out of the car and saw that Donnie was offering out his hand to her. They'd never held hands in public before. She slid her hand into his and together they walked down to the water.

'I think this is the start of the good weather for the summer, you know?' Louise said.

'Let's hope so. The weather in this country depresses me.'

They stopped at the edge of where the water met the shore, and Louise slipped her shoes off before dipping her toes in. The water was freezing but it sparked something in her that she hadn't felt before. A real sense of freedom.

'You joining me in here?'

Donnie shook his head. 'Just seeing you enjoy it is enough for me.'

A few minutes passed and Louise stepped back onto the sand. They found a bench at the edge of where the sand met a pathway and they sat down.

'I've got something I want to ask you,' Louise said. She hadn't imagined it; she saw him tense at the question. 'You don't have to look so worried.'

'You're going to ask me to leave her, aren't you?'

'Well, would that be such a bad thing?'

Donnie sighed, stared out at the water in front of them. He was quiet, and Louise held her breath. Asking him to leave his wife was practically the same thing as telling him she loved him. If she didn't, why bother asking the question at all? Donnie was a smart man, he'd know that.

'We're having fun as we are, Louise. Why spoil it?'

'Spoil it? I want to make things even better between us. I mean, you wouldn't be sleeping with me if you were happy with your wife, would you? The way I see it is, if you want something enough, you'd do anything to get more of it.'

Donnie smiled at that comment, and his shoulders seemed to relax a little. 'I've got a lot to lose, Louise. And no, I don't mean her. I just mean that, well, I have businesses, a home, a reputation. I've been with Layla for a very long time. Everything is split down the middle. If I divorce her, then she gets half of everything that is mine. It could get very, very complicated.'

Louise watched his expression, his narrowing eyes looking far out at the loch, but she knew he wasn't seeing the view. He was imagining the mess of his divorce.

Louise had never asked Donnie outright what it was he did for a living, but these days with the internet, it wasn't hard to find out in her own way. She'd simply googled his name, and the things she'd read about him had made her love him even more. Investing in care homes, being at the forefront of charity organisations, standing up for the community. It had confirmed everything that she already knew about him. He was a good, decent man (even if he was having an affair) who would do anything to help people. She'd also seen Layla in some of those images, on his arm looking beautiful and proud to be next to him. That should be Louise. And it would be, she thought. One day, Louise would be the one standing next to Donnie in designer clothes, with the best shoes and accessories, helping him to continue his amazing work. She couldn't wait for that day to come.

A shitty upbringing in Barrhouse had led Louise and Tam to an agreement from an early age that they wouldn't turn out like either of their parents. Maybe Donnie was her ticket out of that? If they went on to get married, and have children of their own, she'd give her kids a much better upbringing than she and Tam had ever had from their parents. In a better area, with a better home. It wasn't her mum's fault that her dad was a drunk, but she could have done more to protect them from what they'd seen as kids. Now, Helen acted as though things were fine, like their past was that of a normal family. The older their dad got, the more the drink took an effect on him and he slept most of the time. That suited the rest of them. If she'd just divorced him, things would be better now.

'But it wouldn't last forever, the fall out of splitting up.' She slid her hand around the back of his neck and moved closer. 'It would calm down eventually and then it would just be us.'

'And in the middle of a messy divorce, what do you think that would do to us? It would ruin it, Louise.'

'Look,' she said, deciding to backtrack, 'we don't have to talk about this now. You're right. Let's just see this for what it is, a bit of fun.'

Donnie turned and smiled. 'You're an amazing wee thing, you know that?'

Louise allowed him to kiss her, but her stomach sank. A bit of fun was okay, but not what she wanted for her future. She wanted Donnie, more than anything, and she would do whatever she could to get him. If that meant going to his wife and telling her that she'd been having an affair with him, then that's what she would do.

Chapter Thirty

Kev pushed open the entrance door to the high-rise building and headed for the lift. Red and white striped tape lay across the button, a makeshift OUT OF ORDER sign pinned above it.

'For fuck's sake,' Kev muttered under his breath as he turned and made his way towards the stairs. It was a good thing he'd been working out in the prison gym, or he might not have been able to tackle the sixteen floors to get to the flat he was looking for.

After a few minutes and out of breath, Kev stood outside the door of the guy who'd testified against him in court. Steadying himself, he raised his fist and knocked sharply on the door. Listening carefully, he heard the noise from the television inside go quiet as a shuffling of footsteps approached the door.

It opened slightly on a chain and a face appeared between the door and the frame. A widened eye stared back at Kev, and just as the door was about to be slammed shut, Kev stuck his foot between the gap to keep it wedged open.

'I'm not here to cause trouble. I just want to talk to you. I swear.'

The guy behind the door hesitated, but eventually slid the chain off and allowed Kev inside. He followed the guy into the living room and watched as he leaned on a walking stick for support. It made Kev sick to his stomach that people thought he'd been responsible for that.

'What do you want?' the guy said, standing by the window that looked out onto the scheme he was living in.

'I get it, you know. Why you lied in court,' Kev said.

'I didn't lie.'

'Through your fucking teeth, Davie. Donnie Black can be very persuasive, especially when he's flashing the cash in your face, eh?'

Davie turned and stared at Kev, his eyes darkened at the corners. Lack of sleep, or fear. Maybe both.

'You lot are just as bad as them, you know that? I just needed fucking rent money, that was all. I wish I'd stayed clear of the lot of you. I thought once the court case was out the way, that'd be it. But Cammy and the rest of your lot paid me a visit.'

Kev blinked, remembering Cammy informing him of how the Firm had punished Davie after court that day.

'I told Donnie and Steff about it, but they weren't fucking interested. I was left in the gutter like a fucking dog. And I'm still in arrears with my rent. A waste of my fucking time and energy, the whole thing. I'd be better off dead.'

Kev felt a pang of guilt, just for a moment. Then remembered it was Davie's testimony, along with Donnie's set-up, that had helped land him in the jail.

'Well, can't say I disagree, Davie. Now that you've done a job for Donnie, don't expect it to be the last. You're in it for life now. You'll never get away from him unless he ends up doing away with you. Suppose that's your sentence for putting an innocent man away.'

Davie's eyes glazed over as he stood against the windowsill. The pang of guilt had dispersed now, and all Kev felt for the lad was pity. He'd got himself into such a mess with Donnie, and he had no way of backing himself up. At least with Kev, he had his family behind him.

'Good luck, Davie. You're going to need it.'

Chapter Thirty-One

Tam was the first to arrive at the yard aside from the guy who always manned the gate. Crater face let him in, and he drove towards the Portacabin, where he parked up. He'd been summoned by Donnie to arrive at no later than midday and that he'd be met by Donnie himself and Steff, who would send him on the next job. Tam prayed that it wasn't another escort job to a death site.

Tam got out of his car and headed across the yard towards the gate, like he'd been told to do. When he reached the entrance, Crater face turned to him and handed him a piece of paper.

'A note from the boss,' he said, his voice deep and hoarse.

Tam found it hard to believe that Donnie was this guy's boss. By the looks of him, he could crush Donnie's skull with just one hand.

'Cheers,' Tam said, taking the note from him and opening it.

'How'd you get this job then, wee man?'

Tam glanced up at Crater face, surprised that he had more than two words to say. On the two occasions that Tam had been in his company, all he'd done was nod.

'I met Steff Black in the pub, and he offered me cash in hand for odd jobs.' Tam hesitated and then asked, 'How did you end up working for the Blacks?'

Crater face raised a brow. 'I've known Donnie and Steff my whole life. We went to school together.'

'So what? You're their security or something?'

Another nod. 'Aye. I don't let anyone past that hasn't been approved. If anyone tries to get by without my prior knowledge…'

Tam stared at him, waited for him to finish but he didn't have to. Tam got the gist of what he meant.

'I don't know the nature of what goes on in there. All I know is I'm paid to stand here and keep guard.'

Tam said nothing, although he doubted that was the truth. How could the security guy not know what went on?

'I'm Chud, by the way.'

'Tam.'

Tam studied his face a little, and could have sworn he recognised him, but couldn't place him.

They remained silent as they stood awaiting Donnie and Steff's arrival. Tam opened the envelope in his hand, and when he looked inside, he saw eight hundred in notes and a piece of paper. Taking out the message, he read it.

> *Advance payment of the next job. If you complete this, your wage will increase.*

He felt Chud's eyes on him but kept his head down.

'Just a word of warning, wee man, keep on their good side. You'll do yourself a good turn if you just do what they say.'

Tam felt the hairs on the back of his neck stand on end, and he cleared his throat. Neither man looked at one another as they waited for Donnie to arrive, but Tam sensed that Chud knew the meaning of his words. Had he crossed Donnie before, ended up on the wrong side of him? Or had he witnessed someone else who had?

A car approached the gate, and Chud stood to the side to let it pass. It was Steff, looking smug with himself as though he knew he had Tam right where he wanted him. There was no way that Tam could turn down that sort of cash. He guessed he'd already done the worst kind of job in driving that guy to be murdered by them. How much worse could it get?

Donnie was quick to arrive after Steff, and then Chud gestured for Tam to move into the yard while he closed the gates. Tam was inside, on his own, with two of the most dangerous men he'd ever come across and it scared the shit out of him.

'Tam,' Steff said, getting out of his car and moving towards him. 'How's it going?'

Tam nodded, 'Aye, no bad. So, what's this job?'

'Chud gave you the envelope then?' Donnie said, approaching him.

Tam patted the pocket of his jeans where he'd put the money and the note.

'Good. It's good to have a young lad like you on board. No questions asked, just get the job done and on to the next.'

The words that left Donnie's mouth were a warning, Tam knew that. And he took it; there was no way he was going to challenge these two.

'Right, I'm going to give you an address and I want you to go there. When you arrive, you'll meet a guy called Goran. He'll give you an envelope with cash inside, and a key to another vehicle. You've to bring them both back. Got it?' Donnie said with a raised brow, as though expecting Tam to protest.

He didn't.

'And I've to go when?' Tam asked, glancing across at the van on the opposite side of the yard.

'The delivery will be ready in an hour. So just hang about and we'll give you a shout. And you don't need to know the nature of the delivery. Just straight there and straight back, got it?'

'Fine by me.'

–

An hour had passed, and another. Tam had been waiting by the gate, standing next to Chud. At least it was dry and Tam wasn't being paid to stand in the pissing rain all day, like Chud possibly was.

He wondered what Chud's story was, and decided that he would ask him one day, if he had enough balls to do so. He didn't seem as scary as Tam initially thought, having spoken to him earlier.

'Oi, Chud?' Steff called from inside the yard. 'Need your strength, mate.'

Tam turned, glanced at the security man whose expression seemed to fall a little. It was like he couldn't be bothered, or didn't want to go in. Tam wanted to know what he was delivering, but eight hundred quid in cash in his pocket at that precise moment kept him from prodding around in an area that he had been warned off.

'Sounds like you'll be ready to go in a few minutes, wee man,' Chud said before opening the gate and heading inside the yard, but not before closing Tam out. Whatever the delivery, Donnie, Steff and Chud really didn't want Tam to know about it.

He strained to listen as he heard a shuffling of shoes on gravel. Van doors slamming closed. Approaching footsteps.

The gate was pulled open, and Chud took his place at the gate again. 'Donnie's ready for you.'

Tam turned and went back into the yard, towards the van. It was different to the first one he'd driven, smaller. Whatever was in the back, it was smaller than the body he'd transported the last time. Thankfully. Could possibly be drugs this time, or stolen goods? He didn't care this time, so long as it wasn't a human.

'Here,' Steff said, handing a set of keys over to Tam. 'Here's the address. There's a satnav in the van. Goran is expecting you. Like Donnie said, when you get there, he'll give you an envelope and keys to another vehicle. Come straight here and drop both off.'

Tam nodded.

'Good lad, Tam. Like that little message stated in that envelope, you do this well and your wages will increase.' Steff held out a hand, and Tam took it. 'Right, on you go. You've got a long drive ahead of you. There's snacks and stuff in the passenger seat.'

Tam frowned, looked down at the address. 'I'm going to Stranraer?'

'Aye. It's two hours there and two hours back. Problem?'

'No, I just didn't think I'd be travelling that far.'

'That's nothing, wee man. If you can pull this one off, you'll be going a lot further than that,' Steff said.

Tam hesitated, but Steff kept his eyes on him, silently warning him to get in the van. He climbed in and started the engine, typed the address into the satnav and headed out of the yard.

Whatever was in the back of the van was clearly going on the ferry to Ireland.

Chapter Thirty-Two

'He's a liar, Susie. I just know it,' Layla said into the phone.

'Oh, come on now, Layla. Steff is your brother-in-law. You really think he'd lie to your face like that?'

Layla sighed. She wanted to believe that Steff was as loyal to her as he was Donnie, but she knew that wasn't the case. There was no stronger bond than blood. It was just a shame that Layla hadn't worked that out earlier with Kerry. She might still be alive if she had.

'Yes, I do think he'd lie to my face like that because Steff and Donnie are brothers. He'd never tell me if Donnie was having an affair. It's called family loyalty.'

She heard Susie's empathetic tones from the other end of the line and cringed at how desperate she sounded.

'Why don't you leave then? If you're *that* unhappy, just go.'

'I still love him, Susie. More now than I did then. It's just that, well, when I drink it doesn't come across like that.'

'Stop drinking then?'

Layla stifled a laugh. It wasn't as though she hadn't tried. Every day she told herself that she would stop tomorrow. Tomorrow never came in that respect. Alcohol numbed her from the guilt of what happened to Kerry, and the pain from knowing that Donnie didn't love her anymore.

'That's interesting, coming from a woman who owns a pub.'

'That's neither here nor there, Layla. Look, I don't mean to cut you short but I have to go. My taxi will be here to collect me soon to take me to the airport. I've left spare keys at the salon with Darcie. You don't have to go to the house to check things. There's an alarm system for anything untoward. The cows in the field next to it should scare any intruders away.' She laughed. 'I just like knowing that someone can get in if there's an emergency.'

'The good old cows,' Layla laughed. 'Aye, that's fine, Susie. Enjoy your holiday. Three weeks?'

'A month this time. I am spending time with the grandkids out there. Can't wait to just be with the family for a while, away from the shitty weather. I mean, the kids love that I live in a big old farmhouse in the middle of nowhere, but the weather just doesn't match up to that Canary sunshine.'

Layla smiled, wished she could go with Susie, get away from the life she was living. As much as she loved Donnie, she knew that their marriage was over. It had been a long time ago, even if she felt she loved him too much to leave him.

'Look,' Susie said, bringing Layla back from her thoughts, 'why don't you just talk to Donnie? Maybe that's the problem; you haven't spoken to each other about why things have gone so sour. I bet things would get better, and you may even get to the bottom of your suspicions.'

Layla nodded. Susie was right, she did have to talk to Donnie. And that was exactly what she was going to do.

'And if you ever need a friend, or a place to stay until you sort things out, I'm here for you, Layla.'

Layla smiled gratefully. 'Thanks, Susie.'

Layla hung up the phone and stared down at the handset in her hand. She'd told herself over and over that she still loved Donnie. But was she still in love with him? There was only one way to find out. She had to talk to him. Sober.

—

Stepping inside the house, she felt her nerves take over. This discussion could go one of two ways. It could bond them or end them. Layla truly had no idea which was the easier option. They'd been together since forever. Had love turned to habit? It was possible.

Layla removed her shoes and went through to the kitchen, where Donnie was sitting. He had a bottle of beer in front of him and his phone in his hands. Scrolling aimlessly so he didn't have to speak to her, no doubt.

'Hi,' Layla said. 'Can we talk?'

Donnie looked up from his phone, an expectant look on his face. Maybe he didn't have anything to say.

'First of all, I want to start by apologising for the way I've been behaving over the last few...' she stopped. 'Weeks. Months even. I shouldn't speak to you the way I do when I have a drink in me. So, I'm sorry.'

She expected Donnie's expression to soften a little with her apology, but it didn't so she continued. 'Things have been, well, awful between us for so long now and I think there needs to be a change.'

He nodded, again no verbal response. Layla was beginning to feel frustrated but she didn't want to show it, otherwise the conversation would turn into yet another argument.

'So, what do you think?'

'Aye,' he replied. 'I think you're right. There does need to be a change between us.'

Layla felt a weight lift from her shoulders then. Before he could say anything else, she started again.

'I mean, I know things have been bad but I think we can save this, save us. But we need to talk it out. We need to be able to trust each other again, Donnie. We need to get back to the way things used to be between us, like in the early days. You know?'

Donnie remained silent, and Layla kept talking. 'I mean, I know that things started to go wrong before Kerry was killed. She never trusted you or Steff. It was always the reason we argued, wasn't it? She would throw around accusations and spout vile shit about you. I'd always be stuck in the middle. She was my sister, like Steff is your brother. There's a loyalty there that needs to be honoured. But now that Kerry's gone, I need to let things go. I can forget what happened, I really think I can. I think we can start again. Make this work. I'm not saying I can forget my sister, but I'll stop drinking. I'll stop holding her death against you and move on. I'll stop the wild ideas of you cheating on me. I promise.'

She reached across the table, took his hands in hers. Donnie glanced down and reversed the grip. Layla smiled, but her impending happiness was replaced by horror as Donnie gripped her left hand with a force that made her cry out. He began tugging at her wedding ring and pulled it roughly from her finger.

'Donnie, what are you doing?' She winced, staring down at the ring in his hand.

'It's always about Kerry. Always about her, never about me. Layla, we're done. You ruined this, and I can't actually remember any of the reasons why I ever married you.

You're not the Layla you were back then. You're a drunk, a nag and I'm fucking sick of listening to you. Everything you just said, it's too late. So, this' – he held up the ring – 'will be your divorce settlement. When I get the cash for it, you can take it and fuck off. You can stay here until you find somewhere else to live.'

Donnie got to his feet, took a long swig from the beer bottle before shoving the ring into his back pocket and turning to leave.

'Donnie, wait. We can make this work!' Her voice was screechy, and she felt utterly pathetic almost immediately after saying it.

'No, we can't. You're out. I don't want you in my life anymore, Layla. You're frying my nut with the constant accusations of cheating, how it's my fault Kerry died. I've let it go on for too long now.'

Layla froze, couldn't move. Her finger ached from where he'd ripped the ring from its place. She watched him leave, grab his jacket from the hallway and head for the door, and an anger began to burn in her stomach. One that usually came after she'd been drinking.

'You're a fucking bastard, Donnie. I hope you rot in hell!'

'I know you do, Layla.'

The door slammed shut, making her jump. And then her legs gave out from beneath her and she fell to the kitchen floor. Loud sobs escaped her throat as she listened to Donnie's car roar down the drive. She'd thought talking things through with Donnie would be better than Steff's advice to follow him. Turns out that wasn't the case. He'd been the one to initiate a divorce. She'd be left with nothing.

Chapter Thirty-Three

'You're serious? You've told her you're leaving?' Louise asked, staring at Donnie.

'Well, I told her to leave. It's my house.' Donnie smiled widely at her, and it made her heart flutter. 'I told her she could stay there until she sorted something out for herself. But she's out.'

'I can't believe you did it. Did you tell her about me?'

'No. It's none of her business. No offence, Lou, but you're not the only reason I've broken it off with my wife. You're just a bonus factor in it all.'

He leaned over and kissed her, and Louise felt like all her Christmases and birthdays had come at once. She didn't think he'd actually do it. Kissing him back, Louise let her imagination go further than she'd ever allowed it before. A future with Donnie could be on the cards. He might want her to move in with him, and all the things that came with that. She might be young, but she knew that she was in love with Donnie and that she wanted to be with him, no matter what that meant.

'You're happy?' Donnie asked.

'Ecstatic, Donnie. You've no idea. This is so exciting. So, what's next for us?' she asked, almost in one breath.

She watched as Donnie's brow furrowed. 'What do you mean?'

'Well, you've told your wife you don't want to be with her anymore. So where does that leave us?'

'It leaves us right here. We don't need to rush this. Let's just have fun and see where it goes.' Donnie squeezed Louise's hand, and she tried to hide the disappointment from her face.

'Have you ever wanted to travel the world, Louise? Work in different countries and cultures, see what's really out there in the world?' Donnie asked as he tucked a lock of hair behind her ear. His touch set her skin alight.

'I've never thought about it. But I suppose I could go to the moon with you and I wouldn't care.'

Donnie smiled before cupping her chin and pulling her in for a kiss.

She let him. She'd let him do anything he wanted with her if it meant she could be with him.

Chapter Thirty-Four

Kev Barclay stood outside the pub and finished the last of his cigarette before heading inside.

Kev dropped the cigarette onto the pavement, crushed it with his foot and headed inside to the bar where he ordered a pint. He'd have something stronger once the deal was done.

Sitting down at a table in the far corner of the pub, he kept an eye on the front door, willing it to open and for his mates to come flooding through. Just seconds later, that's exactly what happened.

'Barclay! Good to see you out of that shithole,' Cammy shouted from the bar with a huge grin on his face. Kev got to his feet as the other three, Dunny, Mackie and Thomson approached the table. They each shook his hand, gave him a bear hug and slapped him on the back.

'Good to see you, boys,' Kev said as they all sat down.

Cammy appeared at the table with a tray of drinks and he too sat down.

'Thought we'd have seen you sooner than this, cuz,' Cammy said.

'Ah, you know how it is. Got to get some time in with the missus first.' Kev smiled, and the boys laughed.

'How's it going?' Kev asked Cammy.

'Well, as you know we halted the boxing when you went away. But we have gained some new security accounts, just pubs and clubs, a few snooker halls. Got some new guys punting for us out of those places too, so we're making good money. Donnie's been surprisingly quiet. We thought he'd have wanted a fight for territory. But it would seem he has other ventures on his mind at the moment.'

'Things aren't great, Kev. Word has it there's a fucking trafficking ring on the go in the city. All girls fair game, from as young as fifteen,' Dunny interjected.

'Aye,' Mackie said, taking a pint from the tray and taking a large gulp. 'We've got one of those police scanners and the shit you hear on that thing is unreal.'

Kev blew out a mouthful of air. 'That's fucking heavy, boys.'

'Aye,' Cammy said. 'Apart from that, business is good. Can't complain.'

'Good to hear.' Kev smiled. 'So, you think the trafficking shit is to do with Donnie?'

Cammy frowned. 'It's why we left. The business was going in that direction and we wanted nothing to do with it. And because we left, we shut the door on any information on it. Donnie Black is capable of a lot of things, but I didn't think he was truly capable of that shit.'

Kev gave a breathy, sarcastic laugh. 'That fucker is capable of anything. I think we should be keeping a much closer eye on him, boys. Also, I want him to pay for what he did to me. To the Firm. We're not just going to let him get away with that, are we?'

Cammy shook his head and downed his drink. 'Are we fuck letting him get away with it. We were just waiting on you getting out.'

'So, what you got in mind for our old pal Donnie?' Mackie asked.

'I don't know, but it'll be fucking good, that's for sure,' Kev replied, finishing off his pint. 'He left my Darcie to fend for herself. If it wasn't for you boys, she'd have been left in the shit. One thing you don't do is fuck with someone's family.'

Cammy and the rest of the boys nodded.

'But whatever we do decide, we wait. Ignorance needs to be as blissful as possible for old Donnie boy. The quieter we are, the less he'll expect anything untoward. So let him get on with things for now, we'll get to him. Don't you worry about that, Kev. That bastard will be sorry he ever laid eyes on any of us,' Cammy said. 'Good to have my main man back, Kev.'

They all drank in agreement, and Kev looked around the bar, saw that the rest of the punters had gone quiet. When the Barrhouse Firm were present, no one wanted to do or say anything that would send trouble their way. Kev didn't want to hurt anyone, neither did the rest of the lads. But knowing that they had a presence was good for word of mouth. Donnie would soon hear that the Barrhouse Firm were back together and complete again.

Kev felt right at home now, back where he belonged. He should never have gone away in the first place.

Chapter Thirty-Five

There was nothing like a pint on a Friday night, especially when the Barrhouse Firm were in. Although that also usually meant that trouble was lurking in the shadows. Tonight was no different. It was in the air and everyone knew it, but the question was, just what kind of scenario would play out?

Cammy, Mackie, Dunny, Thomson and Kev stood around the pool table and the dart board, drinking their pints and having a good old session, while the rest of the locals kept to their own groups.

'Yer a fucking cheat.' Cammy threw his last dart at the board in a rage.

Kev laughed. 'How the hell can anyone cheat at darts? You can either throw, or you can't.'

Cammy downed the rest of his pint and sat the glass down on the edge of the pool table before his rage turned to humour. 'Aye, I'm shit at throwing darts but I can throw one hell of a fucking punch, so shut yer face, Kev.'

Kev laughed again and held his hands up in mock defeat.

'Good to have you back, Kev,' Cammy said, and the rest of the boys started to laugh.

'You're a fucking big wimp, Cammy. Missed yer cousin, did ye?' Thomson mocked, petting his lip.

Before Cammy or Kev could answer, the door at the front of the pub opened and, like something out of an old western film, the pub fell silent. The singing stopped, the music dropped off from the speakers, and Donnie Black, along with Steff Black, stood side by side. Chud, an ex-mate of the Firm and now one of their security men, stood directly behind them, peering through the gap between their heads.

'Two pints,' Donnie said to the barmaid without looking at her. The sound of her taking a glass from the shelf above and pouring the pint was deafening as the place remained silent.

'Let's go,' Kev said to Cammy quietly.

'Nah. This is our fucking pub. They can crawl back to their own shithole if they want a drink,' Cammy said loudly.

Donnie glared at Cammy and then Kev before letting out a snigger. People around them started to get up from their seats and began heading for the door. For the normal, everyday punter the night was over.

'See you got out then,' Donnie said, raising a brow at Kev.

'You're not blind, then?' Kev remarked, his sarcasm laced with rage.

Soon, the pub was empty, except for staff and a couple of regulars. Tough old guys, born and bred in the Barrhouse area.

'You're out early, though. I heard you paid Davie a visit. How's he doing after you lot done him in?' Donnie asked.

'Don't know what you're on about,' Kev replied.

The sound of pool balls being potted made Donnie's eyes flicker towards Mackie, Dunny and Thomson, who were now inching closer to Kev and Cammy, and as Kev turned in their direction they were all holding pool cues across their bodies.

'You spitting the dummy about having to do some jail time for what you did?'

Steff Black eyed the boys with the cues but didn't say a word, didn't move. That was brave of him, Kev thought. They didn't appear armed, and there were five of them against three. Although Chud was a big lad, he would be a lot slower to attack if it came to it. Kev wondered if Chud would fight against his old mates.

'Do yourself a favour, Black, and fuck off back to your yard. No one around here wants you near them. We all know what you and Steff get up to. Trafficking isn't something this city is going to put up with, and especially not from the likes of you,' Mackie called out across the pub, as if ensuring that his voice was loud enough that the remaining punters would hear it and think twice about sticking around.

Donnie and Steff laughed loudly, and Chud only blinked. Maybe he didn't know what or who he was working for?

'You know what happened to the McAdams, don't you?' Cammy said. 'You want to go down that same path?'

Steff took a step forward, as did Chud. Kev felt the tension in the air shift as the boys next to him raised their cues. This was going to turn nasty and it would happen quickly. Kev hoped that Donnie wasn't armed. From what Kev could remember when working with him, he liked to pull his gun out on any occasion, just to show that he was a hard nut. In truth, Kev knew that the only reason Donnie would pull that gun was because he didn't have another card to play. He was a big boy but wasn't the type to get his hands dirty in a fight; he'd rather leave that to his mates to do for him. He was a nasty bastard and he'd shoot anyone before getting into a fist fight.

'I'll phone the polis if you boys don't take this outside,' the barmaid said.

Cammy glanced at her, gave a reassuring nod, and Kev felt like his chest was going to explode. Donnie was standing right in front of him and all he wanted to do was smash a cue right over his head. He'd set Kev up for something he didn't do. Donnie Black was bottom of the barrel scum, and everyone around the city knew it, even the politicians and the charity workers he shook hands with. But he was their direct line to some serious money. The only people willing to take them on were Kev and the rest of the lads.

'Donnie, if you want a fucking war with the Barrhouse Firm, then you can have one,' Cammy said. 'To be honest, I expected this sooner.'

'Aye, and don't think we're a bunch of fucking pussies, Donnie. We'll cut your throat in your sleep,' Dunny said, turning and pulling a dart from the board before lobbing it in the direction of their rivals. It flew past Donnie's right ear and hit the door behind him, spearing itself in the wood. Donnie didn't seem to flinch.

'Is that right?' Donnie turned, pulled the dart from the door and slid it into his jacket. 'We'll see about that, won't we?'

Steff hadn't moved. Neither had Chud. But before Kev knew what was happening, Mackie had cracked his cue against the table and was launching himself forward at Donnie and Steff, who were now on their way out the door.

Cammy was after Mackie now, and Kev behind him. They were through the door, out on the street. A loud popping sound pierced Kev's ears, and a car shot off in the distance with Mackie chasing after it. Mackie launched the pool cue into the air and it hit the back window.

'The Barrhouse Firm will fucking destroy you, Black, you fucking hear me?' Mackie shouted as loud as he could.

The car came to a halt, and Kev noticed one of the passenger windows lowering. They all knew what was coming and, as quickly as they could, Kev and the rest of the lads dived behind a parked van as shots rang out.

'Mackie, you tool. We're not fucking armed,' Cammy shouted as they took cover. But Mackie was too high on coke to take any notice; he was too busy laughing like a maniac.

Silence fell with the delayed echo of shots ringing out in the distance. The car was gone, and Kev's heart banged hard in his chest.

Kev knew this wasn't just about him, or the fact that Donnie was pissed that he'd got out of jail early. Donnie wanted to shut him and the rest of the lads up, and the only way to do that was to start and finish a war.

'Jesus Christ, Mackie!'

Dunny's voice made Kev look up to see that Mackie had been hit. His lower right arm poured with blood as he sat on the ground, his back to the van.

'I'm fine,' he replied, although Kev could see that he wasn't fine. His face had turned a terrible shade of grey, and his manic laughter had died out.

Cammy got to his feet and went to Mackie, helping him to his feet. 'It's superficial, I think.'

'Easy for you to say, you're not the one with a fucking hole in your arm.' Mackie winced.

Curtains from nearby windows twitched, and Kev glanced up at them. People had seen what happened but would never own up to it. No one around the Barrhouse area would want to get involved with what had just happened.

'If Donnie Black wants a fucking shoot out, he can have one,' Mackie hissed as Cammy led him back towards the pub.

Dunny and Thomson followed behind as Cammy and Kev helped Mackie inside the pub. The barmaid glanced up at them, her eyes wide with terror.

'Oh my god,' she said.

'It's all right, Jenny,' Cammy replied. 'Just get us a whisky and the first aid kit.'

She hesitated, as if unable to move. 'He needs a hospital.'

'No,' Kev replied. 'He needs the first aid kit. And a whisky, like Cam said. And chuck us down a clean towel while you're at it.'

She did as she was told, and Mackie sat down at a table next to the bar. Kev caught the towel and gently wrapped it around Mackie's arm.

Darcie's face entered Kev's mind then. All of their women would be in danger of Donnie Black harming them. That was his style. Kev would have to tell her what happened, and she would be livid with him. All Darcie said she'd wanted was a quiet life when he got out. But Kev knew that wasn't going to happen. Not until Donnie was dead.

'We're going to end that bastard, Kev,' Cammy said, as if hearing his thoughts. 'I fucking swear to it.'

Chapter Thirty-Six

Steff had his foot to the floor, Donnie in the passenger seat and Chud in the back. He hadn't expected the Barrhouse boys to be so irate, but he couldn't say he was surprised either. He and Donnie had fucked Kev Barclay over, had him sent away for something that he wasn't directly responsible for. There were a lot of young lads out there just like him, either in the jail or out and living their lives on the quiet because they'd rather not come across Donnie or Steff again, in case they were dragged into something that would see them back inside. None of them had ever come back and faced Donnie, confronted him. Kev and the rest of the Barrhouse boys were the first.

'Fucking bastards,' Donnie hissed as he lit a cigarette. 'If I'd known Kev Barclay was going to be this much of a pussy, I'd have had him sent away for murder.'

Steff shook his head. 'This could be a problem for us, Donnie. You heard what they said back there. They're not the type to just sit back and say nothing.'

Donnie shot Steff a sidelong glance, unblinking. 'We know who they are, Steff. They used to run with us before they got too big for their boots. What you so worried about?'

'I didn't say I was worried. All I'm saying is they're a distraction. They'll get in the way of business and lose us money.'

Donnie's expression softened a little, as though realising that Steff was right.

'They want a war with us, Donnie. Do you think we're prepared for that?'

'Are we fucking prepared for that?' Donnie laughed loudly. Steff didn't share his humour. This was a lot more serious than Donnie was giving it credit for. 'Like I said, Steff, those bastards back there are small time compared to us. They want to go up against gangsters then they can have their fucking war, but I'm telling you they won't win. You think Goran and his crew are going to stand back and allow them to get in the way?'

Steff sighed inwardly. He knew what Goran was like, the calm before the storm. If he knew that Donnie was at war with what was effectively a street gang, he might just pull the plug on the deal with Steff and Donnie, go elsewhere.

Before Steff could voice his thoughts, Donnie started. 'In fact, you know what? Turn this fucking car around and go back. If you think they're that big of a problem, let's go back and fucking finish them off right now.' Donnie was looking in the side mirror, his eyes wide, taking his gun back out of his pocket. 'I hit one of them back there. Let's go and put a bullet in every one of the wee fuckers.'

'Aye, good idea, Donnie. Let's go and make the street a bloodbath. That won't have the polis crawling the streets. Are you off your fucking nut?' Steff replied. 'I'm taking you back to yours.'

'No, you won't take me home. Just drop me off at the yard. I've got stuff to do; I'll sleep there.'

'Why would you do that? Just go home afterwards.'

Donnie shook his head. 'I've left her, Steff. She's a fucking pain in the arse drunk. She's staying there while she gets her shit together.'

Steff tried to hide the delight from his face. 'Wow. Have to say, Donnie, I didn't see that coming.'

'Fuck it. I've more important things to get on with.'

Steff felt like he was hitting a brick wall. Donnie was often impossible. But he was also his brother. But above all else, they were business partners. That was what their old man had always taught them. Family and business together can be tricky. You have to trust each other and stick together, even if you don't agree sometimes.

'Whatever, Donnie. Just do us all a favour, eh? Keep the head. Those lads will be expecting some backlash. If we just keep things going, business as usual, they'll get complacent and that's when we can deal with them.'

Steff pulled up outside the yard, allowing Donnie to get out. Chud got out too, tapped on the roof of the car and closed the door. Good security man, but never did say much. Steff watched as Chud opened up the yard and allowed Donnie access first, before going in and closing the gate behind him.

'Fucking idiot,' Steff whispered before pulling away from the yard.

When he thought about Goran finding out about the Barrhouse Firm, he wondered if it might be a good thing. Goran might actually decide to get rid of them all, especially if they weren't going to be good for business. And the Barrhouse Firm didn't know anything about Goran, as far as Steff was aware. So they wouldn't see him coming. Pitting the Barrhouse Firm against Goran and his men wasn't something that had crossed Steff's mind until now. It was something Donnie should have thought of, but his brother wasn't clever enough for that it would seem. Steff decided to keep that option in mind. Just in case he needed to use it. It could be the perfect way to get rid of Kev and Cammy. And the rest of them.

Chapter Thirty-Seven

It was two in the morning and Darcie had been waiting for Kev to come home from the pub. When he hadn't shown just after closing, she began worrying about him. But she knew that if he was with Cammy and the rest of them, chances were that Kev would be fine. And he wasn't some daft little kid; he was a man who could look after himself. At least, that's what she told herself to try to keep calm.

When she finally heard the key in the door, she remained in bed, listening for the sound of shoes coming off, the bathroom light clicking on, the flush of a toilet. Instead, silence followed when Kev closed the door. Darcie got out of bed and went out to the hallway to find Kev standing by the door, removing his coat quietly.

'You okay?' she said before seeing the bloodstains on his shirt. Her eyes widened in fear, all sorts running through her head. 'What's that?' Darcie pointed at the stains.

'Mackie got shot.' Kev's voice was low, calm. It set Darcie's stomach into motion. 'He's fine, before you start panicking. We're all fine.'

'What the fuck do you mean, he got shot? Who did it?'

'Take a wild fucking guess.'

Darcie felt a surge of adrenaline course through her veins and something inside escaped her throat, a cry that made Kev go to her.

'It's okay, Darcie.'

'How is it okay? It's far from okay. Is Mackie in hospital? Is he dead?'

'I already told you he's fine. It's superficial. Mackie chucked a pool cue at his car after it happened.' Kev smiled a little as he pulled Darcie in close.

How could he think this was funny? Donnie Black knew Kev was out, had attacked Mackie. Maybe he hadn't meant to shoot Mackie. Maybe that bullet was meant for Kev and he'd missed, hit Mackie by accident. If that was the case, then Donnie would want another shot at his target. She couldn't deal with all of this again. Donnie Black scared the hell out of her, and now that he knew Kev was out, he would only try to torment them more. He was a sick bastard who would take great pleasure in hurting people. She'd heard the rumours about him and Steff Black. People were scared of them, and no one said a word about them for fear of reprisal. The scariest thing about them was their clean-cut appearance. In the papers and all over the internet, shaking hands with politicians, doing community charity work and investing in care homes. Anyone who couldn't see past that was blind.

'Kev, I can't live like this. What if this doesn't stop until someone is dead?'

She allowed him to take her in his arms. She wanted to feel safe with him but having found out what had just gone down at the local, Darcie didn't know if she could feel safe ever again.

'Look, you won't have to live like anything. Cammy and the rest of us, we're sorting it. Donnie Black won't reign for much longer. He thinks he's a gangster, but he's nothing but a fucking cardboard cut-out.'

'Kev, I don't want you anywhere near them, for good or bad reason. If you want this relationship to work, then you have to promise me you'll stay away from them. If Cammy and the rest of them want to deal with Donnie then let them. But you don't have to be a part of it.'

Kev didn't say anything, only held her closer. Darcie wanted to believe that Kev would do what she wanted, but she knew that being one of the Barrhouse Firm, knowing what Donnie did to Kev, she knew it was unlikely.

'Promise me that you'll stay away from him. You're just out of prison for something you didn't do. I don't want you having to go away again for killing a bastard like Donnie Black.'

Kev held her at arm's length and nodded. 'I promise.'

—

Sitting behind the desk at the sunbed shop, Darcie stifled a yawn. She'd barely slept since Kev had arrived home only hours earlier, and the thought of what happened continued to swirl around inside her head like some nightmarish merry-go-round.

Darcie glanced up as she heard the door open, and was surprised to see her boss, Layla, enter the shop. Her face was paler than normal, with very little to no make-up on. That wasn't like her.

'Oh, hi. I didn't expect to see you for a while,' Darcie said, forcing herself to sound chirpier than she felt.

'Just thought I'd come in and see how things were going. Not much else to get on with, really.'

Darcie sensed how Layla's expression was flat, matching her tone. That, coupled with the fact that she looked like she was at death's door, seemed very strange. Layla was usually so chatty, smiley.

'Fine with me. You want a cuppa?'

'Anything stronger back there?'

Darcie shook her head. 'No, sorry. Are you all right?'

Layla removed her jacket and slung it down on one of the chairs in the waiting area, before glancing down at the phone in her hand.

'Layla? What's wrong?'

Layla's eyes glistened, and she looked like she was going to throw up.

'Here.' Darcie got up from her seat behind the desk and moved around it. She took Layla by the crook of her elbow and guided her towards a chair. 'Sit down, you look like you're going to pass out or something.'

Layla allowed Darcie to help and she slouched back on one of the chairs. 'It's all such a mess.'

'What's such a mess?'

'It's my husband. He's left me.'

Darcie felt her brow raise in shock, but she tried to keep her expression composed.

'The bastard. He's nothing but a self-centred, arrogant, cocky bastard.' Tears poured down from her eyes, but her tone didn't match the sadness in them. Her voice was laced with a venom Darcie hadn't ever heard in Layla before.

'I'm sorry, Layla.'

'He's always been a prick, always. I just tried to block it out. My sister tried to tell me years ago not to be with him, and I didn't listen. I'm such a stupid bitch.'

'You're not. Sometimes the heart just doesn't listen to what's good for us,' Darcie replied, still in shock that her boss was opening up to her like this. Maybe she didn't have many friends, other than Susie.

Darcie gave Layla's hand a squeeze and didn't know what else to say. What could she say?

'Shall I go across to the pub and buy a bottle?'

Layla furiously wiped at the tears and took a breath. 'No, I've drank enough of that shit because of him.'

'Fair enough,' Darcie replied.

'And I need a clear head with this. He thinks he can treat me the way he treats everyone else?' Layla spat. 'He might be able to treat everyone else like shit, but I'm not taking it from him. Donnie Black, pfft, he thinks he's the fucking mafia or something.'

Darcie froze. Had she heard that right? *Donnie Black?* As if reading her thoughts, Layla frowned at her.

'What's wrong?'

'You're married to Donnie Black?'

'I take it by that look you've heard of my husband?'

Darcie took a steadying breath. What was she supposed to say to that? She couldn't very well tell her about Kev, or what had happened at the pub the previous night. And going by the fact that Darcie had been working for Layla, it would seem that she had no idea that her husband put Kev away for something he didn't do.

'I've heard of him, yes.'

'The whole city knows him, and he thrives on that. He never used to be like this. He was a good guy when I met him. The power just…' she paused. 'Went to his head I suppose.'

Darcie felt sick. The idea that she'd been working for Layla for so long, without having the faintest idea that she was married to that monster, made her want to throw up. How could she have been so blind? So stupid?

'You never mentioned him before. Donnie, I mean,' Darcie said, her throat feeling drier with every second.

'My business, the shops, are in my maiden name. Although he owns them, so when we divorce it's likely I'll lose the lot.'

Darcie let out a slow and steady breath.

A rush of relief took over when the phone rang. As Darcie was about to answer it, Layla got up and moved towards it.

'I'll get it, if you don't mind? I need a distraction. Why don't you have a break?'

Darcie smiled at her boss and got to her feet. Pushing the door away from her, she stepped outside and allowed the door to close behind her.

What in the *actual* fuck was she supposed to do now?

—

He pulled up outside the shop and left the engine running.

He watched from across the car park as Darcie came out of the shop, but she wasn't alone. Another woman appeared and when Kev saw her face, something inside him surged and he sat forward to get a better look. His eyes weren't deceiving him. The woman with Darcie was Donnie Black's wife, Layla Black.

Kev unclipped his belt and threw the car door open before getting out. He strode across the car park, a rage burning in his throat, but before he could say anything, Layla was already in her car and pulling out of the precinct. Darcie was still locking up the shop when Kev reached her.

'Oh,' she said, turning to face him. 'I wasn't expecting to see you here.'

Her smile softened the rage inside him, but it didn't stop him from wanting to know why she was with Layla Black.

'What the fuck was she doing in the shop?' Kev said, motioning towards Layla's car in the distance.

Darcie's face paled, her expression falling as her eyes followed his. 'Look, let's not do this here.'

'Why was she here? Does she know who you are? Did Donnie send her to threaten you or something?'

Darcie took Kev's hands in hers and stood close, staring into his eyes before pulling him away from the front of the shop towards the car park.

Kev didn't want to get into things in the middle of the precinct, so he moved with Darcie, decided that it would be better for them to have the conversation in private. Now his stomach churned as all sorts of thoughts went through his head. Was Donnie watching them right now?

They got into the car and Darcie sighed, shook her head and stared out of the windscreen. 'You're never going to believe this, but I've literally only just found out today that she is married to Donnie. But that's not the worst thing. She's my boss.'

Kev felt his jaw fall open, but the words in his head wouldn't reach his tongue.

'I swear to god, I had absolutely no idea, Kev. She doesn't refer to herself as Layla Black, otherwise I'd maybe have made the connection.'

Kev cleared his throat. 'How did you not know? I mean, did you not recognise her?'

'I can't recognise someone I don't know, Kev. I'd never seen her before I started working there after you went away. But thanks, it's nice to know you believe me.'

Darcie grabbed the door handle, but Kev anticipated the move and hit the lock button.

She turned, stared through him. 'Let me out. I don't want to be near you if you don't trust me.'

'I never said I don't trust you, Darcie. I believe you. It's just hard to process, that's all. You have to understand that this is mad to me. My girlfriend is working for the wife of a guy who set me up. And what if he shows up to the shop while you're working? He could do something to you to get to me.'

'But he doesn't know who I am.'

'That's not really a chance I'm willing to take.'

Silence hung heavy between them, before Darcie sighed, took Kev's hand and said, 'I'll quit. I don't want to be around her if there's a possibility that he could show up.'

Kev was relieved that he didn't have to suggest Darcie quitting. He wouldn't put it past Donnie to hurt Darcie, just to show his power.

'But if I'm going to quit the shop, then you need to do something for me in return. If we're going to have a future together, Kev, you're going to have to pull away from this life. No more Firm, no more fighting and being in a gang. I need a quiet life. I can't handle looking over my shoulder, wondering what's going to happen next.'

Kev nodded. He loved Darcie more than anything; he would do whatever it took to be with her. 'Fine. Consider it done.'

Kev felt guilty for lying. He had to get Donnie off the streets before he'd feel safe to get on with his life. And the Barrhouse Firm weren't going to let him walk away until it was done.

Chapter Thirty-Eight

Pushing the door open and heading into the salon, Darcie took a deep breath as she readied herself to hand in her resignation. Her stomach rolled as the door closed behind her and Layla looked up from the computer screen.

'Oh, hi,' Layla said. 'You're not meant to be on today, or have I fucked up the shifts?'

Darcie shook her head. 'No, you haven't. But I do have something that I want to tell you.'

Layla was only half listening, her eyes darting between Darcie and the screen. Darcie felt sorry for her; it seemed as though Layla really had no one else in her life other than her husband. But for the sake of her relationship with Kev, she had to do this. It was important.

'What's wrong, Darcie?' Layla asked, as though reading Darcie's expression. 'Are you sick or something?'

'Not sick. But I am giving you my resignation, effective from now.'

Layla blinked, as though doing so would erase the words that had passed between them.

'What?' Layla gasped. 'You're leaving? Why, what's wrong?'

Darcie smiled as genuinely as she could, hoping that her eyes wouldn't deceive the lie. 'Nothing's wrong at all. I'm just going to do something else.'

Layla's eyes narrowed, as though she knew Darcie was hiding something. 'Is this because you've found out who my husband is? You don't want to work for a gangster?'

Darcie felt sick. It was typical of Layla to come to such a conclusion so close to the truth. She forced a laugh. 'No, it's nothing to do with your husband. I don't even know him. It's just, well, if you must know, my partner and I are going into business together. Just a cleaning business.'

It was the first thing she could think of and even she knew it sounded exactly like a lie plucked out of thin air. Hopefully, Layla would fall for it.

Layla sighed and nodded. 'Fair enough, Darcie. But I'll be sad to see you go. I feel we've become friends since you started working here. Are you sure there isn't anything I can do to make you stay on, even for just a couple of shifts a week?'

As much as Darcie liked Layla, and she genuinely liked the job, if she stayed it would be like betraying Kev and his family. She couldn't be that person; Kev had had enough of that in his life since working for Donnie Black.

'If I didn't need to sleep at night, I'd stay in a second and do both jobs, Layla. But I can't give anything other than a hundred per cent to this.' And that was the truth. Loyalty was a big thing when it came to Kev and the rest of the Firm. If Darcie broke that, she'd never be forgiven by any of them.

Layla got up from her seat and moved around the counter, before hugging Darcie. 'Like I said, I'll be sorry to lose you. Will you keep in touch?'

'Of course,' Darcie lied again.

'How about one for the road, then?' Layla smiled as she leaned across the counter and produced a bottle of wine that already had some out of it.

'Not for me. Got a lot on today.'

Layla looked disappointed about the wine; about Darcie's departure.

Smiling, Darcie said her goodbyes and left the shop, before crossing the road and rounding the corner to where Kev's car was parked.

'Done?' Kev asked as she climbed in.

'Yes, done,' Darcie replied, closing the door harder than necessary.

'Look, I know you liked that job, but this is for the best. It's for your safety, Darcie.'

Darcie sighed and turned to pull on her seatbelt. 'I know.' As she clicked the seatbelt into place, she said, 'And you'll stick to your part of the deal?'

'Aye, course I will.' But he didn't look at her as the words left his mouth. Deep down, Darcie knew Kev would never leave the firm.

Chapter Thirty-Nine

It had been a few weeks since Donnie had said that he'd told his wife he didn't want to be with her anymore. In those weeks, Louise had spent more time with him than she ever thought she'd be able to. He'd been attentive, romantic even, taking her to places, nights away here there and everywhere. She was twenty, meaning that she was of legal age to not have to tell her parents any of her business, but she certainly didn't want to tell them the truth. She could just imagine her mum's face when she told her she was seeing a man more than twice her age. It'd likely give her a heart attack. So, she'd lied, said that she was staying over at a friend's house from college. They had coursework to be getting on with that was due in soon. Her mum hadn't questioned her. The truth was, she and Donnie had been spending nights away in all parts of Scotland. She'd expected lavish hotels but Donnie had gone for something more subtle. He'd used Airbnb, and a lot of the time she'd pretended in her head that they were living in their own little apartment together, with no ex-wife or age gap lagging behind them.

Tonight was one of those nights. She didn't even know where they were. Somewhere on the east coast maybe? Not that she cared. Louise was so in love with Donnie now that it physically ached in her chest and that was all she had space for in her head to think about.

'Why don't we go out for dinner tonight?' Louise asked.

Donnie was tapping away on his phone and barely looked up. 'Erm, aye, why not.'

'What's so important on that thing? You're always on it,' Louise asked, trying not to sound like a nag.

'No offence, Lou, but you wouldn't understand.'

'Try me. I might be young but I'm not stupid, Donnie.'

'It's just, well, I've been spending so much time away with you that I've had to deal with my work and business from a distance. I don't want my partner thinking that because I'm away with you that my head isn't in the game, you know?'

Louise regarded this for a moment. He hadn't actually said how he felt about her. Perhaps that was the closest thing she was going to get to him saying that he loved her. Not that she'd told him how she really felt either. She was too scared in case he rejected her. But if he was going to do that, then why would he be with her at all? Why would he tell his wife that he didn't want to be with her anymore?

'Anything I can do to help?' Louise asked.

Donnie looked up from his phone then before tucking it into his pocket. 'Actually, if you're offering?'

'Anything at all,' Louise said, lifting the glass of wine from the coffee table and taking a sip. 'What do you need?'

Donnie got up from the chair and moved through to the bedroom. She listened as he unzipped a bag before returning to the lounge. He stood in the doorway between the lounge and the hall, and in his hand was a small black box. A ring box.

'Jesus, Donnie.'

He must have caught the look on her face and realised what she was thinking. He started to laugh. 'No, I'm not proposing, Louise. Jesus, I'm still married, remember.'

Louise joined in his laughter, even if she was just a little disappointed.

'I need to sell this, but I have a lot of other stuff going on right now, and I really could use some help getting it to the guy that's taking it off my hands.'

Louise got to her feet and approached Donnie, curious as to what was inside. A ring, of course. But what was it like? And more importantly, how much was it worth?

'Can I see it?' she asked.

Donnie opened the box and she looked inside. A large diamond in the middle, with diamonds down the band on either side.

'Is that your wife's wedding ring?'

'Yes. I need rid of it; it's worth a lot of money.'

'I can take it to the person you're selling it to, if you want. I said I'd help, didn't I?'

Donnie snapped the box shut and smiled widely at Louise. 'You're a legend, Lou.'

He told her the address, explained that it wasn't far from their accommodation and that if she went now, she could be back in time for them to go out for dinner together.

There was no point in waiting around. She drank back the rest of the wine from her glass, shoved on her trainers and grabbed the box from Donnie's hand.

'It's worth a lot of money, Lou. Be careful with it. The guy has said that he will transfer the money into my bank account, so make sure you see him do that and then you can come back. Sound, okay?' Donnie asked.

Louise nodded. How difficult could it be? The quicker she did this, the quicker she could be sitting across a dinner table from the man of her dreams.

Chapter Forty

Steff Black handed Tam an envelope. It was stuffed full of cash, and Tam didn't need to count it to guess how much was inside. It had to be well over a thousand. A backdated payment for the last few jobs he'd done over the last few weeks. He'd been flat out, driving around the country, delivering god knew what to different locations. Mostly, his trips were from the yard to Stranraer, but on the odd occasion he made trips down as far as Manchester, meeting people like Goran, doing key swaps and then heading back up the road.

'Thanks,' Tam said as he slid the envelope into the front pocket of his jeans. 'I take it I've got another job lined up.'

Steff nodded. 'Aye. It's a pick-up and drop-off this time though. You'll pick up the next van from the location, and you'll drop it off somewhere else before bringing another van back here. It'll take a while, so make sure you've got plenty snacks to keep you going. No unscheduled stops, remember?'

Tam was made to understand early on that even stopping for a piss without Steff's or Donnie's permission was unacceptable. Whatever was in transit had to get from point A to B without any interruptions, no matter what.

Tam heard Steff's phone sound from his jacket, and Steff took it out, looked down at the screen and nodded. 'Speak of shit and it hits you in the face. That's your next job in now. You need to take one of the vans from here and head out. I'll set up the satnav for you.'

Before Tam could ask any questions, Steff had already disappeared down the yard towards one of the vans. He sighed but remembered the huge chunk of cash in his pocket and thought himself lucky to have a job at all.

Tam pulled out his phone and looked down at the screen. He had been working so much the last few weeks, he had barely spoken to his family. He and his sister were normally close, but he'd barely seen her at all.

He typed out a text message, asking how she was and that he wanted to catch up with her soon. Tam pressed send just as Steff was approaching him with a set of keys.

'Ready?'

'Aye. Can I stop for supplies before I get going?' Tam asked.

'Aye, I suppose. But only one stop, mind. I don't want you stopping at a service station halfway through the journey, and if I find out you do...' Steff trailed off before dropping the keys into Tam's hand.

Tam didn't need him to finish the sentence. He knew what would happen.

'Now, I've got somewhere important to be. Chud will let you out.' Steff got into his car and drove out of the yard.

Tam glanced over at Chud and nodded in his direction. The gesture was returned before Tam got into the van.

'Here we fucking go again,' he said under his breath as he started the engine, hating himself for the work he was involved in. But Tam was in too deep, far too deep and for the long haul. He needed to shift his focus from the work he was doing with the Blacks to the money he was making. This was all for him and Louise to start a new life together, away from their parents and Barrhouse itself.

Chapter Forty-One

Layla was lying on the couch, a glass of wine perched on the edge of the table in front of her, the empty bottle next to it. Weeks had gone by since Donnie had ripped the ring off her finger and told her she could stay there until she found somewhere to live. Not that she'd done much searching. Why should she? It was her home too. She still couldn't believe he'd done it.

'He's a fucking bastard if he thinks I'll ever move out of this house,' she slurred to herself.

'Layla?' A male voice called from the kitchen. She sat up quickly, straightened herself out as much as she could, but her eyes lagged behind with the dizziness from being so intoxicated.

'Layla, you in?' It was Steff's voice, likely here to check up on her so that he could feedback to Donnie. Like a dog and its bloody owner.

'What the hell do you want?' Layla said, attempting to get to her feet. Stumbling forward, she knocked yet another glass over and red wine spilled all over the cream carpet. Shit! She might live in a luxurious home, but she was as well living in a slum the way she was treating the place.

Steff appeared in the doorway and gave a laugh. 'Check the nick of you.'

'Fuck off,' Layla sneered. 'If you're here to check up on me for *him*, then you can tell him from me that he's the king of all pricks and he can jump in front of a train. And make sure you give that as a direct quote.'

Steff laughed again. 'Wow, that wine really does loosen the tongue, doesn't it?'

Layla tried to keep her balance as she reached down to retrieve the wine glass, but instead, she stumbled forward again. Steff rushed forward and reached her in time before she fell face first into the fireplace.

'Jesus, Layla. How much have you had?'

'None of your business. What are you even doing here, Steff?' she hissed. 'And how did you get in?'

'You left the back door open. And I'm here to see if you're okay?'

Layla shrugged him off, and he let go, before stumbling her way through to the kitchen to open another bottle of wine.

'Is that a good idea? By the looks of it, you've had a skinful already,' Steff said, following her through the house.

Anything was better than staying sober, she thought. The drunker she got, the less she'd remember about her shitty husband and her shitty life. Or at least, she could pretend that he was a shit. It didn't seem to matter what Donnie did to her, she just couldn't stop loving him. The bastard.

'Want some?' Layla shook the bottle at him, ignoring his judgement.

'Go on then, if it means you don't drink the entire bottle yourself then why not?' Steff replied.

She watched as he pulled two fresh wine glasses from the cupboard, took the bottle from her and placed the glasses on the counter before guiding her to the kitchen table.

'Why are you being so nice?'

'Believe it or not, Layla, I just want to help you. If I was a girl, I'd be holding your hair back in the toilet of some nightclub right now.'

Layla burst out laughing, but she could feel tears pricking the corners of her eyes.

'I don't know if I can trust you, Steff. You're Donnie's brother. I know you say you mean well, but you're only here to check up on me. I'm not stupid.'

'No, you're not. But you *are* pissed, so your perceptions are way off. I promise you, I'm here as your friend, not Donnie's brother.'

Layla regarded him as he moved away from her, opened the wine and poured some into the glasses before sitting down next to her at the table. He handed a glass to her, and she took it, drank a large mouthful and then set it down on the table.

'If you're here as my friend, then you can tell me the truth. Is he having an affair?'

She was hopeful for two things. One, that Steff would be truthful, and two, that Donnie wasn't being unfaithful. Even though they'd technically separated, it would still hurt. And Kerry's death would kill her all over again, because if he was being unfaithful then she would have been right about not trusting him all those years ago.

'Why do you care, Layla? I mean, look at the state you've got yourself into because of him. He's not good for you. You're not good for each other.'

'That doesn't answer my question, Steff.'

Steff took a glug from his glass and placed it next to hers before taking her hand in his. Glancing down at his grip, she was surprised by it.

'You don't have to know the answer to that question. It'll only hurt you.'

She felt the contents of her stomach begin to spin. 'So, he *is* having an affair? I fucking knew it, the bastard. Who is she, Steff? Do you know her?'

Steff sighed. 'It's not an affair as such. He's not romantically involved if that's what you're worried about. It's just… well, you know what Donnie's like. His eyes are always wandering.'

Layla didn't know what to think. 'Wandering eyes is one thing, Steff. But to act on it? Fuck, I'll kill him.'

'You're separated now, Layla. You're not together anymore. I know that doesn't mean that it doesn't hurt, obviously.'

His grip on her hand tightened a little, a reassuring sense that he was trying to be there for her. She looked at him differently then. Not as Donnie's brother, or her brother-in-law, but as his own person. As Steff. Her friend. Comforter.

'Layla, I've never thought he was good for you. Never. I've always believed there was someone out there far better for you than him and what he could offer.'

Before Layla could stop it, she was leaning in and kissing him. And his response wasn't to pull away. She was already pulling at his clothes.

This would teach Donnie Black not to fuck her over. She might seem like a pathetic little wife who'd been betrayed by her husband, but she was angry. What better way to channel that anger than to have Donnie's brother in Donnie's bed? She'd make sure Donnie knew all about it. She'd have the last laugh.

Chapter Forty-Two

Steff lay on the kitchen floor, Layla wrapped up in his arms, and he smiled to himself. He'd been waiting for this for years, as far back as he could remember. Layla Black had been in his head since the first day he'd laid eyes on her. It was just a pity that Donnie got there first, even if he did know that Steff had his eye on her. That was Donnie all over. Greed was his middle name. Steff was only just able to tolerate Donnie, even if they were brothers. And the more he saw Layla hurt for him, the more he wanted to end Donnie. Layla didn't deserve this. She was a good woman.

'What would you do if Donnie walked in here right now?' Layla asked, bringing him back from his thoughts.

'I don't know.'

'I'd laugh in his face. The bastard deserves it.'

'That's strong,' Steff replied. 'You don't feel a little remorseful?'

Layla laughed a little. 'Not in the slightest. If he can do this to me, then I can hit him with something far worse. I can't wait to see the look on his face when I tell him.'

Steff sat up, glanced down at a naked Layla, took in her scent. 'You can't tell him. Not yet.'

'Why not? He's probably out there right now with his bit of skirt. I'm not going to allow him to think that I'm sat here in this house by myself, pining for him.'

Steff hesitated. That's what she'd been doing when he arrived. She'd been lying on the couch, drowning her sorrows and almost begging Steff for answers.

'Just don't say anything, Layla. It goes further than just you and him. He's my brother.'

'That wasn't bothering you a few minutes ago, was it?'

Layla stared at him, at his pleading eyes, and she sighed. 'Fine.'

She leaned in and kissed him again and for the first time in his life, Steff felt like he had the connection with Layla that he'd always wanted.

This feeling of triumph Layla was feeling wouldn't last, he knew. Donnie would soon creep back into her head and she'd start to feel guilty about sleeping with him. He'd just have to make sure that didn't happen, give Layla a reason to stop thinking about Donnie and focus all her feelings on him, just like he'd done with her for the last two decades. No one ever came close to Layla. It had always been her.

Chapter Forty-Three

Louise walked along the coastal road. She'd been walking for around ten minutes, Google Maps taking her down from the main area of where they were staying, and now she was looking across water. The sun was setting but the air was still warm. She wore a short-sleeved T-shirt, and she glanced down at her tattoo and smiled. The co-ordinates of where they'd first met in the form of a rose stem, with the rose petals at the top. They represented the very spot they met at the boxing event. It was the sweetest, most romantic idea she'd ever heard of.

The sky had an orange glow to it, yet the sun was still so bright that she had to squint to see ahead of her.

Louise stopped walking, glanced around when she realised that she was the only person on the path. The phone in her hand was almost out of battery, but she could see that her app was telling her she was almost at the destination where this person would meet her to buy Donnie's ring. Something in her stomach sat heavy. Worry? Doubt? She didn't feel right.

'Excuse me?' A voice came from behind her. Turning, Louise saw a lad around Tam's age. He was bigger than her brother in terms of build, but around the same height. 'You Louise?'

'Depends on who's asking,' Louise replied.

He glanced down at her hands, looked at the left then the right before looking back up to meet her eyes. 'I'm here for the ring.'

Thank fuck for that, Louise thought to herself. Then she glanced at him and, for a second, thought she recognised him. 'Hey, do I know you?'

The guy shook his head and said nothing.

'Donnie said you've to transfer the money in front of me before I leave.'

The lad nodded and slid his hand into his pocket, pulling out a set of keys. 'My phone's charging in the car. You'll need to come back with me so I can send Donnie the money.'

Louise hesitated but before she could refuse, the lad turned and started to walk away. She had no choice but to follow him. If she didn't, he might not come back. She could lose Donnie a sale. She didn't want to give him a cause to get angry at her. He did say it was worth a lot of money, and it might be the only way to get his wife out of the picture so she could start a proper life with Donnie.

Louise started after the lad, taking bigger than normal strides to catch up with him. Looking down at her phone, she could see that the battery was sitting at just two per cent. Stupid thing. She definitely needed a new phone.

Only a minute or so later, she stood in a small car park. Glancing around, she could see that there were only a handful of spaces, maybe enough for six cars. The lad stood by a small van, opened the door and stared at Louise.

'Do you want to see me transfer this cash or not?' he asked. 'I'm on a schedule here. Come on.'

Louise inched closer to the lad as he reached in for his phone. Just as she did, her own phone beeped in her hand and, as she looked down, she saw the screen die. Then, for some reason, her memory served her right in that very moment.

'I do know you. You're mates with my brother, Tam Bellshaw? I met you once, down at the canal. You were standing talking to him with your dog and—' Before she could finish, the lad pushed her hard.

She was against the van, face first. Her arm twisted up her back, the pain so sudden she cried out. Something was shoved over her face, and the lad held her tightly.

'Don't struggle. It'll make it worse.' His voice was low, menacing.

The terror inside Louise sat in the base of her throat, but the more she tried to scream, the harder it became.

Her legs began to go from beneath her, and all she could think about was Donnie coming to save her. He knew where she was; surely when she didn't return then he'd come looking for her?

'That's it, just relax. It'll be much easier if you just go with it.'

No, she thought I don't want to. But then her head started to ache, her thoughts becoming cloudy.

Help, she thought. Someone, help.

—

The haze that had descended was slowly shifting, but still, she couldn't move. Everything was dark, silent. Somewhere out there, on the other side of her closed eyes, Louise felt movement, a presence. Then a familiar voice that assured her everything was going to be okay.

'What the fuck did you do?' Donnie's voice sounded far away, like she had something covering her.

'I did what you told me. But she didn't fully go under. She was screaming like a fucking lunatic, and I just hit her. I had to do it to get her to shut up.'

Louise tried to force her limbs to work, but the heaviness of them held her still.

'That's going to take fucking weeks to heal. Punters pay for quality, not someone who looks like she's been pulled off the fucking street. Jesus, are you stupid?'

Louise tried to concentrate on Donnie's voice. What he was saying wasn't making any sense. Why wasn't he helping her?

'Sorry, boss. I thought I was doing the right thing. You know, avoiding attention.'

'Aye,' Donnie said, and Louise continued to fight against her dead limbs as she listened. 'Well, just get her to the drop-off point. There'll be someone waiting for you. And make sure she's completely unconscious. If she wakes up mid journey, you'll be the one who has to deal with the polis.'

The rising panic gripped her throat, and Louise wanted to scream. Whatever, whoever was out there with Donnie was going to take her away, and Donnie wasn't going to help her. He'd set her up. But why would he do that? She thought that they loved each other. Tears sprang to her eyes, stinging against her closed lids.

Forcing her eyes open, tears swam in front of her vision. She could just about make out the doors in front of her. She was in the back of that lad's van.

'Right, I've got somewhere to be. Don't fuck this up again. Get it done right, or you'll have me to deal with.' Donnie's voice was a low rumble, and as hazy as she felt, Louise heard every word.

The doors opened, and Louise tried to move her hands, ready to defend herself, but only her fingers twitched. A scream bubbled in the base of her throat but it sat there, stuck and unable to release itself.

Then she saw him through the tears, the love of her life. Donnie stood above her, the other lad next to him. Donnie wasn't smiling; he didn't look concerned or angry. There was nothing to his expression. That scared her more than lying in the back of the van because it meant that she'd fallen for a lie.

She wanted to call him for everything, but her lips remained closed.

'Sorry, Lou. It's just business.'

Donnie disappeared from sight, and the lad covered her face again.

Chapter Forty-Four

Tam had already done the handover of the van and had been given a new set of keys. He headed towards the new van that he had been instructed to take to Stranraer, and his head and eyes were beginning to ache. The bright lights of the oncoming cars had dazzled him, and all Tam wanted to do was lie down across the seats and have a half hour kip. Steff wouldn't like that. It would mean the job taking longer and, at best, Tam wouldn't get paid. He didn't have to think of the worst thing; Steff had left that warning hanging there.

He pressed the button on the key and opened the door before climbing in. Tam glanced at the stereo and smiled when he realised that it was DAB radio.

'Nice one, at least I can listen to Absolute Nineties,' he said under his breath.

Cranking up the volume, he began tapping the steering wheel as Run-D.M.C blared from the speakers. He loved this song. His sister always said that he was born in the wrong year as he was always listening to nineties music.

Tam pulled out of the deserted car park and began his journey to Stranraer. Goran would be waiting and would report back to Steff if he was late.

Glancing in the mirrors, Tam couldn't help but allow the curiosity to creep in about what exactly it was that he was transporting back and forth. Drugs, he told himself.

What else? Tam was slowly learning that ignorance was bliss and it paid well.

The road was dark, and Tam hadn't seen many other vehicles pass by. He lowered the volume in case Steff or Donnie tried to contact him. He didn't want to miss their calls.

A sound from behind his seat caught his attention, and he glanced in the mirror before remembering that he couldn't actually see into the back. He wasn't allowed to look in there. The less he knew, the better. But the sound grew, a scratching, a shifting sound. Tapping.

'Oh fuck,' Tam hissed. He wasn't transporting drugs. He was transporting a fucking human. Again. 'Nah, fuck this, man. No amount of money or fear is worth this.'

What if he was taking another man to be executed by them? He'd blocked the memory of that first night out, but the guy's face was like a permanent scar on his brain.

Tam saw a lay-by up ahead and decided to pull in. He had to look, *had* to see what was in the back. Maybe he was being paranoid. Maybe the tiredness was playing tricks on him.

He parked the van in the lay-by and switched off the engine and the lights. He was in the middle of nowhere, blackness around him. The sound didn't stop; the scratching and movement from the back of the van increased. He got out, stood by the back doors with his phone in his hand. He switched the light on so he could see inside.

With shaking hands, Tam gripped one of the handles and pulled the door open.

'What the actual fuck?'

There he was, standing in the middle of the night on a deserted road, staring into the back of a van that now resembled a dog rescue vehicle. A cage was bolted to the floor, and inside was a girl. She was tied to the cage, her wrists and ankles bound by ropes and cable ties. Her eyes wide with terror, she stared out at him.

'*Louise?* What the fuck?'

Chapter Forty-Five

Her wrists and arms ached as Tam released her from inside the cage. She had no idea how long she'd been in there, but for now she was just grateful that she was free.

Louise fell into Tam's arms as she climbed out of the cage, and they both fell to the ground. She trembled as she clung to her brother, sobbing into his shirt.

'Jesus Christ, Lou. What the hell are you doing in the back of this van?'

Her throat was dry; she'd not had a drink since before she'd left the hotel room she'd shared with Donnie. Opening her mouth to speak, her lips dry and cracked, the only sounds to escape were more sobs.

Tam picked her up and walked slowly with her to the front of the van and sat her in the passenger seat, before closing the door and moving around to the driver side. Shivering, she picked up the water bottle from the dashboard and started to gulp it down. It hurt to swallow, but she savoured the feeling as it wet her throat and lips.

Her mind swirled. How was she here, in this place, with her brother as the driver? Tam wasn't the one who'd kidnapped her, hit her over the head after she'd struggled against whatever it was that was shoved into her mouth.

'Louise... are you okay? What the hell?' Tam said again.

He was in a panic; she could see that. She should be panicking too, but instead she was trying to calm her brother down.

'I was kidnapped by some guy.'

'Who?'

'I don't know who he was, but I recognised him. A mate of yours maybe. I met him before; he had a dog with him. He was working for my boyfriend.'

'Big Jambo? I'll fucking kill him.' Tam hissed.

Donnie's face flashed into her mind then; the bastard had set this up. If he hadn't, then why had he allowed that guy to do what he did?

'Louise... who's your boyfriend?' Tam's voice was panicked, matching exactly how she was feeling.

'I can't tell you, Tam. You'll go mental.'

'Louise, you need to tell me who you're going out with. If it's who I think, then we're both in serious danger. It's Donnie Black, isn't it? That's who you've been seeing.'

Louise felt her stomach lurch as Tam glared at her, his eyes wide and his expression more serious than she'd ever seen it. She felt herself nodding slowly, confirming the answer to his question.

'Shit, Lou. Do you have any idea what the hell you've got yourself involved with?'

'Me? Why the hell are you driving the van I was huckled into?' Louise let out a sob.

'Because I work for the bastard. But I swear, Louise, if I'd known I was transporting girls, I'd never have done it. The guy has me over a fucking barrel. Had me drive a guy to his death and then press the fucking button.'

They were both crying now, Louise more terrified than ever before. To see Tam scared was somehow worse than being kidnapped. He was usually the calm one, so laid back he was almost horizontal.

'We need to get away from here. When I don't show up at the dock, they're all going to know something's wrong.'

Tam leaned over and pulled the seatbelt around Louise, who could see he was trying to compose himself. It was difficult for her to stop the panic coming in waves, but she tried to breathe through it as Tam clicked the belt into place before doing his own.

'I want to go home, Tam.'

'We can't go home. He'll find us there. We have to go somewhere else until I can figure out what to do.'

Tam started the engine and glanced at the mobile phone on the dashboard; the one that Steff had given him. Grabbing it, he threw it out the window of the van before pulling out of the lay-by and onto the road. He heard it hit the ground, and the sound fell into the distance.

'But what about Mum? She's been through enough with Dad being a monster; we can't throw her to Donnie too.'

'Just let me figure out what to do, Louise. I can't think right now. All I need is to get away from here. I'm supposed to be arriving at the dock in thirty minutes, so we don't have a lot of time.'

Louise's mind rushed with everything that had happened. Just a few hours ago, she was with the love of her life in an apartment, thinking about what the future might hold for her and Donnie. The legitimate businessman, who did good things for the community, for charity. It was obvious to her now that was all just a front for something else. What the hell had he planned for her that meant she had to be held in a cage only big enough to fit a dog?

'How long have you worked for him?' Louise asked, still gobsmacked that Donnie was capable of what he'd done. 'How many times have you driven a girl like me to the dock? And what's at the docks, Tam?'

He shook his head. 'I didn't know this is what I was doing. I thought it was drugs being shipped across the water. I had no fucking idea that I was involved in trafficking.'

'Trafficking?'

Tam didn't reply and the silence in the van was deafening. They both knew what it meant. Louise was being sold on to someone, somewhere overseas.

The thought of what might have happened if Tam hadn't opened the doors was overwhelming, and Louise stuck her head out of the window, emptying the water from her stomach that she'd only just gulped down minutes before.

She thought she knew Donnie. She was in love with him. It seemed he was someone else entirely. If Tam hadn't discovered she was in the back of the van, she dreaded to think what would have happened to her. Something so horrific, she wouldn't allow her mind to go there.

Chapter Forty-Six

The masked group stood at opposite ends of the yard, their black outfits allowing them to blend in with the dark night. The still and silence of the place around them meant that Kev could hear absolutely every breath, every heart beat as though the sound was coming through a speaker.

'Donnie Black's security are usually on the door twenty-four seven,' Cammy said. 'But even fuckers like big Chud need to piss.'

Kev nodded. 'You're sure we've got enough time to get this done?'

'Aye,' Cammy said. 'Mackie and Thomson are already set. Mackie would rather set fire to a chair with Donnie on it, mind you, but we can't have it all, can we?'

Kev smiled. This was nothing in comparison to what Kev and the rest of them had planned for Donnie and Steff. In particular, Kev wanted to see Donnie suffer for what he'd put him through. His promise to Darcie sat in the back of his mind. If she knew what he was about to do, she might well leave. He'd have to make sure she didn't find out.

'They're bad bastards, Kev,' Cammy said.

'I know.'

'Naw, I mean bad, *bad* bastards.'

'Like the McAdams?' Kev asked, remembering the stories about Barry, Marcus and Tommy McAdam. The city was run by them at one point, and everyone knew what they were up to but were too scared to say anything against them.

'Aye. But worse. I mean, cross country shit. You know what happened to the McAdams's, don't you? Nothing short of fucking genius if you ask me. This city cannae afford another firm like them. That's why we need to sort Donnie Black out. Obviously he needs paying back for setting you up, that's a given. But with the rest of his shit, he's only just getting started and rumour has it he's responsible for that young lassie going missing, and fuck knows how many more. Folk are saying she's in Europe now, being sold as a sex slave. It's fucking disgusting.'

Kev's stomach churned at the thought. 'If I'd known any of this, I wouldn't have done any of those jobs for him at all.'

'None of us would, Kev. That's why we need to show him that he can't get away with what he's done, or what he wants to do. And nobody shoots a Barrhouse boy and lives to tell the fucking tale.'

Before Kev could respond, he saw Mackie raise a hand, and Thomson threw his bottle across the gate into the yard.

There was a loud pop, then an explosion before the boys bolted from the scene and took their spot in the trees to watch Donnie's yard burn to the ground.

'Let's hope the bastard is in there and he's burning to death,' Mackie said, an evil smile on his face.

This was just the start. A warning to him and to Steff that the city wasn't theirs for the taking.

Chapter Forty-Seven

They hadn't been back on the road for long but Louise could feel her eyes heavy, so she allowed them to fall shut while Tam tried to get them to a safe place. She had just begun dozing off when she felt the van jolt forward, and Tam cried out.

'What was that?'

'Bastards have a fucking tracking device on the van under my seat. They've found us.'

Louise sat forward in her seat and peered into the side mirror. A car behind them, its full beam shining onto the van.

'Is that Donnie?' Louise cried. 'What the hell are we going to do, Tam?'

'I don't know. It could be Steff, his brother. Look in that glove compartment. There might be something we can use to threaten him.'

Louise rummaged inside the compartment and pulled out a screwdriver, a lighter and an empty cigarette pack. She handed the screwdriver to Tam and glanced back in the mirror. The lights were flashing wildly now, and Louise started to sob.

'It's going to be all right, Lou. I'll drive us to the nearest police station.'

That didn't help to ease her fear, but she had to trust Tam. He was her brother, was trying to get her out of this nightmare situation.

Then, without warning, the van jolted again and it careered off the road onto the hard shoulder before coming to an abrupt stop. Tam's head collided with the steering wheel, and Louise put her hands out, braced herself against the dashboard.

—

She screamed for him to wait as he unclicked the seatbelt and pulled at the door handle. He didn't have to throw himself out of the van. She could have made it, could have got them away from the car that was following them. Driving was the one thing Tam had taught her, even though she didn't actually have a licence.

The door swung backwards and forwards as she slammed on the brakes. Getting out of the van, she ran towards where he'd landed on the road. She knelt down beside him and all she could see was the blood pouring from the wound in his shoulder. It was impossible to stop the panic as it clawed its way up from inside her. Their assailants wouldn't be far behind and if they were to survive, she had to get him back in the van.

'Jesus *fucking* Christ.' She placed her hand on the wound where he'd been shot and applied pressure. But it didn't work this time; the blood oozed quickly through her fingers, staining her clothes. 'Why the fuck did you do that? We can get away; we still have time.'

Glancing into his eyes, she could see death was upon him. His laboured breaths scared her. 'Come on, you need to get back in the van.'

'Take it,' he gasped. He gripped her hand. It felt wet and sticky. The metallic smell which hovered between them was so strong it made her feel sick. 'Just take the van and go, get rid of that tracker. If I have to die here to keep you safe then I will.'

She could see he was beginning to fall in and out of consciousness. They were running out of time.

A voice in the distance made her look up. She couldn't make out the words, but they were frantic. Shadows darted around in the street lights down the road. The people who did this to him were on the run, but not in the opposite direction. They were coming to finish the job and to take her away.

'Go. Now!' he hissed, pulling his hand away. She let go and looked down at him. His eyes were full of terror, fear. 'If they catch you, we're both dead. If you go, at least one of us has a chance.'

'I'm not leaving you, Tam.'

'Just do what I fucking say, Lou. Please.'

She hesitated before getting to her feet. Then she ran so fast her legs immediately began to burn. Reaching the van, she jumped into the driver's seat and didn't bother to put her seatbelt on.

'Fuck, fuck, fuck!' Louise sobbed loudly. This couldn't be happening. It had to be a nightmare that she was going to wake up from. Leaning forward, she reached under the driver seat and felt something alien underneath. Her fingers brushed against a small box attached to the underside of the seat. Ripping it from the fabric, she glared at it before tossing it out of the window. She started the engine and glanced up at the mirror. The rear window had been shattered in the hit. That was why she could hear everything. Donnie's voice in the distance, shouting and bawling, incomprehensible words. Tam was bellowing back but she couldn't make it out, even though the voices got louder. Her heart hammered in her chest as she forced the van into gear, released the clutch and pulled away as quickly as she could, all the while sobbing loudly at the very realisation that she was leaving her brother to die.

Then she heard a shot, and everything inside her stilled before she let out a sound she didn't think she was capable of.

A guttural roar left her throat as her blood ran cold. Her brother was dead, likely killed by Donnie. The man who claimed to want to be with her, and yet had orchestrated for her to be kidnapped and had who the hell knew what planned for her.

Her bloodstained hands gripped the steering wheel and tears streamed down from her eyes. Angrily wiping them away, she glared at her reflection in the mirror to see his blood smeared across her cheeks.

Then she turned her eyes to the road and kept driving. There was no going back now. She had no choice but to keep going and hope that, whatever happened, Donnie wouldn't find her.

Chapter Forty-Eight

He opened his eyes, questioning how he was still alive. This wasn't real, he had to be crossing that bridge between life and death and his subconscious was projecting these images in front of him.

If that was the case, he wouldn't feel pain from where the bullet had hit, from where Donnie had shot him and then taken off to find his sister. But not before he'd given him a few harsh blows to the ribs via his foot.

'*You should never have stopped the van, Tam. If you'd just followed the rules, you could have been home in your shitty little terraced house with a beer in your hand. You've crossed a line, boy. No one fucks with my business and gets away with it.*'

Those were the last words Tam heard, and they were already haunting him. Donnie's voice had hissed in his ear as Tam lay on the ground, bleeding from the wound on his shoulder.

He'd gone for a second shot after Lou had disappeared with the van, but somehow, Tam's luck had come in and the gun hadn't worked. He didn't know why. Jammed, or perhaps Donnie had only one bullet? Either way, it had bought Tam some time.

Donnie had lost his shit by that point, had attacked Tam for the second time, all the while screaming at him how his bosses wouldn't take too kindly to losing a deal. A deal, as though his sister was a product. Even in the middle of taking the worst kicking of his life, on top of being shot, the cold reality of what could have happened to Louise had set in. Donnie and Steff had been paying Tam to transport girls to the ferry dock, where they would be taken away and sold for unspeakable amounts of money. Tam had been part of ruining young girls' lives and he hadn't even known it. The thought was worse than the gunshot wound on his shoulder, or the blinding pain from being kicked in the ribs so hard he wondered if they'd punctured his lungs. He'd lain there, perfectly still, once Donnie had stopped. Play dead, or at least almost dead, Tam had told himself. If Donnie thought that Tam was close to death's door, then he might leave. It had worked, to Tam's relief.

Not long after Donnie had taken off, leaving Tam on the side of the road, Tam pulled himself into the sitting position. Ribs aching and shoulder bleeding out, Tam looked around him and realised that any chance of surviving the night was minuscule. There was no one around, the road deserted due to nightfall. And his chances of being seen on this part of the road were slim, unless he stood in the middle of the road and hoped that any approaching cars coming towards him would swerve in time and miss him. If he could just get to the hospital, get himself fixed up, then he might have a chance of finding Louise.

Tam tried but couldn't get to his feet; the pain was excruciating. The bright lights from the approaching car made him squint, but he raised his arm, as painful as it was, and waved frantically for the car to stop. It began to slow and stopped in front of him, although the full beams were left on, shining directly into Tam's eyes.

A door opened, and heavy footsteps approached. Tam tried to shield his eyes from the lights but a shadow fell over them. Tam glanced up at the face of the man who stood over him and frowned.

'What the hell are you doing here?' Tam forced the words out through the pain. He was sure he was going to pass out at any moment.

'You really have fucked yourself, wee man.'

Large hands gripped Tam by his hoodie, but before he could protest, the darkness from the night sky crept inside him until he felt nothing.

Chapter Forty-Nine

Ditch the van, that would be the only way to get away. She'd got rid of the tracker, driven as far into civilisation as she could before the thought had entered her head. The streets were beginning to darken as Louise pulled into a supermarket car park. She didn't even know where she was, not having bothered to take in her surroundings. She wasn't in Glasgow, that was for sure. She had, however, been driving for a while now, so she could be close enough to be able to reach home. She was beginning to panic; the overwhelming sensation that her throat was beginning to close up gripped her firmly, and her blood ran cold. But she wasn't going to allow the panic attack to set in. She was the only person who could save her now. Tam had sacrificed himself to get her to safety, and she owed it to him to keep going.

Climbing out of the van and not even bothering to close the door, she ran towards the entrance. There weren't many people around, and suddenly Louise realised that she was out in the open. Exposed. If there were crowds, she could hide in amongst them and go unseen by Donnie, if he was still on her tail. Louise had no way of knowing if that was the case.

Eyeing the small clothing section, Louise moved quickly through the aisles towards it, keeping her head down to hide the blood smeared across her cheeks. No one seemed to pay any attention to her, although it didn't settle the worry or angst weighing heavy on her chest.

Grabbing a T-shirt and hoodie from one of the rails and gripping them tightly, Louise kept her head down as she moved towards the public toilets.

Stay calm, she thought as she placed her free hand on the toilet door and pushed it open. Upon a quick inspection, she saw that the toilets were empty and thanked the universe that she would have just a few moments alone to do what she needed to do. Locking herself in one of the cubicles, Louise took off her own top and pulled the T-shirt and hoodie on over her head. If she could change her appearance just a little, then it would help her in her quest to get as far away from what the hell had just happened, an event in her life that she still couldn't wrap her head around.

Opening the door, she glanced at herself in the mirror above the sinks and realised that she still very much resembled herself. That, coupled with crimson-stained cheeks meant she had more work to do. She moved across the floor and splashed her face with water, before scrubbing at her skin. Washing away what was left of her brother, she thought. A lump formed in her throat at the vision of what was likely to have happened to Tam, before she pushed the images away and tried hard not to let out a wail of terror. She had to keep it together if she was going to get out of the supermarket without getting caught.

She'd considered going to the nearest police station, but the fear of no one believing her was too overwhelming. Who would believe a stupid little girl over a man like Donnie? A businessman, with a wife and a successful career? The idea was out of her head quicker than it took her to get changed in the bathroom.

She needed something else. A hat, maybe a wig? There was no more time, the hood would have to suffice. Pulling it up over her head, Louise took a deep breath and shoved her own tops into the hand towel bin beneath the sinks and opened the door. Stepping out onto the shop floor, she expected someone to be waiting on her, to ask her what exactly it was she thought she was doing. But to be greeted with empty space – and no one there to question her – flooded her with relief.

She rushed towards the door, fully aware that the alarms were going to go off because she hadn't removed the security tags. Tam had told her how removing them would either set the alarms off before you even got to leave the shop, or ink would explode from the tag and stain the clothes. She'd rather set them off on the way out and try to run as fast as she could. She supposed that if she was caught by security and they themselves called the police, then she would have to tell them why she was stealing clothes, why she was running. There would be no other choice.

Reaching the exit, she passed between the scanners and prayed that they'd remain silent and she would be able to get away unnoticed.

Holding her breath, Louise stepped over the super-market threshold onto the paved footpath outside and waited for the loud, high-pitched sound to come. It didn't. No one seemed to notice that Louise was out of the store, with stolen goods on her back.

Her heart thrummed in her chest as she moved across the car park, weaving in and out of the parked cars. She no longer resembled the girl who'd been with Donnie just hours before. No longer was she the little sister of Tam, nor was she innocent now. She'd been stupid to fall for Donnie Black. But he'd been so convincing that he wanted her. It turned out that he only wanted her to suffer, to gain money from selling her to whoever he'd told Tam to deliver the van to.

Nausea crept up to her throat as she thought about Tam. She couldn't believe that he'd sacrificed himself like that, just to let her get away. They'd both been fooled by Donnie and now Tam had paid the ultimate price. Maybe she could go back for him; maybe he would still be alive? Louise knew she was clutching at hope, when in fact all hope was gone the second she'd set eyes on Donnie Black.

Swallowing the lump in her throat, she forced the nausea out of her mind and moved out of the car park and onto the main road. She was able to stop herself from being sick, but she couldn't stop the tears as they trickled down her face.

'Are you okay?'

The voice startled Louise as she glanced up in the direction of the person who'd spoken. A woman around her mum's age was staring at her with a worried expression on her face.

Louise opened her mouth to speak but didn't know what to say.

'Do you need help?'

Nodding, Louise felt her legs go from beneath her. The woman put her arms out to catch her but missed. Louise sat down, her back against the wall surrounding the car park, and sobbed uncontrollably as the woman crouched down beside her and seemed almost close to tears herself.

'My brother's just died,' Louise wept.

'Oh love, I am sorry. Should you be at home with your family?'

Shit, what the hell was she going to tell her parents about Tam?

'I can't,' she replied. 'The people who did it, they're after me.'

The look of horror which spread across the woman's face scared Louise. 'Did what?'

Louise glanced up at the sky through her tears and admitted defeat. She had to go to the police. There was no other choice.

'Someone killed him and I need to get to the police. Please, help me,' Louise said, failing to compose herself as the woman helped her to her feet.

'Come on, love, my car is just over there. I'll take you to wherever you need to go. Don't worry, you're safe with me.'

Louise allowed the woman to help her to the car, and as she climbed into the passenger seat, all she could think of was the look on Tam's face when she last saw him. He knew he was going to die. Louise had known, on some level, that she was leaving her brother to face a brutal death all on his own.

She would never forgive herself for that, but she would get justice for him. Even if getting it killed her too.

Chapter Fifty

The kitchen floor was uncomfortable, but she hadn't wanted to move in case she woke Steff up. At the same time, the worry of not moving and Donnie walking into the house to find them entangled in one another had a grip on her throat. She knew that even though Donnie had made it clear things were over between them, he'd still lose his shit if he found his wife and brother, his best friend, in a position they couldn't lie their way out of.

She sat up slowly, allowing Steff's arm to fall gently from around her shoulder. Layla got to her feet and the wine headache hit her almost instantly. How could she have been so stupid to think that sleeping with Steff to get revenge on her husband was a good idea? She was never going to get away with this. Donnie would kill her when he found out; he'd kill Steff too. And he would find out. He had a way of knowing things that he shouldn't.

Creeping upstairs to the bathroom, Layla passed through the hallway and chose not to look at the huge, framed picture of her and Donnie on their wedding day. Guilt, remorse and anger coursed through her veins at the best of times because of Donnie's betrayal, but now she was no better than he was. At least he was having an affair with a stranger. She'd slept with the one man that Donnie trusted most in the world. He'd use that betrayal to fuel his rage.

Pushing the door open, Layla stepped into the bathroom and splashed her face with cold water. The sobering thought of Steff lying naked on the kitchen floor snapped her back to reality. He had to leave; she had to get him out of the house.

Just as she was about to go back downstairs, she heard Steff's phone ringing. It would likely be Donnie, asking where he was. Would Steff tell him?

'A'right, mate?' Steff's voice filtered its way up from the kitchen, and Layla's heart was in her throat. She couldn't help but listen in.

'Calm down, what do you mean she's gone?'

Layla froze. Who were they talking about?

'He did what? Jesus! Where are you now?'

Another pause, and Layla worried her heart was going to burst out of her chest.

'Fucking hell,' Steff sighed loudly. 'And you're sure he's dead?'

Layla's hand fell across her mouth as she listened.

'Right, I'll meet you back at the yard. Have you heard from Goran? Does he know?'

Goran? Who the fuck was Goran?

'Donnie, I said I'd meet you at the yard. Calm the fuck down, eh? I'll be there as soon as I can.'

Layla listened as Steff hung up the phone and he cursed under his breath. Patting her face with the fluffy towel hanging on the rail next to the sink, Layla composed herself and walked back to the kitchen, pretending that she hadn't listened in on the phone call.

'Hey,' she said, barely able to look Steff in the eye.

His expression was hard, troubled. But it soon softened as he looked at her. 'Hi. Look, I don't want to leave but I have to be somewhere.'

'Oh? Everything okay?'

Layla tried to disguise the deep breath she took in. Something felt terribly wrong.

'Just work stuff.' Steff pulled Layla in at the waist and kissed her lips. 'I can come back later?'

Layla faked a smile but shook her head. 'No, it's fine. Go and do what you have to do. I'll see you later.'

Steff seemed unaware of how uncomfortable Layla was feeling, but that was a good thing. She didn't want her guilt to shine out from her eyes.

'Can I ask you something?'

'Anything,' Steff replied. He was holding her tightly, as though he knew she wanted to move away but he didn't want to let it happen.

'I overheard your conversation. Who's Goran?'

Steff's expression didn't change, although his eyes did flicker at the question. 'Just a guy we're doing business with.'

'Is Donnie in trouble with him?'

'Why would you think that?'

'Well...' Layla hesitated. Should she come clean that she heard the whole conversation? Would that implicate her in some way if something truly awful was going on?

'You asked Donnie if he was sure someone was dead.'

Steff's cool expression fell then, and it was replaced by something a lot colder.

'Layla, it's best you don't know.'

Yeah, she thought. That was how she'd been throughout her entire relationship with Donnie. She knew he was in on the criminal world, with Donald, their father, being Glasgow's biggest gangster. But she'd always chosen to remain blind to it all; she loved Donnie and that was all that had mattered. She really had been so stupid for twenty years of her life. Layla sighed angrily then.

'You know what, Steff? I think you're right. In fact, I think it's best that I know fuck all about anything Donnie's involved with, including you.'

He frowned, loosened his grip on her waist and took a step back.

'It's really nothing, Layla.'

'Bullshit, Steff! We both know that's not true. I've gone through my life and marriage with Donnie keeping my mouth and eyes shut to the kind of work the Blacks do. I can't do it anymore. My god, is Mel in on all this too? This criminal business you've got going on?' She stopped and took a breath. 'Donnie ending things with me was probably my only way out. I'm sorry, this thing between us' – she waved her hand between them – 'it should never have happened. I thought it would be a good way to show Donnie that I could be a cold-hearted bastard too, but in truth, it's just going to make things so much more complicated than they need to be. I'm sorry, Steff. I shouldn't have used you like that. But overhearing that phone call just put things into perspective for me. I'm just angry it has taken me this long to see things so clearly.'

Steff shook his head. 'I think you're reading too much into this, Layla. It's just a bit of business trouble. No one's dead. I think you've misheard what was said.'

'No, I won't be gaslighted. Not by you or Donnie.'

That seemed to stop Steff in his tracks then, and Layla moved towards the front door. Pulling it open, she stood to the side and said nothing, only glared at Steff.

He knew that she wanted him to leave. 'I'm sorry you feel that way, Layla. I really am.'

Layla parted her lips to speak but refrained from letting her voice be heard for fear of bursting into tears of anger.

As Steff passed by to leave, he leaned in and kissed her on the cheek. She wanted to pull away but was rooted to the spot.

Closing the door behind him, Layla couldn't get the words from the overheard phone call out of her head.

What do you mean she's gone? Are you sure he's dead? Does Goran know?

What kind of business was this?

Chapter Fifty-One

The woman, Heather, who'd come to Louise's aid at the supermarket, stopped the car outside the police station and switched off the engine. Louise felt her chest constrict at the thought of having to go in and speak to an officer about what had happened. She didn't even know where to start.

'Do you want me to come inside with you?'

Louise nodded. She didn't want to be alone; she didn't feel strong enough.

They both got out of the car and headed towards the entrance, the woman holding onto the crook of Louise's elbow.

'I'm sorry your night has been taken up by this,' Louise said, tears filling her eyes once more.

'Hey,' Heather replied. 'I'm not going to abandon a young girl as distressed as you are.' She gave Louise's arm a reassuring squeeze and pushed the entrance door open.

Stepping through and into the reception area, Louise felt like she was going to throw up there and then.

'Can I help you?' the officer behind the desk glanced up.

Louise looked at Heather, who nodded and smiled gently. 'Go on. I'll be right here waiting for when you get out, then I can take you to wherever you need to go.'

Stepping closer to the desk, Louise took a deep breath, swallowed the lump in her throat and looked into the female officer's eyes.

'I want to report a kidnap and murder.'

The officer's eyes flickered, but her expression was blank.

—

Before Louise knew what was happening, she was sitting in a cold and clinical room. Surrounded by white walls and faced with a male and female officer. Two coffee cups sat in front of them, and a bottle of water in front of Louise.

'Okay, Louise. I'm DS Carntyne and this is DS Stewart. You said you wanted to report a kidnapping and murder. Why don't you start from the beginning?' DS Carntyne, the female officer, said. Her voice was gentle and it soothed Louise a little.

'I was kidnapped earlier today. But I got away.'

The officers didn't react, other than to take notes in the books in front of them.

'Do you know who kidnapped you?' DS Carntyne asked.

Louise nodded. 'It's complicated. But yes, I do.'

'Can you give us a name?' DS Stewart added.

'My boyfriend. Well, I thought he was my boyfriend. Turns out he was trying to have me trafficked.' Tears spilled over and her voice cracked as the words came out.

'It's okay,' Carntyne said. 'Take your time.'

Steadying herself, Louise continued. 'His name is Donnie Black. My brother said he was grooming me. And when my brother tried to get me away, Donnie followed us, ran us off the road and then he...' she swallowed hard, unable to bear the words she was about to say. 'Then he shot my brother. He's dead.'

DS Stewart sat forward on his seat, and Louise noticed how his brow furrowed. 'You know this for sure?'

DS Carntyne glanced at him before turning her attention back to Louise.

'Yes, I'm sure. He shot him. Donnie would have made sure Tam was dead so he couldn't tell anyone about what he was planning. And now he's after me.'

Louise wiped her tears away with the back of the sleeve of the stolen hoodie and tried to contain her sobs. Why was he questioning her like that? This was why she hadn't wanted to come to the police, she knew they wouldn't believe her.

'Okay,' DS Carntyne said. 'Can you tell us where this happened, Louise?'

Louise shook her head. 'I don't know where we were. But before Tam was shot, before we were run off the road, he told me that Donnie paid him to deliver vans to the dock at Stranraer, before driving back to the yard with a different van. Tam didn't know that I was in the back of his van. I was tied up and put in a cage. He let me out.'

Louise grabbed the bottle of water in front of her and took a large gulp, trying to stem the urge to throw up. Her body was trying to reject what was happening.

'Can you give us any information on the van? The registration? The colour?' DS Stewart asked. 'It would really help us.'

Louise shook her head again. What a stupid, stupid idiot she was. She hadn't logged any of this information. But then she remembered dumping it in the car park at the supermarket where she'd met Heather.

'I can tell you where I left the van. I dumped it after I got away so that he couldn't find me.'

DS Carntyne gave another gentle smile before nodding. 'Okay, that's good, Louise. We can certainly get some of our officers out there to check that.'

'I'll get an officer on to that right now,' DS Stewart said. He got to his feet; the chair scraped against the floor and caused a shiver to run up Louise's spine. He exited the room, and Louise took another sip of water.

'Are you okay?' DS Carntyne asked.

Louise took a sip from the water in front of her. 'No. I was fooled into thinking Donnie wanted to be with me when he wanted to sell me. It's disgusting. But I don't care about that half as much as what he did to my brother. You have to catch him; you have to put him away. He's so dangerous.'

Louise's words were coming in quick succession, and she was struggling to get a proper breath. Every nerve in her body tingled with fear.

'It's okay, just take deep breaths. You're doing really well. I think we should have you checked over by a doctor. You've been through a horrific ordeal, Louise. It wouldn't do any harm, and then we could proceed with you giving us an official statement?'

Louise nodded as she wiped her hands on her trousers. DS Carntyne's voice was pleasant, but it wasn't enough to block out the thoughts screaming through her head. *Tam is dead because of you, Louise.*

The panic and anguish were building again; she needed some air. Now.

'Is it okay if I go outside? I need some air. I feel like I can't breathe.'

'Of course, Louise. Do you want me to come with you?'

'No, I'll be fine on my own. I won't be a minute.'

Louise left the interview room and walked along the short corridor towards the exit. Bursting through and into the fresh air, she gulped and gasped, bending over and resting her hands on her knees.

The air was still, birds chirped their night-time song in a nearby tree and, in the distance, she could smell the remnants of a barbeque. Why did everything and everyone around her seem so calm while her world was in chaos?

Straightening her back, Louise looked up to the sky and began to count the stars. It wasn't something she'd ever done before but had heard her mum say that she'd done it when she was trying to stop smoking. It helped to take her mind off the constant nag in the back of her mind. *Smoke the cigarette. Smoke it.*

One, two, three... Louise counted a hundred stars before she stopped. Her chest no longer constricting, her palms no longer sweating.

'I don't know, but as soon as I heard your name I was out here calling you.'

The voice was hushed, and Louise couldn't see where it was coming from.

'Yes, her, it's definitely her. Unless you want us all to end up at the bottom of the canal, I'd suggest you get someone over here to take her right now. I'm not fucking kidding, Donnie, this is serious shit. It's bad enough that little bitch Demi Simpson's face is still all over the news. My boss is on us to get results with that case, I don't need another one.'

Louise turned, moved slowly towards the edge of the building and when she peered around, DS Stewart was standing with his back to her, just a few feet away. Her stomach rolled as she listened to his conversation.

'I've covered up enough of your fucking shit, Donnie. I'm not doing more of your dirty work. I'm on shift here. My partner will notice if I just disappear. It'll look too dodgy if I fuck off and she vanishes too. She's in there giving information right now.'

Louise's head began to spin; her hands tingled as beads of sweat formed on her brow. No. Fucking. Way. DS Stewart was on the phone to Donnie, telling him that she was here. He was bent.

She had to go, now. Run. Turning, she saw Heather sitting in her car just ten yards away. She could go without being seen or heard.

'Fine. But I swear, Donnie, this is the last time. I'll sort it somehow. Just give me time to work out how I can get her in the car and I'll bring her to you.'

That was all Louise needed to hear. She turned on her heel and put on a jog, inching closer and closer to Heather's car. Heather looked up, smiled and Louise climbed inside.

'That was quick. Are you okay?'

Louise pulled the hood up over her head and put down her visor so that when DS Stewart appeared from behind the building, he wouldn't see her.

'I'm fine now.'

'What did they say?'

'Nothing much. Can you drop me off now, please?'

She jammed her shaking hands between her knees and kept her eyes on the building. DS Stewart appeared, and Louise watched him shove his mobile into his pocket.

'Of course. Where would you like to go?' Heather asked.

Louise gave her an address and watched DS Stewart walk into the station. He hadn't noticed her sitting in the car. It would take him only a few moments to realise that she was gone, and then he would be back on the phone to Donnie.

If hell existed, Louise had already passed by it and was descending into the depths of the eternal abyss.

Chapter Fifty-Two

Lying in bed, Darcie stared up at the ceiling as the worry crept in, not allowing her to sleep. Kev still wasn't home, and as much as he'd promised her that he would leave well alone when it came to Donnie Black, she knew it wouldn't be the case.

Glancing at the time on her phone, she sighed loudly. There was no point in trying to sleep now, she thought as she threw the duvet off and got out of bed. She made her way out to the kitchen in just a T-shirt and flicked on the kettle. As much as tea wasn't going to cut it right now, she wouldn't have a drink. If something did kick off with Kev and the rest of the boys, she wanted a clear head to be able to deal with it.

The kettle seemed to take forever to boil as she stood by the kitchen window, smoking her cigarette. The night air was cold against her skin, so she went back to the bedroom to grab her dressing gown. As she crossed the small hallway of her flat, there was a gentle knock at the door. It was so quiet that she had to ask herself if it wasn't just her imagination, or her desire for it to be Kev coming home in one piece.

Then it came again, a little more hurried this time. Frowning, Darcie padded across the hall and peered through the spyhole, but the bulb in the communal light had blown and the close was in darkness.

'Darcie, let me in. Please.' The desperation coming from the voice on the other side of the door scared her, but she recognised the person immediately. Unlocking and pulling the door open, Darcie was almost knocked to the floor as the person clung to her.

'Jesus, what's wrong?' she asked, regaining her balance.

'It's Tam. He's dead!'

Darcie held her cousin at arm's length, not quite processing what she'd just heard. She hadn't seen Louise or Tam in such a long time, since just before Kev went to prison. Life had just got in the way for all of them.

'Louise, what the hell has happened? What do you mean Tam's dead?'

Darcie felt the terror rock her as she took everything in. She had to be calm, had to find out what had happened.

'Louise, tell me...' she swallowed. 'What's happened?'

–

Darcie had managed to get Louise into the bathroom before her sobs brought on a need to vomit. She'd never seen anyone so terrified in her life. But what she'd said hadn't made any sense, and since the words left her mouth, she'd said nothing else.

'Breathe, just breathe,' Darcie said. 'Take a minute to compose yourself.'

Louise lowered herself onto the edge of the bath, took long, deep breaths, but still she shook uncontrollably. Darcie went to the kitchen and grabbed water from the fridge before handing it to Louise.

'Drink this.'

Why did people think drinking water was the solution to all problems? It was all anybody ever did in times of high stress.

'Darcie, what the hell am I going to tell my mum?' Louise sobbed again.

'You have to start from the beginning before I can answer that, Lou. What has happened to Tam?'

Darcie might seem strong on the outside, but she was just about keeping the tears at bay herself.

'We were in a crash a few hours ago.'

'Jesus!' Darcie said, giving Louise the once-over. 'When? Where?'

'I don't know. I just drove away.'

'You left the scene of the crash? Where is Tam now?'

Louise shook her head vigorously. 'He told me to leave, so he wouldn't find me.'

Darcie frowned. 'So who wouldn't find you?'

'My boyfriend, and whoever else was trying to take me.'

It was Darcie's turn to shake her head vigorously. 'What do you mean, take you? Did someone try to hurt you on purpose?'

Then Louise composed herself, looked up at Darcie through tear-filled eyes and told her everything, and Darcie felt sick.

'Your boyfriend is Donnie Black?' Darcie asked in disbelief. 'As in Donnie Black, the guy who was responsible for putting Kev in prison?'

Louise looked up at her with wide eyes. 'Donnie was the reason Kev went to jail?'

Darcie didn't bother to go into detail, too busy trying to process everything that she'd just been told.

Every ounce of trouble that had been thrown at their family came from the same source. Donnie Black. He was more dangerous than she could have imagined.

233

Louise sobbed and Darcie held on to her. 'It's okay, Lou.'

'How is it going to be okay, Darcie? Tam is dead because I was too stupid to see Donnie for what he is.'

'He fooled everyone around him into thinking he was a good guy, Louise. That says more about him than it does about you or any of us.'

Darcie tried to keep her emotions under control, but all she could think about was how terrified she was. All roads led back to Donnie Black. Tam was dead because of him, Louise almost trafficked to god knows where and into the hands of foreign gangs. Mackie had been shot.

What the hell else would they all face at the hands of Black?

Chapter Fifty-Three

They'd all gone back to Mackie's gaff and cracked open a bottle of whisky to celebrate starting the war on Donnie Black. It had been one hell of a way to let Donnie know that no matter who he thought he was, Glasgow's top man, gangland boss or the owner of a recycling yard, the Barrhouse Firm weren't going to let him get away with what he had planned, especially not after what he'd done to Kev.

'To blowing the bastard up.' Mackie raised his glass and laughed aggressively.

The rest of the boys raised their glasses too, although Kev silently vowed it would be his last before heading home to Darcie. In fact, he'd managed to make sure that he didn't drink too much of the *mental milk* as Darcie always called it. He wanted to keep a clear head in case blowing up the yard came back to bite them earlier than expected, especially if Donnie wasn't in there when the place went up.

'I'll drink to that,' Thomson said, swallowing back a large mouthful; he was followed by the rest of them.

'You think he really was in there? I mean, it would be too easy, wouldn't it? To be rid of him just like that?' Kev said, placing his glass on the table, avoiding the playing cards and the packs of cigarettes.

'Well, if he was, then job done. But if he wasn't, then it means we get to play more games with him. We'll blow up his fucking house if we have to. Fuck him, and fuck his brother too, and anyone else who thinks he's worth protecting. Once he sees the state of the yard, or at least what's left of it, he'll have nowhere to work from, and a king needs his castle, eh?' Thomson replied.

Kev nodded and got to his feet. 'Boys, it's been a pleasure. But I need to get back to Darcie's. Keep me informed if you hear anything, eh?'

'Aye, Kev. Good man. See you tomorrow,' Mackie said, and the rest of the boys waved him off.

-

It wasn't a far walk from Mackie's to Darcie's flat, so Kev got his head down and picked up the pace, all the while thinking about what he and the rest of the boys had done earlier. It had felt fucking marvellous to take out Donnie's yard, the one place that he operated from. The drugs, the stolen goods, the knocked-off booze... all of it. Then there was the idea of the Black brothers being responsible for trafficking girls out of Scotland. When they'd heard that was the direction the business would be going in, that was when the Barrhouse Firm wanted out. They didn't have concrete evidence of any of it; however, it couldn't just be a coincidence that several girls had gone missing in the city over the last year or so. But there was one thing that Kev knew that the rest of the boys didn't. Back at that field rave years ago, he'd seen Donnie with that girl. He never had been able to get that image out of his head. He'd decided to speak out against Donnie, but then Donald had paid him a visit.

It wouldn't surprise Kev at all if Donnie was trafficking. It would be in keeping with his nature from back then. And as he got older, smarter, he would get away with more. Kev was angry for keeping quiet for so long. If trafficking was what Donnie was into, it could happen to someone like his little sister, just about to turn fifteen. Not that he saw much of her these days, what with her living in Torquay with her mother now. It was a good thing, really; it meant she was away from Glasgow, away from the dangers of men like Donnie Black.

He would tell the boys what happened back then, tell them that he had a gut feeling. But he'd wait until they were sober.

After around a ten-minute walk, Kev reached the front door of the flat. It was already past midnight and he knew Darcie would be in bed by now. Keeping as quiet as he could, Kev pushed the door open and crept inside the flat, but once over the threshold, he saw that the lights were on in the living room. He could hear Darcie crying.

'Babe?' he said, making his way through to the living room.

Darcie looked up from the sofa. It wasn't only her who was crying. It was Louise, Darcie's cousin. He hadn't seen her since before he'd gone to prison.

'Where the hell have you been, Kev? I've been trying to contact you and you've not answered,' Darcie said, her voice quivering as she spoke.

'Sorry, my phone died. What's going on?' Kev asked, eyeing Louise.

'You'd better sit down for this. Something *fucking horrific* has happened.' Darcie's voice cracked, and Louise began sobbing loudly. By the look on her face, it wasn't for the first time that night.

'It's Tam's. He's dead.'

'What the fuck happened?' Kev went to them, sat down next to Darcie and wrapped an arm round her as she comforted her cousin.

'Donnie Black shot him.'

Everything seemed to still around him as the words sank in. Kev looked at Darcie, a wave of confusion rushing through him suddenly. He couldn't have heard her correctly, there was no way.

'Hang on, Donnie killed Tam?'

Louise took a long breath and wiped at her tears with the sleeve of her hoodie.

What Louise told Kev caused something to shift inside him. Hearing what Donnie had put Louise through, how he'd made her think he loved her and then set her up to be kidnapped, made him sick to his stomach. But that sickness quickly turned to anger he'd never imagined he was capable of. But it confirmed his suspicions about Donnie. He'd been right, and now he felt guilty about keeping quiet because Donald had threatened him. He could have stopped this years ago.

'I heard that police officer mention that girl that's been on the news too. Demi Simpson? I think Donnie took her too,' Louise said, finally able to control her trembling voice.

As he processed everything, the first thing that came into his mind was what the rest of the Firm would say. This was only going to fuel their rage even more about Black and what he was getting up to.

'We need to go to the police, Kev,' Darcie said.

Kev shot up from the couch, closed his eyes and shook his head. 'Did you not hear what Louise said? The polis are involved, Darcie. It's probably how the bastard managed to get me sent away in the fucking first place. The filth are in on it all. We can't go to them if they're protecting Donnie.'

'It won't be the entire force across the country; it's just this one guy,' Darcie pleaded.

'We don't know that for sure. Even if that's the case, it only takes just one officer to make things difficult for the likes of Louise and god knows how many others. And what about Tam? If the polis are covering for Donnie, then Tam's body will be long gone. I'm sorry to be so fucking blunt but it's true.'

Louise got to her feet and moved towards the window. She was silent as she looked out across the scheme. Darcie went to her, slid an arm around her shoulder. Kev pulled his phone from his pocket and glanced down at it.

If the police weren't an option, then Kev and the boys would have to take Donnie out themselves.

Chapter Fifty-Four

Standing back, away from the eyes of the police and the fire service, Steff watched as the yard burned to the ground. He knew who would have caused this, it didn't take a genius to work it out. Kev and the rest of the Barrhouse Firm obviously didn't like what had happened in the pub. And Kev would have a grudge because Donnie had set him up for prison. No one else would have the guts to come at Donnie Black like this. No one.

Steff kept back, stepping away from the scene and heading out of the other side of the woodland path towards his car. Once inside, he pulled out his phone and called Donnie.

'Where are you?' he asked, knowing fine well that Donnie had no clue about the yard yet. If he did, he'd have contacted Steff long before now.

'I'm waiting for Stewart. He phoned, said that Louise had rocked up at the polis station. Gave my name, told them Tam was dead. The lot. He's going to bring her to me so I can complete the delivery to Goran and get back to the yard.'

Steff took a breath. 'About that... The yard's gone.'

'Eh? What you talking about?'

'It's been blown up. There's fuck all left of it,' Steff said, almost unable to believe the words himself. Those bastards were going to pay for this.

'Tell me you're fucking kidding, Steff.' Donnie's voice was low, and Steff could tell that he was about to erupt.

'I wish I was, Donnie. It's Kev and the rest of those lads. I'm fucking sure of it.'

'Fuck!' Donnie hissed.

Steff didn't need to hear that they'd lost everything in that fire. Their security accounts, cash, the books for the taxman. Everything was in there.

Donnie was quiet for a moment, and Steff allowed him the time to take everything in. There was no way that Donnie was going to allow the Firm to ruin his empire. No fucking way.

'We're fucked, Steff.'

'Nah, Mel will have backup copies of everything. She wouldn't have left everything in there. She's a Black, learned from the best. She'll have insurance on all this stuff.'

Donnie sighed. 'I hope you're right.' And almost in an instant, Donnie dismissed it all as though it hadn't happened. 'Can you get down here and meet me? Once Stewart drops her off, I want us to make the delivery our fucking selves. There is no way I'm going to let anyone else ruin this fucking empire I've worked so hard to build after the McAdam collapse.'

Steff felt an annoyance begin to build. All Donnie seemed to care about was the fucking McAdam collapse, and how he was going to be Glasgow's next big crime boss; the biggest. Bullshit, it was all utter bullshit. Now that someone had blown up the yard, he'd be the laughing stock of the underworld.

'Fine,' he said.

But Steff had an idea. This was the perfect opportunity for him, now that Donnie was falling. He could swoop in for Layla. With Donnie looking like a monster, he could come in and be her hero.

Chapter Fifty-Five

'What do you mean, things aren't going to plan? We had a deal, Black,' Goran hissed down the phone.

Donnie moved around the car, taking big and hurried strides. This was his worst nightmare, to have to stand there and promise that he'd be able to fix things when, in fact, he didn't know for sure if that was the truth. He hadn't factored Louise escaping into the plan. He never did. It was always simple: the delivery boys would do their job, bring the second van back to the yard and Donnie would get a lump sum for the next girl. It had almost gone wrong with Demi Simpson, but Donnie had managed to pull that one back in the nick of time. And when the delivery had been made, Donnie and Steff had made sure that particular lad never forgot his mistake. Tam had taken care of that, pushing the button himself and inserting himself into Donnie's employment for life at the same time.

But this time, things couldn't be saved. How was Donnie to know that she wouldn't be given enough sedative and she'd wake up mid journey? If she'd stayed out of it, Tam would have delivered his own sister to Goran and Donnie would be paid by now.

'We still have a deal, Goran. I've never not delivered on a deal. Every girl I've said I can get, you've got. Blondes, brunettes, fucking grey-haired grannies. There isn't a type

I can't manage. This will be no different. I've got men working behind the scenes to sort this.'

Goran hadn't specified the type of girls he wanted, and that was what made it more fun for Donnie. He could get his fill from them while making them fall for him before sending them off.

'Men?' Goran asked, sounding confused.

'I've got insiders, polis and that. You don't have to worry, Goran.'

'I don't give a fuck how you do it, Donnie. Just get it sorted. The ferry leaves in two hours. No delivery... well, I shouldn't have to explain what will happen. You think your own form of punishment is harsh? That's nothing compared to what will happen to you if you don't fucking sort this.'

Before Donnie could respond, Goran hung up on him.

'Arrgh! Fucking bitch!' Donnie screamed, his voice echoing out across the vast emptiness of the deserted roadside. 'Where the fuck is Stewart?'

Glaring down at his watch, his blood almost boiled when he saw that DS Stewart was half an hour late. He called the phone he provided Stewart with and when he didn't answer, Donnie kicked the back bumper of his car.

Just moments later, headlights approached and a car pulled in behind Donnie's. He saw the registration and sighed with relief that Stewart had actually turned up.

Approaching the car with caution, he stopped when Stewart got out of the car. He stood by the driver door as it hung open and stared across at Donnie.

'She in the boot?' Donnie asked, moving around to the back of the car to check Louise was actually unconscious this time.

'No, she's not.'

Donnie stopped, stared at Stewart. 'What do you mean, no?'

'She's done a bunk, Donnie. After I got off the phone to you, she was gone.'

'What the fuck happened?'

'I checked the CCTV, and she was listening in on our phone call. She knows I'm in with you.'

Donnie gritted his teeth. That little bitch was much savvier than he ever gave her credit for. 'Where did she go?'

'If I knew that, do you think I'd be standing here empty fucking handed, Donnie? I didn't see her leave. My partner said she went outside to get fresh air while she took a break from giving a statement and just never came back in.'

Donnie wanted to kill Stewart right at that moment, but he couldn't. He needed him, needed all of them in order to continue working with Goran, to keep their business under wraps.

This was completely out of control. Donnie never lost control, but somehow Louise had managed to fuck him over, thanks to the help of her brother, Tam. Well, lucky for Donnie, Tam had been taken care of.

'You know what, DS Stewart?' Donnie spat out his name. 'You are fucking useless. And when someone is useless to me, I don't need them anymore.'

DS Stewart tutted, but when he saw Donnie pull a blade on him, his expression changed. 'Ah, you're one of those gangsters, are you? I thought it was wee neds that pulled blades on each other?'

'Don't push your fucking luck, Stewart.'

'You know you won't, and can't, kill me. I'm a DS, Donnie. Bent or not, the filth would be all over this like a bloodhound. You would never get away with it. And as soon as the rest of us lot hear you did this to me, you think they wouldn't turn on you? You wouldn't last five minutes out there once they found out what you did to me.'

Donnie's mind raced as much as his anger continued to build. He was losing control of everything around him.

'Not to mention what Goran is going to do to you when he finds out you lost a delivery. You're nothing on Marcus McAdam, Donnie, and even he fell from his fucking throne.'

Rushing forward, Donnie raised his arm, ready to slice through Stewart. Just then, another car appeared and stopped abruptly beside them.

Steff got out of the car and put himself between Donnie and the DS.

'What the fuck is going on here?' he said, eyeing the knife in Donnie's hand. 'Put that away, Donnie. You'll do yourself a fucking injury.'

Donnie glared at both men, but more so at Steff. What the fuck was the deal with his attitude? First of all he was short with him on the phone, now he was getting cocky and sarcastic, dissing him in front of Stewart.

'What did you just fucking say to me?'

Steff turned away, faced DS Stewart and shook his head. 'Unless you want a permanent scar, I'd suggest you take yourself back to the station and get on with the rest of your shift. I won't fucking tell you twice.'

Stewart hesitated before climbing into his car and pulling away from the side of the road where they'd all congregated.

'What's your fucking problem, Donnie? You're unhinged tonight.'

'Are you off your fucking head? Or have I been speaking a foreign fucking language all night? That bastard lost her, Steff. You know what that means, don't you?'

Steff nodded but glanced down at the knife. Donnie slipped it away into his inside pocket and rubbed his hand over the back of his head. He couldn't understand what was going on. Things had become chaotic. People seemed to be losing respect for him, including his brother.

'Aye, of course I know what it means, Donnie. But do you think stabbing a polis officer to death is going to help? It'll make things far worse and you've already murdered one lad tonight. What the hell happened to Tam anyway, where's his body?'

'It's been taken care of. I ordered Chud to deal with it.' Donnie frowned, pulled his lips into a snarl. 'You're supposed to be on my side. What the fuck is up with you tonight?'

Steff sighed loudly. 'Look, I don't have an issue. But this new paranoia thing you've got going on is doing my fucking nut in. If Louise isn't here, we're as well going back to what the fuck is left of the yard and try to work out what the hell we're going to do about Kev and the rest of the Barrhouse Firm. Our empire is crumbling around us here, Donnie, and you're standing here in the middle of fucking nowhere arguing with me about whether I have a problem with you or not.'

Donnie processed what Steff had said, took a steadying breath and composed himself. Maybe Steff was right, he had been feeling paranoid. But was there any wonder, what with the issues of Demi almost being compromised, and then Louise's escape?

'You know what, Steff. Fuck it. Fuck it all and fuck the lot of them. I'm done with this shitty fucking day. I'm going back to the house. If Goran wants to come after me then he'll have to wait until tomorrow.'

Donnie climbed into the car and waited for Steff to try to stop him, because that was what he wanted to happen. Steff was always the voice of reason, but for some reason tonight, he was being very stand-offish and Donnie couldn't quite work out why.

Something wasn't right.

Chapter Fifty-Six

It had finally happened. After all these years of loving her, she'd finally fallen into his arms. He never thought it was possible, that all he'd ever wanted in life would happen. Yet almost as soon as it was over, she'd immediately regretted her decision. He could still smell her perfume on his clothes. The light scent of alcohol lingered too, although it wasn't her fault that she drank so much. That was all Donnie's doing. It was always about him, always about Donnie *fucking* Black.

It had been hard living in his shadow all these years, but he'd become an expert at that. Being rejected by her, even when she didn't realise that's what she was doing, was tough. Of course he'd been able to hold it together, make sure that his face didn't show what was killing him inside, that she still loved Donnie, even after the way he treated her.

Steff thought back to their younger days, when Donnie and Layla had just got together. Steff had always liked her from as far back as he could remember. Her smile, the way she laughed, her passion to have fun and go with the flow. All those things were the reason he fell for her. And that bastard of a brother of his knew it, yet he still went after her anyway. It wasn't as though Steff could say anything about it, with Donnie being the more dominant brother. That and the fact that their father had always favoured Donnie over Steff and Mel. Steff had never been in the running for anything he wanted. Layla, the family business. Nothing. Standing back and watching Donnie break Layla down, bit by bit, year by year – it had almost killed him. But he'd thrown himself into the business and tried to forget about it. Not being able to get away from Layla hadn't helped. Now, finally, Donnie had ended things between them. He'd slept with her, and she regretted it. But Steff definitely didn't. He wanted to make her see that it should have been him she married. And he would.

He threw back a large measure of Jack and slammed the glass on the kitchen counter. He hated feeling this way, trapped by his own heart. But there was one way to get rid of Donnie, to stop Layla from wanting him.

Steff glanced at his phone and looked up the number he had stored in his contacts. It was a card he didn't think he'd ever play, but he had no other choice. He was so close to getting what he'd always wanted, he wasn't about to let it slip away now.

He dialled, held the phone to his ear and listened. When the call connected on the other side, he didn't wait.

'I have information about Demi Simpson. I know who's responsible for her disappearance. Can we meet?'

The other person was speechless, so Steff took control of the conversation. He set out instructions of when and where to meet.

'This isn't a ransom. I just want to do the right thing,' he said. He wasn't lying, but in making the call he didn't have Demi Simpson's best interests at heart. Only his own.

Chapter Fifty-Seven

A few hours had passed since Layla had asked Steff to leave. Sleeping with him had been a huge mistake. She'd done it for all the wrong reasons – to make Donnie jealous, to get him to see that they did still belong together and that there were no other women out there who could love him as much as she could. Layla hated herself for considering forgiving him for sleeping with other women. But whether it was a one-night stand or a full-blown affair, she still wanted him. Or was it purely habitual? Sleeping with Steff had felt good, of course it had. He was handsome, he knew what he was doing. But he wasn't Donnie.

She had no idea if Donnie would ever come back to the house. If he did, would she question him about everything? If they were going to work, then they had to lay everything out on the table. And she had to forget the past too, about Kerry, and stop blaming him for her death.

Torn, Layla decided the best thing she could do was go to bed and sleep, wake up with a clear head and perhaps try to contact Donnie, ask if he'd be willing to talk things out.

Placing her foot on the bottom step, she heard a scratch at the front door behind her and her heart lurched. Turning, she watched as the door crept open and Donnie appeared in the hallway in front of her. He looked exhausted, completely washed out.

They stared at each other for what felt like forever but could only have been seconds, before he closed the door behind him and turned the key in the lock. The sound was deafening, along with Layla's pumping heart.

'I didn't expect to see you back here,' Layla said.

'This is my home,' he replied. 'Our home, if you'll still have me.'

It was as though they'd had the exact same thoughts, at the exact same moment. Whatever had happened tonight could be discussed later. Right now, all Layla wanted was to lie in bed with her husband and forget all the bad shit. The affairs, the one-night stand with Steff, the possibility that Donnie had murdered someone. All that mattered was that he took her in his arms and they were together.

Nodding, Donnie moved past her, his hand brushing against hers. She still got that same feeling from when they were first together, before they were even married. That feeling that she got from no one else. That was the first time he'd shown any kind of tenderness or affection towards her in god knows how long. She missed the way they used to be, how he used to go to her for comfort when he was stressed with work. Layla always had a way of calming him, making him feel better. Those days were long gone.

Steff's face flashed into her mind, the image of them entangled together on the kitchen floor. It made her feel sick with guilt. How could she have wanted to hurt Donnie like that? It wasn't in her nature.

Seeing his face now made her realise that he really could do anything to her and she would still have him.

As they climbed the stairs together, Layla vowed to herself that she would start afresh tomorrow. No more grudges, no more living in the past.

All she wanted was Donnie. Always.

Donnie lay snoring beside her, absolutely dead to the world. They'd had sex almost as soon as they were inside the bedroom. It was hurried, frantic, and Layla hadn't expected it. Once he'd finished, Donnie had simply turned over and shut his eyes. Something inside Layla spun around and around. An itch that had to be scratched. He was off, quiet.

She watched him sleep soundly, as if he hadn't slept properly since he'd last been in their bed. Maybe he hadn't.

Slipping out of the bed as silently as she could, Layla moved around to where his jeans were lying on the floor in a heap and removed his mobile from his pocket. As his hand hung out from under the duvet, she slipped the button under his finger and gently pressed it against the tip. The phone unlocked and he didn't flinch. Taking herself out to the hallway and down to the kitchen, she sat at the table and began scrolling through it. Not she knew what she was looking for. A picture, a text, maybe even a voicemail.

She eyed the bottle of wine on the counter, the one she'd opened after Steff had left. She'd only had half a glass from it to settle her nerves. Now she felt like she needed a drink to settle her nerves at what she might find in Donnie's phone. Of course, when he'd arrived home earlier, she'd told herself she wanted a fresh start with him, no more focusing on the past. But in order to be able to move on, surely she had to know everything?

Opening up the gallery of photos and images, she scanned through them quickly. There was nothing suspicious, no girls or women. Coming out of the 'all images' file, she opened up the file marked 'deleted' and took a deep breath, before getting up and reaching for the bottle on the counter. Just one, she told herself. One would be enough to take away the jitters.

And there it was, the images that meant Donnie really wasn't as smart as everyone seemed to think he was. He hadn't fully deleted the images he'd meant to. The girl in the photos had to be under twenty years old and the idea made Layla sick to her stomach. She sank back the small amount of wine she'd poured, before refilling the glass.

She was the polar opposite to Layla. Blonde hair, beautiful. Young. Young enough to spark concern. Maybe she looked older than she was.

'What the fuck?' Layla whispered as she began scrolling through the images. More and more appeared, some with the girl and Donnie posing together, some of her on her own, in very compromising positions. Gazing up at the camera lens, posing in nothing but lingerie. The exact same as one of the sets that Layla had in her drawer upstairs. Then she paused. Could Donnie have taken that same set and given it to this girl?

Getting to her feet, Layla began pacing the kitchen floor. So many images flooded the screen as she scrolled and scrolled until she couldn't look at them anymore. And then a WhatsApp message appeared on the screen. Layla clicked on the message, and as she scanned over the words, she placed the wine glass down on the table before she dropped it.

You have fucked up, big time Donnie. And I will not stand for it. Consider yourself dead.

The message came from Goran, the name she'd overheard Steff mention. Who was this guy? And what in the hell had Donnie done to warrant such a message? Should she message him back, pretending to be Donnie? The idea was out of her head as quickly as it had appeared. That was a ridiculous thing to even think.

She closed down the message from Goran and scrolled down to see a few names she recognised. Steff, obviously. Chud, who'd worked for Donnie for a couple of years now. A big, slightly odd-looking lad who often said very little. There was a recent message from him, around thirty minutes after Donnie had arrived back home. All it said was:

> Tam taken care of. Job done.

Of course, Donnie hadn't replied; he'd been in the process of having sex with Layla at that point. In that instant, Layla decided she would reply to this one. She wanted to know who Tam was and what the hell Donnie had instructed Chud to take care of.

> Good lad. What exactly did you do?

She waited as the little icon popped up at the bottom of the message box, indicating that Chud was in the process of replying.

> What you told me to do, dump him and get rid of the evidence. Like I said, all taken care of.

Layla felt the phone slip from her hand, but she managed to catch it before it hit the floor.

'Jesus, fucking Christ,' Layla whispered.

Getting to her feet, she drained the rest of the glass of wine, grabbed the bottle and headed back upstairs. She stood by the open door of the bedroom she'd shared with Donnie for so many years and felt her stomach lurch.

Whoever Tam was, he was dead because of Donnie. Just like Kerry. Layla was kidding herself if she thought their marriage could ever go back to the way it was. Yes, she loved Donnie, but she hated what he'd become. He wasn't the lad she'd fallen in love with all those years ago. Even Steff had changed. There was something far different about both of them. The three of them had been so close back in high school, and their bond had always remained. Not now, Layla thought. There was no way she could trust either of them. If Donnie ever did anything to upset Steff, he could use the fact that he'd slept with Layla against him, or against her.

'What a fucking mess my fucking life is,' she whispered.

Turning her back on her husband, she moved through to the bathroom, locked herself in and sank to the floor before a silent eruption of emotions came pouring out.

Chapter Fifty-Eight

Two days had passed since it had happened. Two days since her big brother had been taken away from her, all because he was trying to protect her from being sold like an animal in a cattle market. It was all her fault. She should have been the one to die, not Tam. He didn't deserve it.

Lying in bed, she scrolled through the searches on the iPad that was on the bedside table. With everything that had happened, and everything coming to light about what she had almost been forced into, Demi Simpson hadn't really left her mind since. Louise wondered if Demi had fallen to the same fate that had awaited her but hadn't managed to escape. Donnie could have been the secret boyfriend of Demi's that no one knew about, the missing piece to the puzzle of why she went missing. A gentle tap on the bedroom door jolted her from her thoughts.

'Are you okay?' Darcie asked, peering around the door from the hallway. Louise had been crashing at her cousin's house since she'd arrived, hadn't had the guts to tell her mum about what had happened to Tam. How was she supposed to explain that she'd been seeing an older man who'd in fact groomed her, set her up to be kidnapped and trafficked and then, to top it off, murdered her brother when he tried to stop it from happening? Instead, she'd sent a message to say that she was on a trip with college and she would be gone for a week. It would give her time to think about what she was going to do, how she would eventually have to tell her mum what had happened.

'No,' was all Louise could manage, before turning over in the bed and facing away from Darcie, facing away from her problems.

'Cuppa?'

'No, I don't want anything.'

She felt the weight on the mattress shift as Darcie got up and left the bedroom. Louise sighed with relief; she wasn't strong enough to hold it together in front of Darcie today. Would she ever be strong enough to hold it together ever again? With the way she was feeling, it was highly doubtful.

She could feel herself dozing off when she jerked herself awake at the sound of the front door being knocked on from the outside. Louise's nerves were shot to bits. Every little sound was enough to cause her to have a panic attack, set her on edge, fearing that Donnie would come to Darcie's flat and take her away before anyone had the chance to stop him.

Closing her eyes and trying to block out the looming daylight, she listened as someone, either Kev or Darcie, moved towards the front door to answer it. She heard the sound of a chain being released, a lock turning and the handle being pulled down before the door opened.

'What the fuck?' It was Kev's voice, loud and confused.

Louise sat up quickly, straining her ears to listen, all the while her heartbeat picking up the pace.

Then she heard the sound of her cousin, a scream that was so high-pitched, yet short, that it reached the depths of Louise's soul.

The door closed, and Darcie was sobbing loudly. Kev didn't say another word, and Louise flung off the duvet before rushing out to the hall to see what was going on. As she opened the bedroom door, she froze. Stared at the people standing there.

'Lou. Are you all right?'

Tam was standing right in front of her, back from the dead. But before she could answer him, he had to reach out to grab her as her knees buckled and she fell to the floor.

'It's okay. I'm fine, I'm all right.'

She stared up at him, searching his face for signs that it wasn't really him, that she was dreaming and that at any moment she was going to wake up and continue living in the nightmare that was now her life, but as Louise blinked against the tears, Tam's face only became clearer.

Darcie's sobs were muffled as she clung to Kev, who, when Louise looked up at him, looked just as dazed and shocked as she felt.

'You're not dead?' she whispered.

Tam shook his head but winced as she grabbed him and held him tightly. She hadn't even noticed the man standing in the hall with them until that moment. He was a big guy, huge in fact. A lot bigger than Donnie in terms of build, not so much in height. His face took her breath away a little as she glanced over the acne scars, and possible burn marks.

Tam had noticed she'd been staring at the man because he said, 'This is Chud. He's the one who helped me.'

'You're supposed to be on Donnie's side. Is this an ambush or something?' Kev said, his tone aggressive as he pushed away from Darcie and squared up to Chud.

'No,' Tam said before Chud could answer. 'Donnie sent him to get rid of me, but he helped me get cleaned up. Donnie's got a shite aim, the bullet grazed me.'

Louise took a breath, swallowed back the next wave of emotion that she could feel coming over her.

'I'm sick of Donnie Black, Kev. You of all people know what it's like to be under his rule. He's a bad bastard; it just so happens that I've had enough of him. I don't really give a shit what happens to me if he finds out I've kept Tam alive. I just couldn't go through with anchoring him to the bottom of the nearest canal. Especially not when I found out why he wanted rid.' Chud glanced down at Louise, and she saw a gentle glimmer behind that monstrous expression. 'I'm sorry about what he did to you. But I'm also sorry to say that it's not the first time he's tried it, and it certainly isn't going to be the last.'

Louise felt sick at how stupid she'd been. How had she not seen Donnie Black for what he was? Of course he was never interested in her romantically, she was barely an adult. The thought disgusted her.

'You knew about what he was doing and you still worked for him?' Kev spat, and Louise noted how Darcie had a grip on his arm.

Chud shook his head. 'You don't understand. He set me up so that he had a hold on me. But then I realised that what would happen to me was nothing compared to what people like Louise were being put through. So when he gave me the job of getting rid of Tam, that was when I decided enough was enough.'

Tam got to his feet, helped Louise to stand, and the five of them stood in the small hallway of Darcie's flat.

'We're going after him,' Tam said. 'The police need to know what he's been doing and lock him away.'

Louise felt her stomach lurch. It was obvious that even Chud didn't realise the full extent of where Donnie's business ventures lay.

'The police won't do anything about it, Tam. Donnie's in cahoots with them. I witnessed a conversation between a DS and Donnie over the phone when I went to the police station about what had happened to you. The police are working for him; well, some of them are. Certainly the one I met is.'

'Did you know about that, Chud?' Kev eyed him suspiciously.

'No, I didn't, although I can't say I'm surprised. He's dangerous, Kev. You and I both know that first hand. He's got so many dodgy and sinister things going on in the background that I'm sure even the closest people to him don't even know about them.'

Louise wondered how things could get any worse.

Chapter Fifty-Nine

Leaning against the kitchen counter, Donnie took a sip from his coffee mug and stared at the doorway which led to the main hallway of the house. Going home the previous night had been the right thing to do. This house was where he belonged, no question. He couldn't fathom why he'd stayed away as long as he had.

'Morning,' Layla said as she entered the kitchen. It was a friendly greeting; it was almost forced through gritted teeth.

'What's up with your face?' Donnie asked. 'Thought you'd have been glad to have me back.'

Always so full of himself, she thought. Layla didn't say anything in response to the question. Instead, she reached around him for the coffee pot, but Donnie blocked her.

'Oi, I was talking.'

'And I wasn't listening.'

'Here we go again, I'm only just back and you're already tearing me a new arsehole,' he spat. He sat the mug down next to him, harder than he'd intended, and coffee splashed out, just missing his hand.

'I'm not, Donnie. But if you don't tell me what the fuck you've been up to, then I'll tear you more than a new fucking arsehole. So go on,' Layla shouted, 'want to explain the messages on your phone?'

'What the fuck are you on about, you mental case?'

'You know fine well what I'm on about. That Tam has been taken care of? What have you done, Donnie?'

He gritted his teeth, telling himself that he wasn't going to hurt her. But he could already feel his fists tingling. How dare she look through his fucking phone. What was on there was none of Layla's business.

'Go on then. I'm waiting.'

He turned, picked up the coffee mug and lobbed it across the kitchen. Hitting the wall, it shattered and hot coffee sprayed everywhere. Layla jumped and a little scream escaped her lips.

He spun around to face her and grabbed her by the upper arms. 'You know what? I've had enough of listening to your shite. I came back here because I thought it was the best thing. But now I remember why I left in the fucking first place. You think I want to be married to a drunk who spends her nights lying in a pool of her own fucking vomit? Even on a good day I wouldn't have you on my arm, you're a fucking disgrace. I've had enough, Layla, I'm done. I want you out of here. Go and pack a fucking bag.'

Layla glared at him, but he could see past the fake expression of anger. She was terrified. Good, he thought. It might make her sit up and see sense that he wasn't kidding.

'Why the fuck don't you leave?' Layla spat back.

'Because this is my house, Layla. In case you've forgotten, my money has paid for this place. Your shitty little businesses are just the front for all this, to keep the taxman at bay. And I own them too. Now,' he lowered his voice, 'are you going to leave by yourself, or do I have to fucking throw you out?'

He watched as things began to register with her. Finally, she was listening. As much as it did his image good to have a wife on his arm, he'd cope without her. Having Layla in his life was more hassle than it was worth. She was drunk more than she was sober, and was forever throwing Kerry's death at him as though it was his fault. Having the occasional shag with a younger, fitter girl before setting her up for business was better than having a drunk waiting for him every night.

She turned her back on him and walked slowly out of the kitchen and upstairs. He moved across to the shattered coffee mug and began picking it up; all the while Layla was upstairs, slamming doors and screaming obscenities. Not that Donnie was listening. He was sick of listening to her whining and moaning at him constantly. Kerry this and Kerry that. It wasn't Donnie's fault that she'd died; at least if it was he'd accept the jibes and put up with it. Layla's sister Kerry was a bitch, a lippy cow, nothing more and nothing less, but Donnie never ever wanted her dead. Out of the way, yes. But not dead.

He didn't have time to concern himself with a scorned wife. He needed to get on with sorting out business. Louise was still missing and Goran was like a raging bull about it. The last thing he wanted was Goran's gang on his back. He'd get Chud and Steff on the case with finding Louise.

Dropping shards into the bin, Donnie took out his phone and opened up a new message box. As he typed, he thought about lost revenue, and how even though he was pissed off that payments had been missed, getting it all in a lump sum would be a good thing. At least if Louise wasn't found, he could pay Goran off this time.

He'd have fun fucking with this punter. After all, these people were the reason he was sitting in a mansion in the best part of the city.

Turning his attentions back to the present, the first thing he was going to do was sort out the little bastards that fucked with the yard. If they wanted to play with fire, then Donnie was going to blow this war right up.

He pulled a small package from his back pocket and poured the white powder onto the kitchen counter, before taking out one of his bankcards and separating the powder into two lines. Donnie bent down and ran his nostril along the lines, one at a time, sniffing loudly as he did. The coke would give him a clearer mind on how to fix everything.

He could do this and do it well. He didn't need mass amounts of men behind him. He was Donnie Black, son of Donald Black. If he could get Goran back onside, the Barrhouse Firm would be snuffed out by the end of the week.

Chapter Sixty

The text came through. All it said was:

> You owe me! I want what's mine.

He was a bastard was Donnie Black. A cold-hearted, dirty bastard that deserved nothing more than to suffer for everything he'd put people through in order to get to where he was at in life. It was disgusting. *He* was disgusting but he could disguise it well, hide behind that charming smile.

> I've got your money. If you want it, you'll need to come to me.

Switching off the phone and setting it down on the table after the text was sent, an equal measure of fear and exhilaration rose up and into the air. They almost felt liberated.

The door was open, an invitation to let him know this was the place to come to get his money. He'd think it would be as simple as entering, taking his cash before dishing out a bit of a beating if he felt in the mood for it, and then leaving again, before heading off to his next victim.

It was a thrill to have watched the yard go up in flames like that, so quick and easy. His trafficking base burned to the ground, one of his employees turning a blind eye in exchange for a payout. Although it had seemed the lad was already on the turn anyway. He'd had enough of Donnie's ways, too, so it hadn't taken much persuasion.

There were plenty of people gunning for Donnie now. The Barrhouse Firm for one. Louise. Even his own wife had had enough of his shit.

Donnie Black wasn't going to see this coming. Not by a long shot.

Chapter Sixty-One

His ribs ached to the point where he needed to replace his pain relief patch, but even that wouldn't take the edge off the pain. Louise handed him a glass of straight Jack Daniel's and told him to drink it. Not that he would have protested. He needed as much of the stuff as he could drink to block out the trauma of what had happened. He should have disappeared after that first night working for Donnie, when he was instructed to take that guy to the incinerator place. Tam was responsible for that guy's death. And how many others? Surely Louise wasn't the only girl he'd sent overseas to be sold as a sex slave?

'I can't believe this is happening,' Louise said. She sat down next to him and rested her chin in her hands.

'I know,' Tam said. He felt weak, like a lost little boy who didn't know his way back home. 'I just can't believe I was stupid enough to think I wouldn't get into bother working for him. Steff told me in the beginning that once I was in there was no way of getting out. Well, turns out there is one way and I somehow managed to avoid it by the skin of my fucking teeth.'

'You shouldn't think of it like that,' Kev said. 'He had me fooled too.'

Tam sighed, took a large mouthful of Jack and swallowed it hard. The burn in his throat was welcome, it allowed him to forget everything for just a second.

A second without Donnie in his head was better than nothing.

'I should have known not to mess with him. Louise told me about you working for him. I knew you'd gone to prison. I just fell for the bullshit of the story.'

'No one was going to believe me over the polis, were they? I mean, police corruption isn't supposed to happen in real life. It's only meant for the TV.'

Tam winced as he shifted position on the sofa. Donnie really had done a number on him. Nearly killed him. Nearly being the key word. For some reason, he hadn't managed to finish the job. His gun had jammed, yes. But he could have made sure Tam stayed quiet. Could've stamped on his head until his brain was nothing but matter on the side of the road. But he hadn't. Tam wondered why. Maybe he was so used to having his heavies do his dirty work for him that he just couldn't bring himself to do it. Pulling a trigger was a way of disassociating from the act itself. When Tam had had to activate that incinerator, he'd been able to disassociate. It hadn't been him that had cremated that guy. It had been the machine.

A gentle tapping on the door caused Tam and the rest of them to look up, and he felt his sister tense next to him. Darcie got up to answer it.

'I should have stood up to him, Lou. I'm a fucking boxer. I should have knocked him clean off his feet but I didn't. I just took it like a wee guy.'

'No, Tam. Don't think like that. It's my fault we're here. I should have stayed away from him,' Louise said.

'Nah.' A voice came. Looking up, Tam was staring straight at the leader of the Barrhouse Firm. 'He should have stayed away from you. He should have stayed away from all of us. But, here we are.'

Cammy stood just inside the doorway of the living room, and Tam could see the rest of the boys behind him. Mackie, Dunny and Thomson. Kev got to his feet from the sofa on the other side of the room and moved towards them, shook Cammy's hand and greeted the rest of the boys. Then Cammy glanced across the room at Chud with a reserved expression.

'I hear you went on the turn, went against the big boss?' Cammy said.

Chud, who stood by the window smoking a cigarette, simply nodded. 'It wasn't right what he was doing, or what he wanted me to do with Tam.'

Cammy and the rest of the boys nodded. 'And you're loyal to this lot now, are you? It's just, well, you were in the pub with him and Steff Black, weren't you? Like one of those puppies, following its master around.'

'Cam, we can trust him,' Kev interjected. 'He's not a threat. If he was, Tam wouldn't be sitting here now.'

Cammy paused before nodding, as though he accepted that if Kev trusted Chud that was good enough for him.

'Donnie and Steff didn't tell me much, but I overheard a lot of things. They're working with a European guy, Goran. They're basically trafficking as many girls overseas as they can and I don't think Louise here was the first. From what I could hear, there have been a few. I kept my mouth shut because I had to for my own safety. And I'm glad I did. If I hadn't, I don't think me or Tam would be breathing right now.'

Turning, he stared down at both Tam and Louise, his eyes narrow and his expression stern.

'You both all right?'

Louise shook her head. 'Combination of terrified and absolute fire-raging fury. Other than that, I'm okay.'

'Chud, are you absolutely certain about this?' Cammy asked.

'Aye. Dead sure.'

'It seems that there's a lot we didn't know about. Gangs from Europe involved, and we already know about polis involvement. If Tam hadn't looked in the back of that van, you'd be somewhere in northern Europe by now. Lithuania, Estonia? Who the hell knows.' Cammy shook his head.

When he put it like that, Tam felt sick. He took another gulp from the Jack glass in his hands and swallowed hard. Cammy watched his expression, and there was a flicker of sympathy in his eyes before they narrowed once again.

'Cammy, have you spoken to Mel at all? Has she said anything to you about all this? I mean, she is their sister and she does the books. She'll have some kind of knowledge.' Kev asked.

'I've not spoken to her since getting out the jail that weekend those bastards planted the drugs in your van. Even if I had, she wouldn't tell me anything. Donnie and Steff will have her well warned against speaking to anyone out with their family.'

'Always worth an ask,' Kev said. 'Right, I have something that I've been sitting on for years. It could be something or nothing; although, based on what we know, it's probably relevant,' Kev said.

Tam looked up at Kev, as did everyone else.

'What is it, mate?' Cammy asked.

Kev took a breath and glanced down at Tam and then Louise. 'When we were in our late teens, we went to that rave, remember?'

Cammy and the boys nodded. 'Aye, what about it?'

'Well, I found Donnie in a field, away from the action. He was with a girl. But it wasn't Layla. He was' – he swallowed – 'he had his hands around her neck; she was completely out of it. I confronted him about it and, the next thing I know, Donald senior was at my door the next day, a gun to my fucking head, telling me that if I ever breathed a word, I'd get a bullet in the skull.'

Cammy raised a brow, and Tam could tell everyone in the room seemed shocked.

'It's just that, well, I think it speaks volumes for the person he is now. After we know what's happened to Louise, and the fact that Chud has confirmed there is involvement with European gangs, it's looking more and more likely that the trafficking shit that's going on right now all leads back to Donnie.'

The rest of the Firm moved into the living room, and both Darcie and Louise fell silent as they positioned themselves around the room.

'Fucking hell, if I'd told you lot back then, none of this would be happening right now,' Kev said, running his hands over his face.

'Nah,' Cammy said. 'That bastard had you silenced the only way he knew how. Through Daddy fucking dearest. Well, old Donald is long gone now, as is the yard. Donnie's empire is falling apart and he knows it. I never thought I'd say this, but it's a silver lining that Chud jumped ships back then. Otherwise, we'd still be wondering what the hell is going on.'

Chud kept his eyes down and Cammy gave him a reassuring tap on the shoulder.

'Right then,' Mackie said, 'here's what we're going to do about the bastard.'

Chapter Sixty-Two

Knocking on the door of the Barrhouse Tavern, Donnie cracked his knuckles together as he stamped out his cigarette. There was no way he was going to let Cammy and the rest of those plastic gangsters get away with burning down the yard. But he wasn't going to go straight for them. No, he wanted to make them suffer first. Burn some of their income too.

'Donnie?' Pete said as he opened the door. He saw the look on Pete's face. Fear and terror. 'What can I do for you?'

Donnie didn't answer; instead, he pushed his way into the pub and took a seat at the bar. Of course, there was no one else in with it being just after nine. He watched as Pete closed the door and turned to face him.

'How's things, Pete?'

Nodding, Pete moved in behind the bar. 'No bad, Donnie.'

He liked that Pete was nervous. It was nothing compared to how he would feel if he didn't agree to Donnie's request.

'Here's the thing, Pete, I've known you for a few years now, eh?'

Pete kept his eyes on Donnie as he spoke but remained silent.

'Have drank in your pub for many, many years. I've seen what it can get like in here of a weekend. Gets a bit rowdy, folk like to take the piss when there's no authority. I've seen it. But I've never had to say anything because, well, I was here. Folk knew not to mess about when I was present. So I'll cut to the point. You're going to be looked after, you and this pub. Every week, you'll pay me a thousand quid and your pub will be safe, as will you. Safety isn't something those Barrhouse lads can offer you, not properly.'

Pete licked his dry lips and took a breath before he spoke. 'I've already got security, Donnie. I pay a monthly fee to Cammy McNab and the Barrhouse Firm. It's covered. Sorry.'

Donnie sniggered. 'You're not really hearing me, are you, Pete?'

He got up, moved around to the other side of the bar and pulled a glass down from the shelf before pouring himself a measure of Jack Daniel's. He drank it back greedily and slammed the glass down on the bar top.

Pete jumped and looked away.

'A thousand a week, or you won't have a fucking pub to be looked after at all. I'll blow the place up, just like those bastards did to my yard.' Donnie moved so that he was in Pete's face, giving him no other option but to look him in the eye. 'You hear me now, Pete?'

Pete refused to answer, and Donnie's patience was wearing thin, so he picked up the glass and lobbed it across the bar. It smashed against the door and rained down on the doormat. 'You've got one week to switch over from them to me, or your precious fucking tavern will be nothing but an inferno.'

Donnie walked towards the door, and the glass crunched under his shoes. Once outside, he pulled out his mobile and searched for DS Stewart's number. Why did he say to Pete that he had a week? He needed that money now. Right now.

'Fuck!' He hissed as DS Stewart's phone went to voice-mail. 'It's me. I need you to do me a favour. I need you to do some digging, find me a young lassie. A vulnerable one, easy to manipulate. I don't have a lot of time. Goran's on my case. I don't know, get me a name of one of the prostitutes you've lifted or something, just anyone. Do it, Stewart, or I'll make sure that when Goran comes for me, I'll drag you down with me.'

He hung up and stared up at the sky above him. His old man would be spinning in his grave right now if he could see the mess Donnie had got himself into.

Chapter Sixty-Three

'Cheers,' Cammy said, sliding the envelope of cash into the inner pocket of his jacket. 'Things going good here, Pete? Door staff keeping an eye on things?'

Cammy knew the answer to the question. Of course his boys were doing their job properly. Cammy and the rest of the Firm had instructed them of their duties. It was all part of the agreement with each premises. Good security for a no interest, fixed monthly rate and the Barrhouse boys would be able to operate their drug business from each place, no questions asked. It had been a deal each owner had been willing to do. Their only other option was to have Donnie and Steff Black on their cases, high rates of interest that couldn't be paid other than having their premises attacked and burned to the ground. Losing their livelihoods wasn't an option.

'Aye, Cammy. All good. Boys do a great job,' Pete replied. 'Although, it would've helped if they'd been here this morning.'

Cammy glanced at Pete, whose eyes were wide yet blinking rapidly. He was worried about something.

'What happened?'

'It's Donnie Black. He paid me a visit.'

Cammy felt his jaw clench. Although he couldn't say he was surprised at all. Donnie Black was a businessman, just like Cammy – a failing businessman at that. And after what he and the boys had done to him because of Kev's prison sentence, was it any wonder he'd visited a Barrhouse Firm business?

'Oh aye? And what did he have to say for himself?'

'He threatened me and the pub. Told me that if I didn't switch over to his security company within the week, then I wouldn't have a business at all. Demanded a thousand a week.'

Cammy took a calming breath and closed his eyes for a moment. 'A thousand a week? That's cheap coming from the likes of him.' Cammy caught Pete's expression, knew that he was thinking a thousand a week is far from cheap to someone like him. Cammy ignored it. 'He must be desperate. I wouldn't say you've got anything to worry about here, Pete. I'll let the door staff know about this, get an extra couple of guys on to your premises. Donnie Black won't be threatening you again.'

Pete looked unsure. 'How do you know?'

Cammy frowned. 'Because I'm telling you. You pay us for security, and I give a full service. I couldn't give a shit what Donnie Black thinks he's going to do, but it's not happening on our watch. And you'd do well to trust me, Pete. You don't fucking pay us for nothing.'

Pete nodded quickly. 'Of course, Cammy. I do trust you. It's him I don't trust. The dirty bastard that he is. You've heard the rumour that he's responsible for the disappearance of that young lassie, Demi Simpson. I know some of the family too. Fucking shame so it is.'

Cammy patted Pete on the shoulder. 'Aye, Pete. We know. Like I said, Donnie Black won't be threatening you again. He's getting desperate, so he'll do anything to keep himself in this game.'

Cammy exited the office and out to the main bar area, where Mackie was sitting in with some of the locals having a game of poker. When Mackie locked eyes with him, he was on his feet, abandoning the game.

'What's up?'

Cammy motioned for Mackie to follow him outside. A few of the older punters stood outside, smoking pipes and talking horse racing. They hadn't even noticed that Cammy and Mackie were there.

'It's Black. He's threatened Pete. Told him that if he doesn't switch over to him for security that he's going to burn the place down. Demanding a grand a week off Pete.'

Mackie sniggered. 'That's pennies to him. He's only saying that because of what happened to the yard. He's bluffing.'

'I don't think so. We need to move fast, get him off the streets and settle the unrest surrounding the rumours. He's a dangerous bastard, Mackie. If we don't act fast, another girl will go missing. He'll have Louise to replace.'

Mackie lit a cigarette and nodded. 'Aye, your call. But aren't we waiting on the green light from—'

Cammy shot him a look, and Mackie fell silent. 'Aye. But keep that quiet. Anyone overhears us and the whole plot could fall apart.'

Mackie took a long draw on his cigarette and smoke billowed from his nostrils.

'When I get the call, you'll be the first to know.'

Mackie had resumed his game of poker, Dunny stood at the back of the bar next to the puggy machine and

Thomson and Kev were outside, chatting with the door staff. Their presence alone would be enough to deter Donnie.

The man had lost his yard and hadn't even come after the people he knew were responsible for it. Neither had Steff. So what the hell was going on with them? Had their bollocks finally deflated and now Cammy and the rest of the Firm were seeing them for what they were? Fraudsters? Yes, Donnie Black was minted and a well-known gangster, but the level of respect that people didn't have for him nowadays was laughable. He wanted to be like the McAdams, to claim the city as his own. But he was failing miserably. The McAdam clan had something that Donnie didn't. Ferocity, class. Even though Cammy and the rest of the boys hated them for what they stood for, it was clear that Donnie was never going to be a match for what they once were. And as for demanding Pete pay him a mere grand per week, maybe his finances weren't all that great. Maybe the Black empire was falling a lot faster than any of them realised.

His phone pinged in his pocket and Cammy pulled it out, stared down at the screen and refrained from smiling.

All set.

He forwarded the message to the rest of the boys. And as the messages pinged up on each of their phones, one by one each of his brothers and cousins looked up. They all knew it was time.

Chapter Sixty-Four

Drunk wasn't the word she'd use to describe her condition at that particular moment. Smashed wouldn't even cover it. Paralytic. Layla could barely see straight as she made her way along the hallway towards the bathroom. She felt like she was in a dream, a very fast-paced one that was beginning to make her feel sick. Why did she have to drink so much? It wasn't as though the alcohol was going to change anything. Her marriage had been a failure from day one; her husband was everything she hated in a man, even though she still loved him; her sister was dead and there was no explanation as to what happened. And now, she was lying in the house that Donnie was going to take off her, out of her face and barely able to make it to the bathroom at all.

The blackouts were infrequent; sometimes they would happen without her expecting it. Sometimes they were so bad that she could remember nothing from before she passed out. Layla knew she should stop drinking, but that didn't make it any easier.

Being married to the man she blamed for her sister's death wasn't easy. Of course, no one pushed her in front of that car. No one made her do that. However, if Kerry and Donnie hadn't been arguing, then she wouldn't have stepped out at all. She would still be here, alive and giving

Layla all the support a sister would give, like she used to do.

Knowing that Donnie had failed to be faithful during their marriage made her feel like shit, which drove her to want to block that feeling out. Now that Donnie had confirmed he'd wanted her out of the house, and having discovered those messages on his phone, Layla wondered if she could class this evening's drink binge as a celebration of her freedom.

A wave of sickness washed over her then and she tried to rush along to the bathroom quicker.

–

The pain in her head was what woke her up. It throbbed more than she thought possible. Opening her eyes, she discovered that she was lying on the bathroom floor. How long had she been there? Hours?

'Jesus fucking Christ!' Layla hissed as she stared down at her shaking hands. She swayed on her feet, just about managing to stand. Dried blood stained her cuticles, fingernails torn from the edge. Slowly raising her eyes towards the mirror, she barely recognised herself.

'What the actual fuck?' The words barely a whisper, she gripped the edge of the sink to steady herself as she took in the sight. Blackened eyes from smeared mascara, a bang to the head. What had happened last night?

'Donnie?' she called out, the sheer effort to use her voice making her feel like she was about to be sick. 'Donnie, what the hell happened last night?'

Turning on the tap, she bent down and splashed her face with cold water, before beginning to scrub her hands to get the bloodstains off. They must have had another one of their fights. It was the only way to explain it. It was always the way to explain it.

'Donnie?'

Drying her hands on the towel she'd pulled from the rail next to the sink, she stepped out of the en-suite bathroom and stared into the bedroom she shared with her husband. But he wasn't there. The bed hadn't been slept in. Waking up on the bathroom floor just a few minutes earlier had meant she'd not slept in their bed. Of course not, she never did when she got herself into a drink-fuelled state, usually because Donnie would make her up a bed in the bathtub because he couldn't bear to be near her, and he'd take up the superking to himself. Although not this morning, it would seem.

'*Donnie!*' she called again, this time more forceful. If they had had one of their drunken arguments last night, then the bastard would be giving her the silent treatment. And that's when she remembered that Donnie had left. She hadn't been with him when she'd been drinking. They hadn't argued. Thinking back to what could have caused her to end up where she did, she searched through the drunken and hazy memories. A slight recollection of stumbling to the bathroom, crying about Kerry. Did she simply lose her balance and fall? Glancing at the edge of the toilet and seeing the blood smear confirmed that. The broken towel rail on the floor with bloodstains on it. She'd tried to save herself from the fall.

'You're an idiot, Layla,' she scolded herself.

Pulling the bedroom door open and glaring down the hallway towards the staircase, she noticed that the large, framed wedding photo of them had been knocked off the wall and was lying in its smashed state on the carpet. A blood-smeared handprint in its place. Something in her gut rolled as she cautiously approached the top of the stairs, careful not to step on broken glass. As she got closer to the picture of her and Donnie, she noticed how the white dress was stained pink and red. That wasn't what disturbed her the most. Staring down at the picture, an icy chill crept over her entire body. Donnie's smiling face no longer smiled out at the lens of the camera. The high-quality print had been destroyed, Donnie's face scored and slashed in what looked like a frenzied manner.

Layla stopped and fell to her knees, not caring that the glass surrounding her could pierce her skin. Her eyes wide with horror, she read the words which had been scrolled across the centre of the image in red paint.

SCUM GET WHAT'S COMING!

Chapter Sixty-Five

Kev scrubbed the blood from his hands as he listened to the rest of the boys laugh about what they'd done. He hadn't wanted to go through with trashing Donnie's house when Layla was still inside by herself, but the rest of his cousins hadn't given him much of a choice. He'd wanted to help Layla, but he knew that if he'd called an ambulance, the police would eventually start asking questions. And with Kev not long out of prison, it could have landed him right back where he didn't want to be.

'The bitch has what's coming to her. She's not dumb, she would have known fine well what her husband was up to,' Cammy sneered as he lit a cigarette.

'Aye. And it's not like she's going to remember who did it. She was barely conscious when we broke in,' Mackie chipped in.

Kev sighed, shook his head. 'She's still a woman, though. Imagine Donnie did that to Darcie.'

Cammy shot him a look. 'It's a fucking good thing he didn't. I personally would have shot the bastard long before now if that was the case.'

Dunny and Thomson laughed loudly as Tam sat at the round table, dishing out playing cards. He was part of the Barrhouse Firm now, and trashing Donnie's house had been a way of initiating him into the Firm.

'You're family now, wee man. You'll need to show me some of those boxing moves, see if I could take you on.' Cammy sucked on the end of his cigarette, and Tam laughed.

Something didn't feel right. He genuinely believed that Layla was an innocent victim in Donnie's life. Just like Louise and whoever else who may have been unfortunate enough to come into contact with him.

Kev wondered if they were all just as bad as Donnie, allowing that to happen when Layla was still in the house, unable to even lift her head. That was why Kev had gone to check on her. He hadn't expected there to be blood, but when he'd knelt down to check her, touching her head had been a big mistake. But Cammy had thought it would be a nice touch for Donnie.

'Smear it on that canvas. Right across his smug face. When he next sees it, he'll know he's got nothing to fucking smile about,' Cammy had said.

At the time, Kev had liked the idea. But now he was wracked with guilt. Not about Donnie, but about Layla.

'Kev, you getting in on this or not?' Dunny asked.

Kev turned, nodded and sat down at the table.

'What's up with your face? Cheer up, Kev. This is all because of what that bastard did to Darcie's family. *Your* family. Now, get a fucking whisky in you and let's play some poker,' Cammy said.

Kev was worried about how far this was going to go. Innocent people could get caught in the middle. Wasn't that what they were trying to prevent from happening in the first place?

'Once Donnie's dead, we can begin to get back to real business, without the fear of him coming after our girls,'

Cammy said. 'I'll be happy to pull that trigger. We just have to wait on the go-ahead.'

Chapter Sixty-Six

Walking along the road, Donnie Black smiled to himself as he thought of how he was going to retaliate against the Barrhouse Firm. They were more like toddlers than gangsters. They'd never amount to more than they already were and that was nothing without Donnie behind them, putting cash in their pockets, and they certainly didn't have the balls to go where there was real cash to be made. It was just a shame that Louise had made such a fuss, otherwise Donnie would be sitting on an extra fifty grand right now. He'd get her back; he always managed to sort out his troubles. Visiting Pete at the pub was one of those troubles, and he'd already made a start on dealing with that. Cammy and his little Firm of rodents would be furious. Good, let them be angry. It was nothing compared to what they were going to get after they ruined the yard.

He spotted Louise's house, just twenty yards from where he was standing. It was a long shot, but if she answered the door, he would be able to snatch her up quickly, get her drugged and get her to Goran himself. She'd be no match for Donnie physically. He knew her frame. She was petite, vulnerable up against his size.

Donnie's phone vibrated inside his pocket, and he took it out to answer it. 'Chud?'

'Boss...' there was a moment of silence, and Donnie stopped walking along the street. His voice sounded off, like he was going to deliver bad news.

'Yes?'

'Don't look behind you.'

Donnie strained to listen, but before he could process what Chud had said, the line went dead. Donnie pulled the phone away from his ear and glanced down at it. Pulling up Chud's number to call him back, a sudden force knocked him forward, and he couldn't stop himself from falling to the ground, his phone flying forward and skiting along the pavement.

As he tried to turn, a blow to the back of his head stunned him into stillness. Hands gripped tightly around his ankles before pulling him back along the street. He wanted to reach into his pocket, but he wasn't carrying. Why had he chosen to leave his gun behind on this of all days?

Donnie twisted his body, tried to get a look at his assailant, but as he attempted to turn another blow came, this time to the side of the face. His cheek felt like it had exploded, and his ears rang.

'Don't fucking move.' The voice came from behind him. A male voice that he possibly recognised. Could have put a name to it if he wasn't so dazed.

Donnie resisted the pull from the person behind him, but then he felt a second pair of hands on him and a third blow to the back of the head. He was barely conscious, but before he passed out completely, he glanced up at the blurred faces. Inside he was seething, but on the outside he was paralysed.

'Are you sure about this?' One voice said. It was female.

'Never been surer of anything in my life. He's a bastard, always has been. He deserves everything he gets. Why are you even asking that? He's responsible for your niece going missing.'

There was silence after that, and that's when Donnie recognised his attackers.

Then he was pulled into the cage inside the back of the van, and the doors slammed him into darkness.

–

A thick blanket of darkness enveloped him, and he felt like he couldn't breathe. There was a smell, very specific, like old damp clothes. Then he realised that the scent was coming from him. A mix of stale sweat and piss coated his skin, like snail trail across dry soil.

He tried to speak, but the words seemed to catch on the roof of his mouth, just like his tongue. Dry, so dry, he thought.

'Don't try to say a word,' a voice came from somewhere nearby, so quiet that he almost didn't hear it. Was he imagining the voice? He was so badly dehydrated that it was possible.

He tried to move, but the skin on both his wrists pinched. Cable ties, he realised. But not just cable ties. Rope. It burned his skin as he struggled against the place he'd been secured to. Piping of some kind. Thick, iron pipes that at the present moment were stone cold yet seemed to burn against him.

'And don't bother trying to move either. You're not going anywhere,' the voice said again, although this time it came from a different direction.

He listened to the movement around him, wondering if there was more than one other person present. He couldn't be sure if he recognised the voice; he'd been under the blanket of darkness for some time now. Hours? Days? He wasn't sure.

'Do you *know* you're going to die? Maybe not here. Maybe not today. But you will. The question is, will it be quick, so you don't even know it's happened? Or will I choose to make you die slowly, painfully? That's the bit I haven't decided on. Because that's what you deserve, isn't it? After everything, after it all, the only thing that would put things right would be if you never saw the light of day again.'

He shook his head as the words sank in and he tugged at his restraints. There was no way he was going to let this happen. This was not how he was going to die.

—

The thumping headache woke him. He tried to stretch out, but he was tied down. Ankles, legs, wrists, arms. Opening his eyes, he waited for them to adjust to the darkness. Donnie didn't know where he was, but he was no longer in the back of that van.

'Oi, let me fucking up,' he shouted, although the effort it took to get the words out caused his head to throb even more. He winced.

'Shut up,' a voice came from somewhere in the room.

'I'll fucking kill you,' Donnie said, wriggling inside his bindings. 'You hear me, I'll fucking kill you.'

'Now, now. You wouldn't do that to me, would you?'

A figure emerged from the shadows in the far corner of the room. As Donnie took in what he was seeing, a laugh almost began to build.

'This is a wind up, isn't it? Fucking hell, just untie me, you arsehole.'

'You're the arsehole, Donnie. For ever trusting me.'

Donnie glared at his face. 'What the fuck is this all about, Steff?'

Steff smiled. 'It's purely business, Donnie. You of all people can understand that, surely?'

Donnie's mind whirred. What in the hell was going on here? Why had Steff done this to him?

'You've turned on me? Why? What business could possibly cause you to turn on your brother?'

Steff didn't answer. There was a moment when everything was silent, so silent that Donnie thought the blows to the head had caused him to suddenly go deaf. Then another figure appeared next to Steff. Donnie remembered that there were two people involved in his attack when he was pulled off the street.

'*You?*' Donnie almost laughed again. 'Jesus Christ, the lengths people will go to not to have to pay their fucking debt!'

Susie Fowler gave a menacing smile. 'The only person in debt here is you, Donnie. You're indebted to me now. And if you don't tell me where my fucking niece is, I'm going to make sure that you die a very long, torturous death.'

Donnie frowned. 'I don't know what the fuck you're on about, Susie. You and him' – he glanced at Steff – 'you've fucking lost it.'

Steff eyed Donnie in earnest. 'You're the one who's lost it, Donnie.'

'You're a traitorous bastard, Steff. I mean, what the fuck is this all about? You're not still pissed that I stole your bird back in the day. Still spat the dummy that she'd rather shag me than you? Is that it?'

Steff balled his fist by his side but flexed his fingers and remained where he was. Donnie let out a laugh, not in humour but defence.

Susie rushed forward and slapped Donnie, causing an iron taste to coat the inside of his mouth.

'Demi Simpson, you fucking prick. She's been missing for months, and it's all because you took her like she was some sort of possession. I won't say it again. Where is my fucking niece?'

Before Donnie could respond, he felt the sharpness of the cold blade against his throat, and the look in Susie's eyes told him that if he didn't answer her question, she would slit his skin and allow him to bleed out.

Chapter Sixty-Seven

She stared at the gap in between the door and frame for what felt like forever, not daring to move in case it was all some kind of test. Daylight shone through the crack in the door and a feeling of hope took over.

'I promise you, it's not a trick. You don't belong here,' he said. It was her punter, a regular punter since she'd got here, a punter who she'd built up some kind of weird relationship with. He'd never wanted to sleep with her. Only hug, talk. She'd found it very strange, but also a relief from the relentlessness that was the other brutal male punters she was made to deal with on a daily basis.

'I can't trust you,' she said.

'Yes, you can. I've never hurt you, never made you do… that. You don't belong in this world. I'm giving you a chance to get out. Take it.'

The voices on the street were distant but not so far that it made her think she couldn't do this. It had to be worth a shot. If she was caught, she'd be dragged back here and possibly killed for the act of trying to claw back her freedom And he would be killed too. Maybe being dead would be better than what she'd had to endure for the months she'd been kept captive. Hundreds of disgusting men paying money to the people at the top to do whatever they wanted with her, a lot of whom didn't even speak English. Some of them didn't even look at her.

She'd imagine each and every one of their deaths during each ordeal. Some would be hit by a train, others a car. She even imagined slitting their throats. It was the only way she'd survived this long.

Holding her breath, Demi Simpson slowly got to her feet and crept across the floor of the dark and dreary room she'd been kept in. Staring down the short corridor, she saw that the front door had been propped open and light flooded in and down towards her own room. There was no one around. No one seemed to be patrolling the hall. There were usually two men who didn't speak English other than to tell her to get back when they opened her door to pass in some food and water. She wasn't allowed out of her room. Ever.

'They'll kill you,' she said.

'I'll get away. They won't see either of us ever again,' he replied.

Letting out her breath slowly, she strained to hear their voices. The place seemed deserted. But why? Had something happened? Not that she cared. All she needed to know was that she could get out of the building. If she could just get onto the street, she could ask someone to help her.

When she'd arrived, they'd taken her shoes and jacket from her so she wouldn't be able to run. And up until now, she hadn't wanted to risk it. Today was different. Today was the first time she'd seen daylight in months. She didn't care that she had no shoes or jacket, worse things had happened to her than going outside barefoot.

'Just go, now. Before it's too late and they come back. You won't get a chance like this again.'

Swallowing the lump of fear in her throat, she gave him a sideward glance, mouthed a thank you and slipped between the gap and into the hall, treading carefully along the cold tiles towards the open door. She was careful not to breathe too quickly so as not to alert anyone that she was out of her room. Music blared from one of the rooms upstairs, and she could hear men laughing, cackling at something lurid most likely. The sound made her speed up a little and, soon, she was by the exit. Peering out, the bright white sky hurt her eyes and she blinked against the light.

The street just a few yards away was busy with people. She had no way of knowing if anyone would help her, but she thought that if someone saw her in the street with no shoes, barely any clothes and covered in bruises, then they would know something was wrong with her.

Turning back to make sure that none of the male guards were behind her, she breathed a sigh of relief when she saw an empty hallway, before turning her attention back to the street and slipping through the gap and into the alleyway.

The air was cold against her skin, but it was the freshest feeling she'd felt in so long. She didn't know if she had the energy to run, but she was going to give it her best shot.

Moving along the alley quickly, Demi felt the concrete against her feet pierce her skin. She didn't let it stop her as she moved closer to the end of the alley. Reaching the end, she was met by a locked gate. She needed to climb up and over, so pulling herself up, Demi swung her leg over and dropped down the other side. Looking to her left and then to her right, she noticed that no one seemed to pay any attention to her. They were all too busy sitting at their tables, eating their food and drinking their beers. All but one couple, who were staring at her with a look of concern. She rushed over to them, crouched down beside the female and smiled at her.

'Do you speak English?' Demi asked, her voice almost failing her. She'd barely spoken in months since she'd been taken.

'Yes, I do,' the girl said. Her accent was from home and Demi's voice cracked. 'Are you okay?'

'No. Can you help me?'

The girl looked across at the man with her. They were both in their twenties, Demi guessed. They couldn't be much older than her. He looked as terrified as Demi felt and a pang of guilt hit her by dragging them into her ordeal. But she had no other choice.

'Please. I don't know how long I have before they realise I'm gone.'

The girl got up from her seat and took her hand. 'Wait there,' she said to the man who was still sitting down.

The girl picked up her bag and pulled her through the café towards the toilets. Demi kept her head down, said nothing and made eye contact with no one. Once inside the bathroom, the girl pulled Demi into one of the cubicles and locked the door.

'What's happened to you?' she whispered.

Demi shook her head as tears formed in her eyes. 'I was taken by a foreign man and brought here.'

The girl's shoulders slumped. 'You're a victim of sex trafficking?'

Demi nodded and the tears spilled over.

'Do you have your passport?'

'No. I wasn't exactly brought here legally.'

'Right,' the girl said. Demi could see that she was emotional but trying to hold it together for her sake. She lowered the toilet seat gently and placed her bag on it. 'I went shopping today and bought some clothes. Get changed into them. There's a hairbrush in there and make-up. Try to do yourself up as best as you can. We're going to try to get you some help. Okay?'

Demi sobbed silently. She couldn't believe that this girl had taken her at face value and was going to the lengths she was to help her. Demi wasn't out of danger yet. They could still find her. It was highly unlikely that she would get away unscathed.

'Thank you,' Demi whispered as the girl handed her the bag. 'I don't even know your name.'

'It's Lucy.' She smiled, and then suddenly she hugged Demi close to her. 'We're going to get you away from here. Together.'

Demi sighed and clung to the girl. She really wanted to believe her.

—

Demi looked at her face in the mirror after Lucy had done her make-up and hair. She still looked like herself, but less shocking. The clothes, the hair and new face might be enough to disguise her to get through the streets.

'Allan is finding out where the British Consulate building is from here. As soon as we know, we'll take you there. Okay?' Lucy said.

She nodded, glanced at Lucy in the mirror. 'Why are you being so kind?'

'You asked us for help. We couldn't just leave you there on the street. Something terrible has happened to you. What kind of person would I be if I abandoned you when you had no one else to turn to?'

Demi hadn't spoken to Lucy about her ordeal, only that she'd been abducted. She'd kept everything in, too terrified that if she spoke of the truth, the terror of escaping might hold her back.

Lucy's phone pinged in her pocket and, as she looked at her phone, she nodded and glanced at Demi.

'Allan has found where we need to go. Are you ready?'

Demi nodded, and Lucy took hold of her hand.

'You're going to be fine, Demi. I promise, we'll get you home.'

Demi felt her heart lurch as Lucy opened the cubicle door and stepped out, holding her hand and gently pulling her out. They moved through the café and out to the terrace, where Demi could see Allan standing up at their table. He looked anxious as he wrung his hands together.

'Ready?' Lucy asked him.

'Aye, but just sit down for a minute, eh?'

'What's wrong?' Demi immediately began to panic. 'They're here, aren't they?'

Allan took a breath. 'There were men walking up and down in groups. A few of them, maybe three or four in each group. Staring at everyone, looking inside the cafés and pubs. It might be nothing to do with you but I don't want us looking suspicious. So just sit down, we have one more drink. You sit with your back to the street and then we go.'

Demi felt her stomach drop. They knew she was out and they were looking for her.

'I can't.'

'Hey,' Lucy said. 'Yes, you can. You look entirely different now to what you did when you got here just half an hour ago. They won't recognise you.'

'I can't take the risk. If I sit here and one of them recognises me, we're all dead. Lucy, please.'

Lucy glanced at Allan, who nodded.

'Okay. Try not to panic. There's a taxi rank over there. We walk together, slowly. We don't want to look like we're in a rush. Okay?'

Allan moved out from the table and laid down some cash before they all moved across the street.

Reaching a taxi, Demi climbed in and Lucy was behind her. Allan got into the front. Just as Allan was about to shut the door, the sound of Demi's name being called across the street made her heart stop.

'Ignore it,' Allan said, closing the door. He told the driver where to go and as the taxi pulled away, Demi trembled in her seat.

'It could have been anyone,' Lucy said.

'It was them. I know it was.'

She wanted to turn, to look out the back window to see for herself. But if she did that, then they would see her. They'd chase the taxi. The driver, Allan and Lucy would die, and Demi would too.

'Lucy,' Demi started, but before she could ask her to check if they were gone, the taxi came to a sudden halt.

'What the fuck?' the driver said as he slammed on the brakes. And that was when something inside Demi Simpson sank.

She watched as two men got out of the car in front of them and walked towards the taxi. Allan turned, glanced at both her and Lucy in the back.

'That's them,' Demi said, unable to tear her eyes from two of the men she recognised from the brothel. 'They've found me.'

The taxi driver reached for the handle, but before he could do or say anything, there was a loud popping sound, and Demi threw herself to the floor. Lucy screamed and fell silent. Demi noticed blood spatters on the seat beside her, and when she glanced up at Lucy, she'd stopped screaming, her body slumped against the back door. She was dead. So was Allan.

By some miracle, the driver managed to slam his foot to the floor and the car jolted forward before screeching down the street.

Demi threw her hands over her head and clung to the seat in front of her where Allan's body lay lifeless. Gunshots rang out behind them as the driver picked up speed.

'Jesus fucking Christ,' he screamed as he weaved in and out of traffic. Demi didn't have to look up to know they were being chased.

The sirens grew louder in the distance. The police were coming. She prayed to every higher being possible that they got to her before Goran and his men did.

Chapter Sixty-Eight

'Hey, calm down,' Steff said, gripping her shoulders and holding her steady. 'It'll just be some chancer hoping to have found a few quid in the house.'

Layla shook uncontrollably in his arms. 'No, Steff. You didn't see the mess. The message scrawled across the canvas at the top of the stairs. *Scum get what's coming to them.* It was a threat, Steff. And I was in the house when it happened, completely oblivious to what was going on because I was lying pissed out my head.'

The panic in her chest constricted and she felt like she couldn't get a breath. Her skin tingled, and a hot flash rushed across her cheeks.

'Well, Donnie does have a lot of enemies. You don't get through his line of work without gaining a few of those. Could have been a punter he's cut off due to debt?' Steff suggested. He let go of her and pulled her close.

'No, it's not that. There's something else going on and I've been kept in the dark about it. Steff, if you knew anyone who would do this, you'd tell me, wouldn't you?'

Layla pulled away and looked up at Steff.

'Of course I would tell you, Layla.' Steff sighed. 'If something is going on that I don't know about then I've been kept in the dark about it too.'

Layla nodded. Donnie had always had a secretive side to him, but Layla had been one of those wives that kept her mouth shut and said nothing over the years just to keep him by her side. Now that this had happened, that whatever shit he'd gotten himself into had spilled into her home, Layla wasn't going to put up with it anymore.

'Why don't I get you a drink?' Steff said.

She hesitated, knowing that alcohol was never a good mix with her, especially when she was feeling so low and paranoid. Against her better judgement, Layla nodded, and Steff disappeared into the kitchen.

Left standing in the hallway of Steff's house, she realised that over the years she'd only been there a handful of times. Steff was either always at her and Donnie's place, or at the yard. Glancing around, she noticed how minimalistic it all looked. Plain, crisp white walls, no photos in frames. It was very much a man's house. No woman's touch here.

The sound of Steff's phone ringing made her glance into the kitchen, and Steff smiled apologetically as he answered it, holding up two fingers to tell her he wouldn't be long. Smiling back, Layla took it upon herself to look around the house. All on one level, with several doors off the main hallways, she spotted that out of all seven doors, only one of them was closed. She could see into the living room, bathroom, kitchen, main bedroom, office and utility room. But that one door piqued her curiosity. Taking a few steps forward, she stood outside it, holding onto the handle. When she pulled on it, it didn't budge. The door was locked.

Glancing around, and without knowing what was urging her to do it, Layla looked for the key hook that most homes had these days. Spotting it outside the utility room, Layla went to it and found a lone key hanging on one of the hooks, along with envelopes stuffed into the little shelf below. It was attached to a keyring that

Layla had given to Donnie and Steff when they were all eighteen. An image of them all at the Irn-Bru Carnival in Glasgow, before things got complicated and messy. It made her smile but didn't deter her from taking the key in her hand and moving back to the locked door.

Steff had closed the kitchen door. She could hear him talking but couldn't make out what he was saying. Not that she was interested. Something pulled her to that door.

Sliding the key into the lock with a bit of force she was able to unlock it. Maybe it had been locked for years, she thought.

Quietly pulling on the handle, Layla pushed the door open and when the room revealed itself to her, she froze. Her eyes fixed on the photo frame on the bedside table. Inching closer, she glared at the image, a photograph of her in her wedding dress. She remembered that photo from the album she'd had made up. But she wasn't alone when it was taken. Donnie, her new husband, was standing beside her when the photographer took it. Although, in the image that was in the frame, it wasn't Donnie who was standing next to her. It was Steff.

'What the fuck is this?' she whispered, picking up the frame and staring at it closely. Donnie had been cut out of the image and a folded image of Steff had been put in his place.

'Fucking hell,' she gasped, the frame falling from her grasp. Turning, Layla went to make for the door, but was stopped in her tracks when Steff's shadow fell upon her.

'What are you doing?' he asked, his voice calmer than it should have been.

Swallowing hard, Layla took a breath. 'I could ask you the same thing.'

Steff didn't answer. He simply stepped inside the room, closed the door and Layla heard a loud click. She'd left the key in the door. And now he had it.

'Steff, what is that picture all about?'

He kept his back to her, and she watched his shoulders rise and fall just ever so slightly, before he turned slowly and faced her.

'Steff, it's fucking weird.'

'It's not weird, Layla.'

'It's not weird? You've manufactured a wedding photo to look like it's us who are married. Is this a joke? Or are you some kind of psycho that sleeps with a woman and then pretends you're married to them?'

Steff shook his head. 'I...' he stammered. 'I don't know.'

Layla stared at him blankly.

'I'm sorry, Layla. I never, ever wanted you to find out this way. The thing is, I love you. Always have. But you never, *ever* acknowledged it. You knew – only an idiot wouldn't. But you only ever used me as your security blanket for when Donnie had done something you didn't like, or when you couldn't stand the arguments about Kerry. And for a while I was okay with that. But I needed more from you and you couldn't give it to me.'

Layla frowned, terrified that what she was imagining could possibly be true. 'What the actual fuck are you on about, Steff?'

'No one else knew, except Kerry.' He gritted his teeth. 'She almost fucked it all up. She was going to tell you about me, tell you that I was sick in the head. That you were better off without me and Donnie. I couldn't let that happen.'

She felt her eyes widen. No, she thought. This couldn't be right. Steff was the good one. Always the kind one, whose shoulder was always there if she needed it.

'I had to stop her from telling you. I had to stop Donnie from finding out. But then I saw you after the car hit her, and I realised that I was the reason you were hurting, why you were in so much pain. I never wanted to hurt you, I promise.'

Her shoulders fell as she listened. Layla let out a gasp.

'*You?* It was you. Oh my god. You were there, you comforted me. You had your murderous fucking hands around me as I sobbed. Jesus Christ. You arranged to have her taken out.'

Layla's heart thundered in her chest as she thought about her sister. Her beautiful, funny, loyal and caring sister.

'Let me explain,' Steff said.

Layla turned to leave. All she wanted was to run. But before she was able to get any pace on, she felt his hands on her, pulling her back.

'Layla, don't run.'

She opened her mouth to scream, but his hand fell across her face and muted the sound.

Chapter Sixty-Nine

Susie sat on a chair opposite Donnie, the knife gripped firmly in one hand and a mobile phone in the other. She'd pulled the blade away from his neck after shitting out of actually killing him. That wasn't the kind of person she was. Susie Fowler was just a woman who owned a pub. Nothing more and nothing less. He knew a woman like her wouldn't have the balls to kill him. If it was the other way around, Susie would be dead by now.

Steff had disappeared not long after Susie had changed her mind about slitting his throat. Donnie still couldn't believe that his brother had betrayed him like that. What he couldn't work out was why.

'I don't have to be the one to kill you, Donnie. There are plenty of people who want you out of the way. Pete at the Barrhouse Tavern for a start.' Susie's voice broke through his thoughts.

Donnie sniggered. 'Are you pub owners in some sort of weird club where you talk about your problems with each other?'

'Then there's your wife too, I suppose. She probably hates you. Although I'm still not convinced that she didn't know what you were up to. Living with scum like you, she had to know, surely?'

'Shut your fucking mouth, Susie.'

'Or what? Oh that's right, you can't move, so you're not going to do anything to keep me quiet, are you?'

Donnie struggled, his hands bound behind his back. If he could just loosen his hands enough to be able to wriggle free, he'd kill Susie on the spot.

'Not that you ever do any of your killing with your own hands. You always make someone else do that for you. I get it. If I was a man in your position I would do the same. Not getting your hands dirty means keeping out of prison. A man like you wouldn't last in prison. What is it they say about fake gangsters? Plastic?'

Donnie glared at Susie. 'So plastic that the polis never found Demi?'

That shut her up. She leaned forward on the seat, tossed the knife in the air and caught it perfectly by the handle, before getting to her feet and rushing at him.

'You've got poison running through your blood, Donnie. We need to get that out.' She placed the blade on the surface of his right forearm and began to tear at his flesh.

Donnie screamed in pain and jumped so hard the chair flew up, toppled, and he landed on his side.

'What the fuck is going on here then?' A voice came from the other side of the basement.

Donnie glanced in the direction of where the voice was coming from.

'You took your time,' Susie said, moving away from Donnie.

His arm felt like it was on fire as blood dripped onto the concrete floor.

'Jesus, Susie. If you kill him, you'll never find out what happened to Demi.'

It was Cammy McNab's voice. Donnie watched as he approached and lifted Donnie's chair back into the upright position.

'I'm not going to kill him. Not yet, anyway. I will not let him die until he tells me what happened to Demi.'

Gritting his teeth at the realisation that his brother, the boys from the Barrhouse Firm and Susie had come together against him, he swallowed hard. It seemed everyone was against him.

Cammy knelt down in front of Donnie and glared at him, baring his teeth in a sinister, yet somewhat triumphant smile. 'You're not quite the gangster you thought you were, eh Donnie?'

'He won't say a word about Demi,' Susie interjected. 'I can see it in his face. It's the only control he has left. His fixation with making money from trafficking has lost him a lot of business and respect. His standards have slipped. But he won't speak about Demi.'

'Well then,' Cammy said, 'we'll just have to make you speak, won't we?' Cammy smirked. Getting to his feet, he produced a blindfold from his back pocket and tied it around Donnie's head, covering his eyes, but not before showing him a pair of pliers.

'I'm not fucking scared of you, Cammy. You're nothing.'

Cammy laughed loudly. 'You don't need to be scared of me to make you talk. If I need to bleed the information out of you, then I will.'

Donnie felt the cold metal clamp down on his fingers, and a thick film of sweat formed on his forehead. He'd never been one to show weakness or fear, but at that precise moment he wanted to scream and plead for his life. He was the son of Donald Black, and in his world, showing fear wasn't something that was thought of, let alone shown. He would have to keep that trait going, so he clamped his mouth shut and prepared himself for the pain.

Chapter Seventy

Layla stood with her back pressed against the door and stared blankly at Steff. His expression was hard to read, but he kept his eyes on her, like he was waiting for her to speak.

She parted her lips, felt her tongue peel from the roof of her mouth. 'All these years I was blaming Donnie for Kerry's death, for our marriage falling apart because the drink turned me into a bitter and paranoid bitch, you were sitting on this in silence.'

The whispered words sat heavy between them, and Steff blinked. 'You don't understand, Layla.'

'You're damn fucking right I don't understand, Steff. You'd better start explaining.'

He adjusted his balance, from one foot to the other, his shoulders loose and his eyes narrow. Then he took a step forward, and Layla's instinct was to draw back. With the wall at her back, she couldn't move further away from him.

'Kerry was' – he paused – 'being difficult. You see, she hated the thought of you and Donnie together as much as I did. We were planning to make you see that he wasn't good for you. We had your best interests at heart.'

Layla frowned. 'What do you mean you were planning to make me see? Make me see what?'

He moved closer again. 'That you were better off away from him. Donnie, he's always been bad news.'

'You're supposed to be his best fucking mate. Why would you try to sabotage his life like that?'

It was Steff's turn to look confused. 'Because you deserved so much better, Layla. You weren't put on this planet to be a gangster's wife, especially not when the fucker treats you how he does.'

Layla expelled air and pushed him away. 'What gives you the right to make that decision? And what the fuck did Kerry have to do with all this that caused her death?'

Steff shook his head; a look of despair crossed his face. 'She found out.'

'Found out about what?'

'She saw this. I dunno, Layla, she just kind of lost the plot, told me I was sick in the head and that she was going to tell you that I was some kind of weirdo who was obsessed with you. But in doing that, you'd be left with no one to protect you from Donnie. You'd be stuck with him by yourself.'

Layla felt tears sting the back of her eyes and anger burn in her throat. 'So you thought you'd arrange to have her murdered?'

'It wasn't like that.'

'Jesus Christ, Steff,' she screamed. Then she stopped, composed herself and thought about how she was going to get out of the house without him trying to stop her. She had to be calm, had to make him think that she agreed that what he'd done was for her benefit.

Her heart thrummed in her chest; she was unsure if she was going to be able to pull it off.

'Look, I'm sorry. It's just a lot to take in, that's all. Can you understand that?'

He nodded slowly, before reaching out and taking her hand in his. 'I didn't ever mean to hurt you.'

She swallowed the nauseating lump in her throat and forced a smile. 'I'll be fine. I just need to go home, process all this and try to calm down. I've not been to the salon in a while. I'll pop in there and check on things.'

Turning, she made for the door handle but felt Steff grip her arm, spinning her back to face him.

'All this, it's not real. I love you. I always have done. Isn't that all that matters? I don't want you thinking badly of me.'

Layla felt instantly sick, like she was going to throw up all over him. She hid her true feelings. 'I don't. I promise.'

'Why don't I come with you? To the salon, I mean.'

'You don't have to follow me, Steff. It's not like I'm going to the police. I'm married to a gangster. They'd love that.'

Pulling herself from his grip, she smiled, leaned up and kissed him on the cheek and refrained from gagging, before opening the door. He followed her out to the street, right at her back. Every instinct in her body was telling her to start running, start screaming at him to get away from her. If she made a scene, he'd leave her alone for now, surely? But the fear inside gripped her like nothing she'd ever experienced. As much as her marriage to Donnie was over, all she could think about was what he would say if he knew that Steff had done this. Or did he already know? Maybe he was in on it?

'Layla, I'm sorry.'

She took a steadying breath but didn't stop walking. 'I know you are, Steff.'

Reaching the sunbed shop, she pushed the door and almost fell inside, gasping for air in the hope that she wasn't going to be sick. Sobbing, she made her way through to the bathroom at the back of the shop and stuck her wrists under cold running water to stop the impending panic attack.

How the hell had she missed this? There'd been red flags all over the place with Steff and she hadn't seen them. Now that she thought about them, they were blatantly obvious. Whenever she talked about, or even mentioned, Kerry's name he always subtly changed the subject. Of course he wouldn't want to talk about Kerry; he'd arranged to have her silenced in the most brutal of ways, and Layla had been forced to see it.

The loud, gasping sobs spilled out, and Layla allowed the grief and guilt of what happened to Kerry to take over. She had to let it out. How could she have been so blind to it all? Was she that stupid?

After a few moments, she remembered what Susie had said to her before she'd left for Tenerife. If she ever needed a place to stay if things didn't get better with Donnie, then she could go to Susie's.

Splashing her face with cold water, she rinsed the tears away before heading out to the front of the shop. Darcie's sudden resignation had meant that the shop had no one else to run the place, and Layla was only there some of the time. The place was going under, it wasn't hard to work out.

She opened the safety deposit box from under the counter and took out the set of keys Susie had left with Darcie. Layla couldn't stay in that house now, not after it had been trashed. Not after everything. She'd take Susie up on her offer.

Dialling Susie's number, it rang a few times before going to voicemail. She left a message, letting her know that she was going to take her up on her offer of using the house as a place to stay until she was able to sort out some new accommodation. Surely Susie wouldn't have offered if she hadn't meant it?

Layla spoke aloud to herself, talked herself through what she was about to do next. She'd go home, pack some things and head to Susie's. Wherever her husband was or whatever he was doing, he'd made it clear that he wanted her out of the house. So that's what she was going to do.

Two of the men she'd grown up with, trusted the most in the world, were now like complete strangers to her. She needed to reassess a lot of things.

Chapter Seventy-One

'Fuck!' Donnie screamed, the only way he could cope with the pain. He started to drift in and out of consciousness, his brain protecting him.

Somewhere in the distance, he heard a high-pitched sound. The shrill ringing of a doorbell. Knocking. Maybe someone had heard his cries and phoned the police.

'Are you going to answer that fucking door?' Cammy said, although his voice sounded muffled.

'No,' Susie replied. 'It'll be a cold caller.'

Then a phone rang from somewhere in the room as Donnie slumped to the side, almost falling from his chair and onto the floor.

'Shit. It's Layla.'

Donnie tried to open his eyes. If Layla was here, then maybe she could get help. Parting his lips to speak, Donnie made an attempt to call out to her, but Cammy's hand fell across his mouth.

'Unless you want to lose another finger, I'd suggest you keep that fucking mouth of yours shut, Donnie.'

Cammy's breath was hot against his ear, his voice vibrating against his skin as he lifted Donnie's hand once again before clamping another finger inside the pliers.

'No. Please,' Donnie said, feeling pathetic that he was begging, but desperate not to be put through the ordeal of losing another finger.

'Then shut the fuck up.'

Donnie watched through heavy eyes as Susie headed out of the basement, closing the door quietly behind her.

Chapter Seventy-Two

'Susie?' Layla said, after ringing Susie's number for the third time. 'Hi, I don't know if you got my message, but I wanted to take you up on your offer to stay at yours for a while, since you're away?'

Susie was quiet on the other end of the line, just for a moment. Long enough for Layla to know that something was wrong.

'It's just that, well, your key isn't working. I've tried it a few times, wondered if there was a knack to it?'

'You can't stay.' She finally responded. 'I'm having work done to the house.'

Layla frowned, glanced up from the front door at the building and then around the grounds of the driveway. Something felt wrong.

'Really?'

'Yeah, there's workmen everywhere. Roof is being repaired, and the house can't be lived in while the work is going on.'

Layla took a step back from the door and glanced around while holding the phone to her ear. Why was Susie lying to her?

'Strange. It's just that, I'm standing outside your house right now. There's no one else here apart from me.'

Susie sighed heavily, and Layla shook her head, a bubble of emotion growing in her throat. Attempting to hold it together, Layla said, 'It's fine. You know what, I've had enough folk lie to me over time. Forget it.'

As she pulled the phone away from her ear to hang up, tears sprang to her eyes. Maybe it wasn't the people in her life who were the problem. Maybe Layla was the issue here. She seemed to be the common denominator: everyone was lying to her.

Turning her back to the house, she moved down the drive but stopped when she heard a click behind her. The front door had been opened. Glancing back, she saw Susie's face staring out at her.

'Wait,' she said, stepping over the threshold and pulling the door over behind her.

Layla stared at Susie in confusion. 'Aren't you supposed to be in Tenerife? Why did you lie to me?'

'I'm not lying. Well, not in the way you think I am.' Susie responded.

Layla frowned. 'What does that even mean?'

'Look, Layla, you're my friend. I don't want to hurt you, and if you come into this house right now, then you're going to end up just that.'

Layla stared at Susie for a few moments, trying to work out in her head what the hell she could mean by that.

'Susie, I've had a really fucking shit day so far. You wouldn't believe the half of it. So if you're sitting on something that I need to know, then just tell me. I've had enough of everyone's shit; between my husband and his fucking best mate, I don't think I can hold it together much longer before I erupt.'

Susie's eyes flickered, but her expression remained. She wasn't going to tell Layla anything.

'Okay, I'll start guessing, shall I? Let's see.' Layla rubbed her hands together sarcastically. 'Oh, I know. You're having an affair with Donnie. He's in the house and that's why you won't let me in?'

Layla watched her friend's expression falter, and her own stomach started rolling. 'Oh shit. Is that it, Susie? Are you the one I suspected Donnie was having an affair with?'

She moved towards the door before she'd even thought to, but Susie stood in her way.

'Don't be so bloody ridiculous,' Susie hissed, holding her hand up to stop Layla from going any further.

'Then why won't you let me in? I need a friend, Susie. I'm fucking desperate here.'

Susie closed her eyes momentarily, and as she opened them, a blood curdling scream came from somewhere inside the house, so suddenly that both Layla and Susie jumped.

'What the fuck was that?' Layla said, peering over Susie's shoulder.

'Nothing. Layla, just do yourself a favour and go home. You don't have to be a part of this.'

A second scream erupted, louder this time. It was clear, precise. The voice carried Layla's name through the air.

Layla glanced at Susie, whose eyes twitched as she tried not to blink, before pushing her out of the way and rushing into the house. The voice continued to scream her name, again and again, as she followed the sound down the hall towards the basement.

'Layla, don't!' Susie called after her. It was too late; she was already moving down the stairs in the direction of where her name was being called from.

'Don't come any closer.'

She stopped, not because she was told to, but because of the scene unfolding in front of her.

'Jesus,' she whispered. The metallic stench of blood was overwhelming. She raised a hand to cover her mouth as she stared at the blood on the floor, tracking it with her eyes towards the man sitting on the chair a few feet away.

'Donnie?'

His eyes were wide, wild with terror, sweat pouring off his face. The man standing behind him was familiar. She recognised him, vaguely. He stood behind Donnie, rubbing at his fingers.

'Dirty bastard fucking bit me,' the man hissed, before slipping his fingers around Donnie's neck and lifting a pair of pliers with the other hand to rest on Donnie's shoulder. That was when she saw them. Two fingers lying amongst the pool of blood at Donnie's feet.

She took a step forward; instinct to help the man she'd been with since she was a young teenager took over.

'I said don't come any closer, Layla,' the man said again.

She stopped again. 'What are you doing to him?' Her voice quivered inside her throat. Was she about to watch her husband's murder?

'Nothing he doesn't deserve, Layla,' Susie said from behind. 'There's a lot Donnie has been keeping from you, Layla. It's time you knew what you were married to.'

Watching everything happen in front of her, Layla felt as though she'd been cemented to the floor. Her entire life was a lie.

Chapter Seventy-Three

Louise sat with her back resting against the sofa and switched on the television. Not that there was anything that she would be able to watch that would take her mind off what was going on in her life. As soon as she read the caption at the bottom of the news channel, she bolted upright and shouted for Darcie.

'What is it?'

'Have you seen what's going on in Amsterdam?'

Darcie sat down next to her and read out the caption. 'Suspected gang attack near Red Light District.'

'Jesus,' Louise whispered.

Kev and Tam appeared in the living room, putting on their jackets as they stood by the door. 'What's up?' Tam asked.

But Louise couldn't take her eyes off the screen. The reporter spoke, but his words jumped around inside her head and she was unable to process them properly. All she could do was watch the carnage unfold. Something about the way it was described as a gang attack near the Red Light District sat heavy on her chest.

'*It's believed the incident is gang related, although police are still to comment,*' the reporter said.

Louise got to her feet and moved closer to the screen, staring at the amateur footage which was clear had been filmed on a mobile phone and used by the broadcaster.

She wasn't watching the crowds of people fleeing for their lives, or the shooters themselves, of which there were two or three. Louise had her eye on the car, and the three individuals approaching it. Two female, one male. Someone shouted a name and one of the females seemed to react, yet she didn't turn.

'Jesus Christ,' Tam said, 'how is the channel even allowed to show this?'

Louise ignored him, continued watching. She gasped when loud shots were fired and people started screaming.

'Lou, turn that off, eh? You've seen enough shit over the last few—' Tam said, but she held her hand up to silence her brother.

The footage went back to the beginning, and Louise grabbed the Sky remote, pausing it when she saw the females again. 'No, there's something about this that doesn't sit right with me.'

'Louise, what is it?' Darcie prompted, her tone implying that she knew Louise had seen something significant.

She got to her feet, turned and pointed at the screen. 'That's Demi Simpson.'

Darcie's knitted brow changed quickly from confusion to shock. 'Oh my god.'

'Lou, don't be silly,' Tam said. But as he spoke, Kev pulled out his mobile phone and started tapping away on the screen.

'That's not Demi Simpson, Louise. It looks nothing like her,' Kev said, holding up his phone for all of them to see.

Louise looked at the phone, then back to the screen. 'Of course it's not going to look like that picture her family put out to the press. She's been missing over a year,

Kev. If she was trafficked as a fucking sex slave, she's not exactly going to look her best now, is she? And I recognise her for sure. We went to school together. I saw her every single day.'

Darcie got to her feet and looked at the picture on Kev's phone, before taking the phone in her hand and holding it next to the paused image on the television. They were all quiet for a few moments, until finally Darcie turned and looked at Louise.

'You're right. It's her.'

Kev grabbed the phone from Darcie before holding it to his ear. Louise's hands were in her hair as she began pacing back and forth in front of the TV. This could have been her. She could have been the one being shot at in Amsterdam. The poor girl must've tried to escape. But she'll be dead now, surely?

'Cammy, there's been a development. Demi Simpson, we think she's in Amsterdam.'

There was a moment of silence as Kev listened to Cammy on the other end of the line. Louise held her breath, all she could see was that girl, Demi. The girl before her whom Donnie had managed to fool into believing that he loved her. Just like he had with Louise. The only difference between them was that Louise was lucky enough to have been found before it was too late. It could easily have been Louise's face on that television screen, trying so desperately to make a bid for her freedom.

'Right,' Kev said, hanging up the call to Cammy. He turned to face Tam, gave a nod in the direction of the door and moved out to the hallway. Tam followed.

'Where are you going?' Darcie said, following them out. Louise was close behind her cousin, wondering what was happening.

'We're going to see Donnie. Cammy wants as much backup as possible. The more people against the bastard, the more likely he is to cave and tell us everything. And after what he did to me, Darcie, I'd happily pull the fucker's eyeballs out and ram them down his throat.'

Louise watched as Darcie winced at the words coming from Kev's lips. Donnie had turned everyone's thoughts to venom. Including her own. She'd be willing to watch Donnie suffer for what he was responsible for.

'You two need to stay here. Don't attempt to leave. You're both safe if you just stay hidden. I mean it, Darcie,' Kev said.

'I'm coming with you,' Louise started, but Tam shook his head.

'No, the last time you were with Donnie Black he almost killed us both. I don't want you anywhere near him. Do what Kev said and just chill here until we come back. By the end of the day, Donnie Black will be long gone from all of our lives and we'll be able to get back to normal.'

Kev and Tam left, closing the door behind them. Louise was surprised to hear the key in the lock. She rushed to the window and looked out, watched Kev and Tam climb into Kev's car and drive away, before rushing back out to the hallway and grabbing Tam's car keys from the hook near the kitchen door.

'What are you doing?' Darcie asked.

'I'm following them. I'm not going to stand back and do nothing when that bastard is out there. He tried to kill my brother, arranged to have me sent overseas to be sold as a sex slave. If anything, the least I can do is punch him in the fucking face.'

Darcie hesitated, gave a look of disbelief. 'Are you being serious? This isn't a case of punch Donnie Black in the face and teach him a lesson, Louise. He's a full-on nut job who is going to be taken out. You don't really want to be a part of that, do you? Haven't you been through enough trauma as it is without being witness to that?'

Louise moved past Darcie towards the front door and pulled on the handle. 'Bastards really have locked us in,' she whispered.

'Well, I'm glad they have, otherwise you'd already be on your way to confront a gangster. Seriously, Louise, I don't know what goes on inside that head of yours.'

Louise frowned. 'What's that supposed to mean?'

Darcie sighed. 'I mean, getting involved with a guy old enough to be your dad. A married man for fuck sake. And you really believed that he wanted a relationship? I thought you were smarter than that.'

Louise felt her jaw drop open as she listened to what her cousin had to say. 'Translation; what you really meant was what else would a man like Donnie want with a stupid little girl like me? Jesus fuck, Darcie. My confidence is already in bits and you throw that at me?'

Silence seemed to swallow them up then, but Louise wasn't about to stand around and wait for Darcie to apologise. Instead, she went to the coat pegs on the wall and pulled Tam's car key from his hoodie pocket and then headed out to the small veranda in the living room.

'Look, Louise, I didn't mean it like that. I'm just trying to get you to see that Kev and Tam are right. We shouldn't go anywhere near Donnie. It's not safe.'

Louise wasn't listening. Instead, she opened the veranda door, stepped out onto the concrete platform and climbed over the railing. Glancing down at the grass below, she guessed that she was only around twelve feet off the ground. She could jump that without hurting herself, she thought.

'Louise, don't even think about it,' Darcie said, her hand gripping Louise's arm.

Louise shrugged her off and forced herself away from the railing; her stomach leapt to her throat, and she fell through the air. She landed on the grass and fell to the side. A pain shot through her left ankle, but she knew that was nothing compared to the pain that Demi Simpson would have had to endure over the last however many months.

'Fuck!' Darcie shouted. She landed next to Louise. 'I'm sorry. I shouldn't have said that up there. I don't think you're stupid. I just wanted to protect you, that's all. It came out wrong.'

Louise nodded and took Darcie by the hand before rushing across the road towards Tam's Renault Clio.

'I hope you know how to drive?' Darcie asked, a hint of humour in her tone.

'Enough that I was able to get away from Donnie Black in the first place.'

–

They drove along in silence, following Kev's car, Louise imagining what was going to happen to Donnie. They always said there was a fine line between love and hate. Louise had certainly crossed that line as soon as Donnie had her thrown into that cage in the back of the van and made Tam drive it to the dock.

Louise followed the car, far back enough that they wouldn't be seen. They turned left and headed up the narrow track. When a house came into sight, Darcie gasped.

'Fuck. This is Susie's house. The woman who owns the pub across from the sunbed shop. Why the fuck would they be coming here?'

'Is Susie a millionaire or something? Look at the size of that thing.'

Darcie instructed Louise to pull into the passing point on the track so they could walk the rest of the way. 'We can't exactly park in the drive. The boys will see us.'

As they started to climb to Susie's house, Louise could sense that Darcie wanted to ask her something.

'Just ask. It's not like talking about it is any worse than when it happened.'

Darcie took a breath. 'Did he hurt you?'

Louise thought about the short relationship she'd had with Donnie. That first night she met him at Tam's debut indoor fight seemed like a thousand years ago.

'Actually, no. He was always very...' she paused to think of the word. 'Gentlemanly. Kind. Passionate.' Louise sighed. 'A good actor, I suppose. He always said he wanted to leave his wife for me. But there was always an excuse, like it wasn't the right time, let's not put pressure on ourselves, he needed funds. Turns out by funds he meant he had to sell me.'

Darcie took Louise's hand and gave it a gentle squeeze. 'I'm sorry he put you through all this, Lou. He gets everything that's coming to him.'

Louise smiled. 'He always used to say that whenever he looked at me, his heart would stop. Today I'm going to make that happen so that he can't hurt anyone else.'

Chapter Seventy-Four

Layla moved cautiously forward, inching closer to Donnie. She knew the movement alone could cause her husband some serious harm, but in a strange way she didn't care. Although she would have preferred Steff to be sitting in the chair in front of her with a few of his fingers strewn across the floor.

'I said don't come any closer or he's going to die, and it'll be your fault.'

'It won't be my fault. I didn't make Donnie do whatever it is that's angered you so much. If anyone's to blame for his death, it's him.' She was surprised by how cold her words sounded. Maybe that was due to living with Donnie for so long. Being surrounded by bad things, bad situations had turned her heart icy cold.

'You're smart,' the man said.

'Cammy,' Susie said. 'Tell her. Tell her what that bastard has done.'

'You're about the only one who doesn't know what he's really like, and you've been living with him for the majority of your life. Do you expect us to believe that you were in the dark about him?' Cammy asked. Before Layla could answer, the door opened and two more lads entered the basement.

'Cam,' one of them said. He stopped and glared at Layla. 'Ah, you must be Layla Black. Sunbed shop owner.'

Layla glanced at him and then Susie, whose eyes shone with empathy.

'Layla, this is Kev. He's Darcie's partner. Donnie set him up and he was sent to prison. Darcie had to support herself when he went away, so she ended up working for you, although she didn't know you were married to that.' Susie pointed to Donnie.

Layla felt like her head was going to explode. That must have been why Darcie had left the shop so abruptly.

'Aye, this bastard here didn't like that we were going out and doing things for ourselves,' Cammy said. He clamped the pliers down on Donnie's fingers, and Donnie let out a grunt. 'He knew that Kev was training some of our lads and organising the events, basically growing the name of our firm. So he decided to plant a stash of cocaine in the back of Kev's van and get his mates down at the polis station to pay Kev a visit.'

Donnie wriggled in his seat but Cammy didn't let go.

'You don't have to hurt him like that,' Layla said. She didn't know what else to say. Yes, Donnie deserved to be punished. But like this, in front of her?

'Then there's Demi Simpson. Poor young Demi was groomed by this bastard.'

Kev, and the other lad who had appeared with him, were now standing at the other side of Donnie. The younger lad was staring intensely at him, and Layla could see the venom in his eyes.

'It wasn't just Demi though. My sister too. Difference is I was able to get my sister away.'

Layla didn't know where to look, who to focus on. So much was coming out about her husband, and she still had Steff's lies to face too.

Chapter Seventy-Five

They reached the entrance to the driveway and saw Kev's car parked outside. Darcie stopped walking, but Louise kept moving in the direction of the door. Darcie might be the older of the two, but Louise definitely had more balls than she did. Darcie was terrified of what they might be walking into. They could end up complicit to murder, something that would change their entire lives.

'Louise, I don't think we should go in there. I think we're safer out here.'

'You don't have to come inside. You can stay here, or you can go back to the flat. You weren't the one thrown into a cage in the back of a van, destined for fucking god knows what. I need to see Donnie's face, look him in the eye and ask him what the fuck he thought he was playing at.'

The venom in Louise's voice made Darcie understand just how much hatred she had for Black. About the same amount that Kev had for him, most likely. And Susie.

'I can't leave you to go in there by yourself.'

'I won't be by myself. My brother is in there, so is Kev and I'm sure the rest of the Firm are too.' Louise stopped in front of the door and peered through the letterbox. Darcie forced her legs to move again and she stood next to Louise.

'Can you hear that?' Louise asked, pressing her ear to open the letterbox.

Darcie felt her heart freeze. It was a sound like she'd never heard. A torturous scream coming from somewhere inside the house.

'Jesus,' Louise said, standing up and staring at the door.

Darcie stepped back but turned when she heard footsteps behind them. She felt sick when she saw Steff Black walking towards them, and out of instinct she pulled Louise by the arm and moved her so she was standing behind her.

'You've come to join the party then?' he said. A sinister smile crept across his face, and Darcie shuddered. 'Don't worry, I'm not here to hurt you. I'm the reason your man in there is being held.'

Darcie frowned, and Louise pulled away from her grip.

'What do you mean? Why would you betray him like that?'

Steff moved around them and pulled a key from his pocket before opening the door. 'I didn't like how business was going.'

Darcie suspected it was all bullshit, but he didn't seem to notice as he walked into the house and along the hall, before stopping and glancing back at them. 'I assume that you're here because you want to see him suffer, Louise? Or do you always just stand outside people's houses and stare through the letterbox?'

He disappeared out of sight then, and Louise stepped into the house. Darcie followed her quickly, and the screaming from before grew louder as they made their way down to the basement. Steff opened the door and, instantly, Darcie could smell blood.

'Fuck,' she gagged, placing her sleeve over her mouth and nose. Louise didn't seem to flinch at the scent and, as they emerged into the space, the first thing Darcie saw was Donnie Black, tied to a chair, with a pool of blood at his feet. He was sweating, groaning and crying.

'I fucking told you to stay at home,' Kev said to Louise. Then he locked eyes with Darcie and his expression turned from anger to fury.

'You shouldn't be here,' Tam said, trying to grab for Louise. But she was too quick for him. She was already in front of Donnie, crouching down in front of him. Cammy was next to him, but he'd taken a step back, almost as though he was allowing Louise time to do whatever it was she wanted to do.

'Donnie?' Louise said as she stared at him. He looked up at her, although Darcie couldn't see his face.

'Darcie, what is your part in all this?'

Darcie shook her head. This was all such a mess. Just as Darcie was about to speak, respond to her former boss, Kev was by her side and pulling her across to the other side of the basement.

'You can't be here,' Kev said.

'Why? Because you don't want me to witness the Firm murdering one of their rivals? Kev, this is all sorts of fucked up.'

Kev stared at her with a sadness in his eyes. He hadn't wanted any of this to happen.

'Not because he's a rival. Because of what he stands for. Louise is your cousin; you saw the state she and Tam were in because of that bastard. You can't honestly stand there and take the high ground, Darcie.'

The room fell silent and all eyes moved towards Louise. She and Donnie were staring at each other, and Louise's expression was cool and composed. Darcie noticed how Layla looked utterly lost and terrified, but she wasn't watching Donnie and Louise. She was staring at Steff Black, who had one eye on Donnie and one eye on Layla.

'Donnie,' Louise said, her voice a whimper. 'You told me you loved me. I felt like you did. You were the first guy I ever slept with. Is this what you did to Demi? Did you make her think you loved her too?'

Donnie didn't answer her.

'Does it hurt?' Louise asked, her voice falling to a whisper as she glanced down at the blood on the floor.

Darcie couldn't help but follow her gaze, noticing the severed fingers.

His head rose as he took in her words, before nodding. Louise blinked, her eyes closing for a second longer than normal.

'Good. It'll hurt even more when this guy cuts the rest off, you sick, disgusting bastard.'

Chapter Seventy-Six

Fighting the urge to gag at the sight of the blood and the sounds of Donnie's merciful screams, Layla took the stairs two at a time to escape the hell that she was surrounded by. Susie followed her, close at her back.

'This is insanity, Susie. I'm calling the police,' she said, pulling her phone from her back pocket.

Susie grabbed the phone from her hand and held it tight. 'You think that's a good idea? Donnie had the police on his fucking payroll. And even if he didn't, you really want the police coming here and seeing that we're all part of this? We'll all go to prison and I'll never get fucking justice for what happened to Demi. If it hadn't been for Steff finally having a conscience, I might never have found out. But Steff doesn't know what happened to Demi.'

The shock crept into her chest immediately before doubt quickly took over. 'Or so he says. Can you really trust Steff?'

'Why would he lie? Donnie's his brother.'

Layla knew why. It would have something to do with her; she knew, having just found out what she did about Steff. He'd be using this as a way to get rid of Donnie.

'I think they're both as bad as each other,' Layla replied.

'They're Blacks, poison runs in their blood, I should know, what with them taking security money off me for over a year now, along with what Donnie has done to

Demi.' Susie replied, and then she hesitated. 'You really had no idea about him, did you?'

'I thought he was having an affair. But I had no idea this was the sort of shit he was into.'

Layla wiped at her tears angrily. Kerry had been right all along about Donnie; he was dodgy. Bad news. But she hadn't bothered to listen because she was just a smitten, stupid little girl at the time. Both Donnie and Steff were to blame for Kerry's absence in Layla's life. And now Susie's niece was missing, and this Louise had almost been next. If she hadn't been so blind, she could have stopped this.

'I'm sorry,' Layla whispered.

'I am too.' Susie hugged her. 'But you can't contact the police. You just can't. He'll end up being the one that walks free, and I'll never get justice. Our Demi, she was… is just a sweet, young girl. She doesn't deserve this, Layla. Donnie needs to rot for what he's done. If he has the police in his pocket, we have to deal with him.'

Layla sobbed and Susie held her tight. When she looked up, she saw Steff standing at the top of the stairs, staring at her with concern.

'I won't call the police,' she said to Susie. 'But I can't stay here and watch this.'

'I'm not asking you to. You were never supposed to be part of this.'

Pulling away, Layla headed for the front door. 'Tell that girl downstairs that I'm sorry for what Donnie put her through, and I'm sorry for Demi too. I really am, Susie.'

Susie nodded, smiled sadly. 'I will.'

Steff was by her side as she reached for the handle. 'Let me come with you.'

She glared up at him. 'You stay the fuck away from me. I mean it.'

Steff frowned; his eyes glistened. 'Please, Layla.'

'She said no,' Susie said from behind. 'Whatever it is you've done to upset her, she's asking you to leave her alone.'

Steff turned to Susie and his gentle manner changed. 'This has got fuck all to do with you, Susie.'

'Is that right? Well, you're in my house, and I'll throw you out before her. And I'm sure I don't have to remind you that the Barrhouse Firm are down there, your enemy? Regardless of the fact that you fed me information about him for money, they'll fucking end you if I tell them to.'

Steff stared at Susie for a few long moments before silently admitting defeat and turning to head out the door.

'Please, I just want to talk.'

'Kerry wanted to talk and look what happened to her. Susie, did you know that Steff was responsible for my sister's death? Yeah, she found out Steff had this weird obsession with me and when she threatened to tell me, he paid to have her run over in the street in front of me.'

Susie gasped, stared at Steff in horror.

'And I found out about it just earlier today.'

As Steff stood between both women, Layla's heart thrummed in her chest and beads of sweat trickled down her back. She felt like she was in some kind of horror movie.

'You're no better than Donnie. Get the fuck out of here, Steff.'

'If it wasn't for me, you wouldn't have that bastard down there bleeding all over your floor,' Steff raised his voice. 'You wouldn't know that he was responsible for Demi.'

'You're both responsible. You *let* him do it. You stood back and said fucking nothing,' Layla screamed so loud her throat burned. 'You told me that Donnie wasn't having an affair, so to speak. You knew fine well what he was doing with that other girl, Louise, and you let that happen too. You're just as bad as he is.'

'What's all this about?'

Layla saw three of the men from down in the basement appear at the top of the stairs. They took a step forward, their presence threatening.

Steff didn't respond; he simply turned and attempted to walk out of the house, but he was stopped by one of the lads from the Firm.

Layla sobbed louder than she ever thought possible, and as her legs buckled, Susie caught her.

'It's okay,' Susie hushed.

She couldn't stay in the house. Not with the people who were torturing her husband. Not that she loved him. After this, how could she? But it didn't stop her from grieving the life that she used to have, grieving the husband that she thought she was going to get when she'd married him.

'I'm fine,' Layla sniffed as she stood up.

One of the men glared at her and then looked at Susie. 'Can we trust her?'

'You're asking if I'm going to call the police? I was, but now' – she paused. – 'I couldn't care less if he bleeds dry down there.'

The man nodded. 'Fine. But you're not leaving this house. Not until we're done with him. I mean it. And that goes for you as well, Black. Whatever beef you've got with her, I don't want it fucking this up. If you didn't want to be part of this, you should've thought about that before you grassed your brother up for cash.'

'Dunny, I don't think—' Susie started, but the man held up his hand.

'Lock the doors. All of them. No one leaves until Cammy and the rest of us say so. Got it?'

Layla didn't have enough fight in her to try to convince them to let her out. What would be the point?

Breathe, she told herself. Breathe in the moment, try to push them all out of your head. It was an impossible thing to do when she was surrounded by them.

'Why don't you go into the kitchen, get a glass of wine or something?' Susie suggested. 'There's plenty there.'

Alcohol seemed like her only option to block it all out. It's what she had been used to doing all these years.

The three men standing in the hallway shoved Steff back down towards the basement, and Susie attempted a reassuring smile although it came across as desperate. Almost as though she was silently begging her to keep her mouth shut.

Slipping past Susie, Layla headed along the hallway towards the kitchen. If she could sink enough wine to help her pass out, then maybe she wouldn't hear what was going on down there.

Reaching the kitchen, Layla opened the fridge and eyed two bottles of Pinot Grigio. That'll do nicely, she thought. Time to numb up. Pulling one of the bottles out from the fridge, she chose not to bother with a wine glass. No point trying to look sophisticated when her aim was to be passed out on the floor as soon as possible.

As Layla unscrewed the lid, she heard a phone ringing somewhere in the house, then Susie's voice as she answered it. There was silence for a few moments as Layla glugged back the cold wine. She almost dropped the bottle when Susie screamed.

'It's the police. They've found Demi!'

Placing the bottle down on the counter, Layla moved closer to the kitchen door. She didn't have to strain to hear the sounds of footsteps rushing back to the basement, Susie's screams of elation echoing around the house.

'They've found her.' Pause. 'She's in Amsterdam, at the consulate.'

Everything inside Layla froze when she heard Susie's sobs. She wanted to see Donnie's face now that he'd heard the news. That's if he hadn't bled to death down there.

As she crept down, and everyone came into view, she noticed how still they all were. How they allowed Susie the time to speak. Even Donnie was quiet. Or dying.

'Thank you. Thank you so much. I'll get in touch with them.'

Layla stepped off the last stair and onto the floor. She watched Louise, who'd placed herself in front of Donnie again. His back was still to the door, so she couldn't see his face.

Susie hung up the phone and glared at Donnie, her expression a mix of elation and rage.

'You'll go to hell for what you did to her, Black. I'll make fucking sure of it.'

Chapter Seventy-Seven

Donnie's mind swirled with the news that Demi had been found. Cammy was still stood next to him with the pliers in his hands; pain interrupted his ability to think at all. He knew his time was up, that was for sure.

Somewhere behind him, he heard Susie screaming, crying and cursing him, along with thanking god that Demi was all right. Louise moved out of his line of sight but Cammy remained.

Cammy lurched forward and rummaged through Donnie's pockets. He pulled two mobile phones out and stared at them in his hands. 'Two phones? It doesn't take a genius to work out why you have two. One for your fucked up trafficking venture. You're a dirty fucking pervert, Donnie. Demi's barely a fucking adult! You groomed her then threw her at a pack of European wolves. If there's one thing I can't stand, it's people like you. You deserve everything that's fucking coming to you.' Cammy's words hissed through his teeth.

Donnie couldn't speak, could only shake his head in an attempt to deny everything, although he knew it would do him no good. He felt weak, like life was draining from him slowly. He knew he had to defend himself, to protect the truth of what was going on. Demi, Louise, it all ran so much bigger than them. But all he could think about was the burning pain in his hands.

'Scum!' Susie screamed. 'You're fucking scum. How could you do that to a young girl? Last year in the eyes of the law she was just a child.'

Donnie closed his eyes, took as deep a breath as he could. He thought about Demi, about Louise. About the rest of them that no one seemed to know about. There were half a dozen or so dotted around the world. If they knew about those girls, he'd be long dead by now.

'If you're going to kill me, just get it over with,' Donnie muttered. He tried to sound as though he didn't care. Of course he did. He didn't want to die. Not like this.

'Not yet.' Layla's voice spoke above him. 'I need to ask him some questions.'

A hot slap across the face jolted him, and he opened his eyes. His wife in front of him.

'How long have you been doing this? Trafficking young girls? There has to be more than just two. How many?'

Donnie shook his head. 'They've got it all wrong.'

Another slap, harder this time. 'You think these lads are bad? They're nothing on me, Donnie. I'll take those fucking pliers and cut your balls off unless you tell me what I want to know.'

He believed her. He'd been with Layla for so long now that she'd become just a little bit like him. Ruthless when she needed to be.

'How long?'

Donnie said nothing and gritted his teeth as another surge of pain coursed through him.

A third slap, so hard this time that she almost knocked him over onto the floor. 'Don't you dare ignore me, Donnie. You're sitting here, bleeding to death, with almost half your fingers missing. For once in your fucking existence would you just tell the truth.'

He wanted to open his eyes, to look into the depths of Layla's soul and silently beg her to get him out of this situation. But he felt so weak, yet in so much pain that he couldn't do it. Donnie simply shook his head once more and said, 'This has nothing to do with me.'

'You're a lying cunt, Donnie. You were never who I thought you were. I should never have married you. I should never have gone anywhere near you or Steff. You've both ruined my life, and fuck knows who elses.'

His breath was laboured and he sensed Layla getting to her feet. He wanted to tell her to wait, but the words seemed to jumble inside his head.

A solid blow to the back of the head knocked him forward. He didn't know where or who it'd come from. Just before he hit the floor, a switch went off in his head. A loud ringing began sounding inside his ears, a sensation like warm trickling water could be felt in both ears.

Then there was nothing.

Chapter Seventy-Eight

No one moved. No one made a sound. It was as though every one of them stopped breathing. Steff stared down at his brother and didn't know how to feel.

He glanced at Layla, whose expression was blank, yet her skin pale. She did not blink. Did not move. Neither did Louise. None of them did.

'What happens now?' Layla said, glancing at Cammy, who still held a pair of pliers.

'You, Louise and Darcie take yourselves away. Go home, get cleaned up and pretend that what you saw here today didn't happen.' Cammy blinked, and when he refocused, he was looking at Susie. 'You, deal with the stuff you have to in order to help get Demi home.'

Steff's palms began to get clammy. He wiped them on the insides of his trouser pockets. He knew what Cammy was doing, he was getting the basement ready for a cleanse. Shit, Steff thought. Now that this was actually happening, now that Donnie was actually dead, he felt sick. He hadn't truly believed this day would come. He was responsible for his own brother's death. The reality of that was sickening.

'You,' Cammy said, and Steff caught his gaze. 'You're going to help us sort this.'

Steff didn't exactly have a choice in the matter. He was the one who gave Donnie up, but for good reason. It was the only way he was ever going to have a chance to be with Layla. He'd almost made it, but the guilt had found her. He glanced at Layla then, his heart aching at the pain she was clearly going through at that moment. Steff hadn't meant for her to find out about Kerry, or about how intensely he loved her. But now, it was out there. There was no way of changing that. And now that things were in motion, he realised that the only thing he was going to take away from any of this was his life, and that was if Cammy and the rest of the Firm let him live. If they did, the Black empire would be no more. The rise of the Barrhouse Firm would be too much for him to stand up against on his own. And the Firm would use this if they had to. They'd somehow let Mel and his mother know that Donnie was dead because of him. In this decision he'd made, he'd fucked up everything.

'Fine,' Steff said, 'I'll help.' Then Layla caught his eye and he softened his expression. 'I want to take Layla home first. You guys left her house in a fucking mess. The least I can do is help clean it up.'

Layla's eyes widened. 'Are you kidding? I don't want any of you lot anywhere near me.' She started to move, and the rest of the Firm said nothing; they only moved out of her way.

'Layla,' Darcie said. 'Are you okay?'

Layla didn't stop, didn't answer. In a very calm manner, she climbed the stairs. Darcie and Louise followed and the door at the top of the staircase closed.

Steff felt his heart sink, but his stomach bubbled with anger. How dare she treat him like that? If it wasn't for him, Donnie would still be fooling her. He'd still be alive.

'Whatever you did to her, I'd be careful,' Cammy said. 'Seems as though she's got a heart of fucking stone. I've

344

never known a woman to see this amount of gore and be okay with it.'

'You might be next on her list,' Dunny laughed. No one else matched his humour.

'Shut the fuck up, Cammy. Just make a plan so we can get it over with and I can get the fuck out of here.'

Steff noticed how the Barrhouse Firm lads surrounded him. Mackie and Thomson had been quiet the entire time. Much the same as Tam and Kev. That didn't mean they weren't as fierce as Cammy and Dunny. As for Chud, well, he didn't know where to put himself.

'You,' Steff said, glaring at him, 'do you even know whose side you're on?'

Chud raised a brow and smiled slightly. 'Do you? You were the one who brought Donnie here. You're the reason he's lying there dead.'

'I didn't kill him,' Steff bit back.

'But the polis won't know that, will they? I mean, you've already grassed him in to Susie. Polis will think you've got good enough motive.'

'DNA?' Steff said smugly.

'Who do you think the pliers belonged to?' Dunny smiled widely. 'You didn't notice they were missing from the yard? Oh that's right, the yard's not there anymore, is it?'

'Do what we say, and you might get off lightly. Remember, Steff, you stood back and allowed this bastard to arrange for young girls to be trafficked to Europe. And the only reason you fucking said anything was so you could get your dick wet. It doesn't exactly take a genius to work it out. But if you help us to make this murder scene go away, as if it never happened, then we'll make sure that information never sees the light of day.'

Steff considered Cammy's words and looked at every single member of the Firm. Young Tam was the one who stood out most. The youngest, a skilled boxer who was responsible for a death back when he pressed the button on that incinerator. It had been Steff's and Donnie's way of making sure they had something on him if he ever chose to leave. Steff could play that card, threaten to grass him up to the police, but he knew it wouldn't get him very far. The Firm would have him in the same position Donnie was now: dead in a pool of his own blood.

'You going to be a good boy and do what you're told then?' Dunny said, his tone irritating Steff to the point where he thought he might fly across the room and smack him across the face. *Might* being the key word. That was another thing he'd never get away with.

'Looks like your plan to grass Donnie boy up so you could get your hands on his missus has backfired. Now,' Cammy said, eyeing Steff with a warning glare, 'you're going to help us get him moved or you'll end up in the same spot as him. And to be honest, I'm not so fucking certain you deserve anything less.'

Steff pulled his gaze away from Cammy and glanced down at Donnie's lifeless body.

'You can start by bagging up those fucking fingers.'

Steff wondered how he'd never noticed just how evil Cammy was. Donnie was a pussycat compared to him.

Chapter Seventy-Nine

She stood stock-still; the only movement was her chest as she tried to breathe normally. Susie stood next to her, cupping the crook of her elbow with her hand. The mere touch of Susie's skin on her own made her flinch.

'Are you okay?' Susie asked. 'Layla, look at me.'

Layla's skin prickled with fear. 'He's dead.'

A sob made her glance to her left, and she saw the young girl next to Darcie. She was crying, sucking in long lungful's of air as she clung to Darcie.

'A man like him deserves nothing else, Layla. You know what he is now. You know what he did to my Demi, to young Louise here. They're barely adults, Layla. Prison would never have been enough for him.'

Layla tried to block out Louise's sobs, but they were too loud. They only echoed the truth of what Susie said. Donnie was the mastermind; he made sure young girls were sent overseas, never to be with their families again, their innocent and simple lives snatched away from them, all in the name of money.

'Louise,' Darcie said, 'breathe. Just breathe.'

Layla turned, pulling away from Susie's grip and taking Louise's hand in her own. 'Louise, you need to pull yourself together, sweetheart. What you saw in there, it didn't happen. It wasn't real. Donnie's not dead, okay?'

Louise shook uncontrollably, and Layla could feel Susie's and Darcie's eyes on her. A line formed between Louise's brows as though she didn't understand what she meant.

'A man can never be dead if he never existed in the first place. Okay?' Layla said, nodding slowly to make sure that Louise understood. Then she slowly turned her gaze to Darcie and Susie. 'You two agree, don't you? That Donnie's not dead. He just never existed.'

Susie gave Darcie a sideways glance and took a breath. They all had tears in their eyes – and blood on their hands if they didn't go along with this.

'No one in this house wanted Donnie to get away with what he'd done. He's ruined us all in his own way,' Susie said, seemingly taking control of the situation.

Layla felt a little relief. These girls were just young. Darcie in her middle twenties, and Louise didn't look old enough to have a drink in a pub. Layla and Susie had to be the adults, to make clear and concrete decisions.

'Darcie, your Kev is down there. You know what those lads are capable of. They'll deal with this, right?' Layla asked.

Darcie nodded furiously. 'Kev wanted Donnie dealt with as soon as he got out of prison, but I tried to talk him out of it. But Cammy and the rest of them are his family. They won't allow another one of their own to fall victim to Donnie again. No way.'

Layla was glad to hear that.

'Good,' she said. Even though she wasn't one of the Firm, far from it, she was the one who had smashed his skull with the closest thing to hand as she'd walked behind him. She hadn't planned it. But as soon as she'd seen the hammer lying on the floor, she'd automatically picked it up and swung.

'Darcie, I need you to take Louise away from here. Now. Take her home, make sure she is okay. And say nothing to anyone. Don't stop to speak to anyone. Here,' Susie said, reaching into her handbag and pulling out a handful of cash.

'No, we drove here,' Darcie said, glancing down at the money. 'And you don't have to worry about us talking. This is a family affair. Kev and Tam, and the rest of them. We're all family.'

Layla forced a smile. 'Then no one has anything to worry about.'

Louise tightened her grip on Layla's hand. 'Thank you.' She whispered the words so quietly that if Layla hadn't been focused on her she may not have heard.

Susie walked them out of the house, and Layla turned, heading back for the door which led to the last place Donnie was alive. Just as she was about to open it and step down into the depths of hell, she was met with the face of the leader of the Barrhouse Firm. Cammy McNab.

'You a'right? That was some fucking blow you delivered down there.'

'That was the whole point. The world is a better place without bastards like Donnie.'

Cammy nodded. 'You gonna do the same thing to Steff Black then?'

Layla regarded him. 'Why do you say that?'

'You told him you didn't want him anywhere near you. I'm assuming there was a reason for that?'

Layla sighed and noticed how her hands trembled. Shoving them in her pockets, she shrugged and headed towards the kitchen where she'd taken the wine out of the fridge.

'I get if you don't want to talk about it, although I'm not sure anything you say about Steff could be any more brutal than how Donnie just died.'

Layla was surprised by how forward and upfront Cammy was being. But he was right, and she had nothing else to lose by telling him.

'My sister was killed a number of years ago by a hit-and-run driver. That driver was paid by Steff to kill her.'

Cammy failed to hide the shock on his face. 'Jesus.'

'It gets worse. The reason he did it is because she found out that Steff had doctored a wedding photo to look like I was married to him instead of Donnie, and she said she was going to tell me.'

Cammy's expression didn't change, only grew more shocked.

'I only found the photo today myself. My whole fucking life with them has been a lie. We grew up together, the three of us together all the fucking time. I fell in love with Donnie and married him. Steff was our best man for Christ's sake.' Layla grabbed the second wine bottle and opened the lid, but Cammy pulled it from her grip.

'So you're a gangster's moll,' Cammy said. 'Molls don't act like victims when they're betrayed, do they? They retaliate, like you did. You took your shitty situation and got rid of the core problem.'

Layla scoffed. 'This isn't a fucking gangster film, Cammy. This is real life.' She reached out and wrapped her fingers around the bottle. 'All I need are two things. To know that you and the rest of the lads will finish the job I can't.'

'Done,' Cammy said. 'Already in motion. We want no comeback either. We have the resources to deal with this.'

'Good,' Layla said, pulling the bottle from his grip and unscrewing the lid.

She stared at him and took a glug from the bottle, condensation from the cold glass making her hand work harder to grip it. Layla noticed her hand trembled. The same hand that held onto that bottle was the same hand that she used to kill her husband. Something that she never thought she'd ever be capable of. Layla might have been married to a gangster, but she wasn't a bad person. In fact, killing Donnie might have been the only good thing she'd ever done.

'What's the second thing?' Cammy asked.

'A shit ton of drink to forget Donnie and Steff ever existed.'

Chapter Eighty

Louise slammed the door so hard that the entire car shook. Darcie clicked her seatbelt into place and shuffled in her seat to face Louise.

'Are you okay?' Darcie asked.

Louise said nothing. All she could think about was Donnie's lifeless body lying on the floor of that basement, fingers spread out on the floor unattached to the hand.

'Lou?' Darcie pressed, and Louise glanced up at her.

'It was like a massacre back there,' she said, the words echoing in the small car.

'I know. I feel sick.'

The words were an understatement. When she thought about it, the most brutal thing she'd ever witnessed in her life was her brother's boxing matches. Bare-knuckle fighting was often bloody and the injuries were horrific. She'd seen Tam with a broken nose, fractured cheekbone and countless black eyes. But to see a full-grown man, a man she'd been in love with, lying on the cold floor of a basement in a pool of his own blood, surrounded by men and women he'd betrayed was something she just couldn't get her head around. No woman at the age of twenty should have to see that. No woman at all should have to see that.

'I should have listened to Tam; I should have stayed at the flat.'

Darcie was quiet, almost as though she was holding back the inevitable 'I told you so' remark. But she would have been right to say that.

'I'm such a fucking idiot for thinking he could have ever wanted me for me. I was just a fucking product to him.' Louise rolled up her sleeve and revealed her wrist, showing Darcie the tattoo Donnie had made her get. 'I've kept this hidden, even from Tam. But finding out about Demi, I wondered if he'd done the same with her. Made out he was in love with her? Did she get a tattoo of the first place they met too?'

Darcie glanced down at Louise's wrist, and her eyes filled with tears at the sight of the tattoo across her skin.

'What are those numbers?' Darcie asked.

'It's the co-ordinates of where we first met. But now that I know what he had planned for me, I'm not so sure that's true,' Louise said.

Darcie wiped away her tears and took Louise's wrist in her hand. Staring intently, she read them aloud. 'Well, let's check.' Pulling her phone from her pocket, she typed them into the search engine.

Louise watched her, wondering what she thought she might find.

'Fucking hell!' Darcie turned the phone, and Louise stared down at the screen.

52.3735°N, 4.8956°E – Amsterdam Red Light District Tour/Co-ordinates

'The bastard basically put an address on you,' Darcie said, her hand falling over her mouth. 'Why didn't you show this to us sooner?'

Louise shook her head as the tears began to fall again. 'I don't know. I didn't think about it. I'm ashamed of what

I'd fallen for. He made me feel like I was the best thing in the world, and then he snatched it away the second he sent me out to sell that stupid fucking ring. It was all a plot to get me here.' She pointed at the tattoo.

Darcie leaned over and took Louise in her arms. 'Are you going to be okay to drive us back?'

Louise took a breath, nodded and wiped her sleeve across her eyes. 'I can't ask Tam to come and take us home. He's busy getting rid of the body of a devil. I've driven under worse circumstances.'

She thought back to that night Donnie had run them off the road. The night she thought Tam had been murdered. Nothing could make her feel worse than she did in those moments.

As horrifying as it was to witness Donnie's murder, she was glad he was dead. It was what he deserved.

Louise started the engine, put the car into gear and drove away from Susie's house.

Chapter Eighty-One

Tam Bellshaw stood back and took in the sight. A body wrapped in tarpaulin. Chud mopping up the blood spills on the floor, and Steff Black standing in the corner with a bag of fingers in his hand. It wasn't exactly a scene he thought he'd ever be faced with. Getting involved with Steff and Donnie for some extra cash had been the biggest regret of his life; however, if he hadn't, his sister would be in Europe right now.

'You a'right there, wee man?' Cammy said, standing up after tying the last of the rope at the bottom end of the tarp.

'Aye, fine.' It was a lie. He wasn't fine. He felt a little sick, but not because of the dead body, the severed fingers or the blood. But because of what could have happened had he not found his sister. The sound of Susie realising that her niece had been found had sparked a reality in Tam that if he hadn't found Lou, things could have been very different. Tam could have continued working for the man responsible for his sister's disappearance, and he'd have been none the wiser until it was too late to do anything about it.

'She's fine, you know? Safe now this piece of shit is dead, thanks to his loving wife,' Kev said, patting Tam on the shoulder.

'Aye, I know that. I just can't believe it happened at all.'

Tam imagined getting in a ring with Donnie and Steff. He imagined what it would be like to punch both of them to death. It would only take a few blows in the right place and their lives would be snuffed out. That's what he thought he should have done as Louise's big brother. Wasn't that what he owed her?

'It's finished now. We're putting an end to this, right here. See that mound under that tarp?' Kev pointed. Cammy, Dunny, Mackie and Thomson all stood around it. Chud had stopped mopping, and Steff was staring down at his brother. Steff wasn't quite the gangster he'd made himself out to be. More like a lovesick puppy. 'That's where evil goes to die.'

'Question?' Mackie said. 'Where exactly are we going to send evil to die, as you so put it?'

Tam glanced down at Donnie and then up at Steff. An idea had popped into his head, and he couldn't believe he hadn't thought of it before.

'Steff knows a place. Don't you, Steff?' Tam said.

Steff looked at him, a knowing glint in his eye that told Tam he knew what he was going to suggest.

This was Tam's perfect revenge.

'Do I?'

'Och, don't give me that shit. You know exactly what I'm talking about.' Tam paused. He wanted Steff to suffer during the silence. But he couldn't hold it in for long. 'Westlands Agricultural and Waste Management ring any bells to you?'

Steff shook his head; a sarcastic snigger came out. 'You're a wee bastard, you know that?'

'Oi,' Kev said. 'Watch that mouth of yours, eh?'

'Nah,' Tam replied. 'It's okay. I just know I've hit him where it hurts. You see, these two fuckers made me drive a man – who was still alive by the way – to this agricultural place. An animal incinerator plant. They put this guy into this machine and made me push the button.'

The men spun to look at Steff.

'Aye. And you did it. There's footage of it too,' Steff said.

'What did you just say?' Mackie bellowed. 'You threatening him? You think you're in a position to be able to do that? You want to lose a couple fingers? Because it can be fucking arranged, Black.'

Steff and Mackie squared up to one another, but Steff threw the first punch. The bag containing Donnie's fingers fell to the ground, and Chud's gloved hand picked them up and handed them to Cammy.

Mackie retaliated quickly, and as he swung his fist and it connected with Steff's nose, the nose exploded. Blood poured down Steff's face and dripped onto his shirt.

'Tam here might bare-knuckle box, but I certainly don't,' Mackie said, pushing his face into the side of Steff's head before forcing his weight against him and knocking Steff to the floor.

Steff clutched his face and groaned.

'Mackie,' Cammy sighed. 'Was that really fucking necessary? It couldn't have waited?'

Mackie held his hands up in mock defeat, the knuckle-duster displayed on the middle finger of his right hand.

'Chud,' Cammy said, 'find something to stop the bleeding. Steff here needs to get himself together. We've got a body to move. Tam, you remember where this place is?'

Tam nodded. He could never forget.

'Right. Steff is going to get himself sorted and is going to drive Donnie to the incinerator. We'll follow behind. That way if he gets stopped by the polis, we're not involved.'

Tam looked around him. Chud nodded at him. 'Told you the Firm would sort this shit out, didn't I?'

Chapter Eighty-Two

His nose hadn't stopped bleeding for what seemed like hours. Luckily, the skin between his nostrils was still intact, but he knew his nose was broken. That Mackie was a bastard, but Steff had been backed into a corner with this situation. With Tam having told the Firm what he and Donnie had made him do on his first job, it was no wonder they'd retaliated.

'You better not take the piss out of us, Black. Drive this van straight to the fucking place. No stopping, no detours. We'll be behind you. Any funny business and we'll chuck you in that fucking machine too. Got me?' Cammy said.

Steff nodded and gritted his teeth. He had no one to call on to help him here; he really was chained to doing this.

Steff took a breath and pulled away from Susie's house. Looking in the side mirror, he saw Susie standing at the door, watching him go. When Demi came back to Glasgow, and with Donnie dead, Steff knew his game would be up. He'd not live to see the end of the year.

–

Approaching Westlands, Steff felt his stomach flip. He drove into the plant and parked in their usual spot in front of the main door. The staff weren't around. The place looked closed. But Steff had a key, which he always kept in his wallet. Of course, this wasn't the first time visiting. He and Donnie had got rid of a lot of people here.

He killed the engine and glanced in the mirror. Cammy and the rest of the Firm got out, and Steff looked up at the CCTV camera. It wasn't flashing to indicate it was working. It never was, not since Donnie and Steff had set up payment to the owner. They paid for his silence and their anonymity. They'd fooled Tam into thinking that they had evidence of his involvement of the first job he ever did for them. Steff sighed; he wouldn't have the footage he needed to prove he was being forced into getting rid of a body.

Cammy rapped on the window with the knuckles of a gloved hand, and Steff got out of the van. Cammy stared at him for a moment and then smiled. 'Nose a'right?'

'Let's just get the fuck on with this so I can go home,' Steff said, moving around to the back of the van.

He opened the doors and helped the rest of the lads – all except Tam and Chud – to pull Donnie's body out. Steff opened the door, and they all went inside. Carrying dead weight even with the help of four other men was tough.

Steff saw the machine and began guiding them towards it.

'This place fucking stinks,' Mackie said.

No one responded to the comment. What else was there to say? He was right. It smelled of death.

They put the tarp down on the ground, and everyone stood still, catching their breath. Tam went to the machine and opened it, but then he froze on the spot. Everyone did.

'What the fuck?' Chud said, crouching down next to the tarpaulin-wrapped body. 'Did you hear that?'

A groan, so quiet Steff may have missed it had he not been silent himself. A second groan, a little louder. Laboured breaths.

'Jesus,' Chud said. 'The bastard's still alive.'

Steff felt sick to his stomach.

'So?' Cammy said. 'You think he gave a fuck about Demi or Louise, knowing what was going to happen to them when he had them caged up on their way to fucking Amsterdam? I don't think so.'

Another groan, louder this time, along with a slight movement. The sound was drowned out by the incinerator starting up.

'Right,' Cammy said. 'Let's do this.'

'No fucking way,' Steff said.

They ignored him as they all lifted Donnie towards the machine and placed him inside. Tam shut the door, and they all turned to Steff.

'You know where the button is,' Tam said, gesturing towards the very button he had been forced to press.

'I said no,' Steff said. 'You lot can fuck right off.'

Tam sniggered and shook his head before taking a step close to him. 'You'll press that fucking button or end up in there with him.'

Steff fell silent. He wanted to knock Tam out. But he was outnumbered and the young lad was right. He fully believed that they would put him in next to Donnie if he didn't co-operate.

'Don't think for one second it won't happen, Black.' Cammy's voice echoed around the plant, and Steff closed his eyes briefly.

'Just think of him as a big deed coo.' Dunny laughed, and Thomson sniggered.

Steff moved past Tam and stood in front of the machine. This was it. He was sending his brother to death in the worst possible way. This wasn't right. Steff didn't know a life without Donnie in it. Growing up and Donnie being the oldest, Steff always felt like he lived in his brother's shadow. And Mel was always competing for their dad's attention, but she was never good enough. Not one of them was. Donnie was the golden child. All Steff had wanted was to be with Layla. Maybe he could still have that chance.

'Push the fucking button!' Cammy shouted.

Steff had been warned enough. As much as it pained and humiliated him to take orders like that, he realised that it was the only thing keeping him alive at that moment.

'We're not an unreasonable bunch, Steff. We'll give you a week to pack up your shit and fuck off after you cremate what's left of your brother. Any longer than that…' Cammy left the words hanging.

Steff didn't need an explanation.

Tam stood face to face with Steff, pushing the boundary of personal space. Steff was forced to stand back against the machine, but Tam didn't let up. He pushed closer, and Cammy, Dunny, Mackie and Thomson followed. The only one of the Firm not to join in the intimidation was Chud. He was always the softer one of them all. The biggest, yet the quietest. A gentle giant.

'Fucking do it, now!' Cammy shouted.

Reaching out, Steff pressed the button and turned his back on the machine. The sound it made as it started to burn his brother inside was something he'd never forget. The one thing he couldn't get out of his head was what his old man would have thought of him. He'd have called him for everything, allowing that to happen to family.

Steff tried to avoid eye contact with Cammy, but his enemy made sure to get the last words in.

'There, that wasn't that hard. Was it?'

'Just remember, Steff, you're the one who murdered Donnie. The weapon that smashed him over the back of the head was delivered by your hand, or so DNA will suggest. And you knew about his business. So if you want to keep yourself out of the spotlight, I'd suggest you keep your fucking mouth shut and don't bother showing your face around Barrhouse again. Or Glasgow for that matter.'

Chapter Eighty-Three

'Okay?' the officer asked Demi as they stepped off the plane. Demi nodded and ran a hand over her face. As much as she was glad to be away from the hell of Amsterdam, and back on home soil, Demi couldn't shift the strong feeling of anxiety that sat heavy on her chest. What if Donnie knew she was back and came to find her again? He might be angry enough to kill her. She knew he was in with the police, that no matter what he did he'd get away with it.

'You're safe here, Demi. You don't have anything to worry about now that you're home. We'll do absolutely everything in our power to make sure that you never have to go through any of that ever again.'

Moving through the Arrivals terminal at Glasgow Airport, Demi couldn't stop her eyes darting from side to side, looking for him. Donnie Black had ruined her life, taken every opportunity to be happy away from her. She wanted to know for sure that he was never going to be able to hurt her again. Ever.

Passport control let them through, and once they'd collected their luggage – not that Demi had much – they passed through the doors and out to the main terminal building. She'd been warned that the press would be waiting, that their cameras would flash and people would be firing questions at her left, right and centre. Demi had been instructed to ignore them. To keep her eyes focused on the door and get out to the car that would be waiting to take her home.

When she emerged into the open crowd, the first thing Demi saw was her family. Mum, Dad and Aunt Susie. They were actually there, waiting for her arrival. All three of them were sobbing as they saw Demi, and she dropped her bag and ran to them, falling into her dad's arms. Her mum's and Susie's arms enveloped her too, and, for a few moments, she couldn't hear the noise of the press, couldn't see the flash of the cameras. All she could do was sob into the arms of her family and be forever grateful that she survived Donnie's plan.

She was alive. She was home. She was safe.

Part Six

Six Weeks Later

Chapter Eighty-Four

'Here's to success, happiness and, above all else, safety,' Cammy said as he stood above everyone else at the table. He raised a glass of Jack Daniel's and everyone mimicked him.

The Barrhouse Firm's next indoor boxing event was set to go ahead in one week, with Tam being the main attraction. Things were definitely looking a lot brighter since Donnie's absence.

'I just wanted to say a few things myself.' Kev stood up and then glanced over at Susie who was standing behind the bar. 'Susie, another round for everyone. And get one for yourself and join us.'

Susie smiled and got to work pouring drinks before Kev turned his attention back to the table. He glanced down at everyone. Cammy, Mackie, Thomson and Dunny. Chud, Tam, Darcie and Louise. They were all there, looking up at him, waiting for him to continue.

'First of all, I want to pay tribute to Tam here. It's been a tough few months for him and Lou, and I want to acknowledge how hard he's worked to get back in the ring. He's hard-working, determined and a fucking warrior when it comes to boxing. We're going to make sure you soar, Tam.'

Everyone raised their glasses in unison and drank to Tam, whose face flushed a little. Kev swallowed back his whisky and continued. 'And I want to congratulate my fiancée, Darcie Wright, in buying the sunbed salon. That place is going to be a huge success because of you.'

Darcie smiled up at Kev and drank from her champagne glass. Louise clapped loudly and hugged her cousin tightly.

'And here's to the Firm. May we continue to thrive and keep Barrhouse and Glasgow a safe place.'

Susie appeared at the table with a tray of drinks and set it down between them all. 'I'll drink to that.'

As Cammy and the rest of the group reached for their drinks, Louise glanced up at Susie and smiled. 'How's Demi?'

'She's getting there, one day at a time. It's all still raw for her, you know? She's just in the back, unpacking some deliveries for me. She wants to keep busy, keep her mind off things.'

Louise felt a lump form in her throat. 'Can I meet her?'

Susie nodded. 'Follow me.'

—

As they moved through to the stock room, Louise's stomach spun. She felt sick at the thought of meeting someone who knew what it was like to be in the hands of Donnie Black. Demi was much more damaged than Louise ever could be; she'd gone through worse and had been away from home for such a long time, not knowing if she'd ever get back.

'Demi,' Susie said, pushing the stock room door open and allowing Louise to step inside. 'This is Louise.'

Demi stood still, facing Louise, and her face paled. 'You're Louise?'

Staring at the girl was like looking at herself, but a more fragile version. Her eyes were dark, and Louise couldn't imagine what they'd seen. Louise was so thankful it had been Tam driving that van. Otherwise, Louise would be in Amsterdam right now, living the hell Demi had gone through.

'I'm so sorry for what he did to you.'

Demi took a short breath and closed her eyes, before rushing forward and hugging Louise. 'I'm sorry for what he did to you too.'

Louise glanced up at Susie, who shook her head. It was an indication that Demi didn't know what had happened to Donnie. No one outside the walls of Susie's house that day knew what had happened, and that was the way it was going to stay.

'Do you fancy a drink?' Demi asked, pulling away from Louise and wiping at her tears. 'I've heard we've got tattoos to compare.'

Louise laughed at the joke and nodded. 'I'd love a drink.'

It seemed that Demi knew only that Donnie had been dealt with. Not that he was dead. She'd find out eventually, of course she would. But right now, she had to focus on recovery.

'I hear you escaped him?' Demi said, handing Louise a glass of wine.

'Yeah,' she breathed. 'But only by the skin of my teeth. My brother saved me.'

'Yeah, my aunt Susie told me that. You know, I never thought I'd be here. When I got out, and I escaped that gang shooting at me, I genuinely couldn't believe how lucky I was to be alive. How can one person cause so much horror in another person's life?'

Louise shook her head and took a sip and had absolutely no words left to say.

Chapter Eighty-Five

Glancing down at her handbag, gripped firmly between her fingers, Layla stood on the street and looked down the road towards Susie's pub. The precinct which housed the pub, the salon she'd sold to Darcie for a steal just to get it off her hands, and the rest of the retail places, had been part of her life and home for a number of years. But now that Donnie was dead, and she knew what had happened to Kerry, Layla knew it was time to move on with her life. The house hadn't taken long to sell, even though there were extra legalities involved due to Donnie's disappearance. She'd managed to get around those being Donnie's wife.

She took a deep, cleansing breath and watched as Steff appeared from the footpath that led to the flyover into the lesser popular Barrhouse scheme from the estate. It was where Donnie and Steff had grown up. Where they committed their crimes.

'Don't go,' he said. 'I need to talk to you.'

'I'm not going anywhere. I want to hear what you've got to say for yourself.'

Steff nodded. 'Should we go inside for a drink?'

'The Firm are all in there. You sure you want to go in and sit in their company?'

'I won't be sitting in their company. There's more than enough space for us to sit in another spot where we won't even have to look at them.'

Layla sighed and turned before heading into Susie's pub.

Susie looked up and smiled, but when she saw Steff enter behind her, her smile fell.

'What the fuck is she doing in here with him?' Darcie whispered, although Layla heard her loud and clear. She ignored the comment, ignored all of them.

Cammy McNab got to his feet but remained behind the table, and Layla ordered herself a drink and headed for a table as far away from them as she could get. She didn't want anyone to overhear their conversation.

Steff attempted to pull her seat out for her, and at first she was going to protest, but instead allowed him to do it. Layla sat down and took another steadying breath as Steff sat opposite her. He looked like shit: heavy, swollen eyes and nose and a pale complexion. Good, she thought. He should feel like shit.

'You've got five minutes. As soon as I finish my drink, I'm out of here,' Layla said.

'Okay,' Steff said, shifting in his seat. 'I never meant for you to find out, Layla.'

'You never meant for me to find out what? That you killed my sister or that you were obsessed with me? Or that you and Donnie were running a trafficking organisation?'

Steff shook his head, his eyes pleading with her to see things from his point of view. 'I'm sorry you found out about me being in love with you the way you did. I should have told you long before that.'

Layla felt sick. He wasn't sorry for the right reasons, about the right things. He wasn't sorry for doing what he did. All she cared about was his part in Kerry's death, and how she hadn't seen it all the years she blamed Donnie.

'It wasn't an accident, Steff. You paid someone to run her over in the fucking street so that your sick little secret would stay in the dark. You call yourself a man? You can't even tell someone you love them properly; you have to make it so fucked up that someone dies because of it?'

'I didn't want to tell you because it would hurt you.' Steff's tone went up, his volume too.

'No, Steff. You're missing the fucking point. It hurts me that you did this and you played the part of my friend afterwards. You and Donnie, you're cut from the same fucking cloth.'

'I'm nothing like him. I always had your best interests at heart.' Steff got to his feet and slammed his hands on the table. Layla jumped but stayed in her seat, lifted her glass and drank it down in one go. She promised herself it was the last drink she would ever have. She was going to get sober and get her life together.

'Problem here?' Cammy said, appearing from around the other side of the pub. Kev and Dunny stood either side of him.

'No, Steff was just leaving,' Layla said, getting to her feet. She pulled her phone out of her pocket and glanced down at the text. She replied with a simple smiley emoji and placed the phone back in her bag. 'And so am I.'

Steff shook his head and stared at Layla with a sadness in his eyes. He wasn't remorseful for anyone but himself, and deep down she'd known this before she even saw him today.

'You know what, Steff? I can't even look at you. You make me sick. Donnie's dead and I wish you were too.

You don't deserve to be fucking breathing after everything you've done. I hate you.'

Steff's eyes glazed over and tears pooled in them. Layla turned away, not willing to watch the *pity me* act.

–

Exiting the pub, she waved to Susie and tried her best to swallow the lump in her throat. Susie was her only friend in the world, but Layla couldn't stay in Barrhouse. There was nothing left for her there.

Steff walked off across the precinct, taking slow steps as though he was waiting for Layla to call him back.

Cammy appeared by her side and stared at Steff too.

'You know that Donnie was still alive when we took him away from Susie's house that day?' Cammy said, so quietly that Layla had to strain to listen.

'Fuck sake,' Layla said. 'So, where the hell is he then?'

'Steff cremated him up at Westlands.'

Layla turned sharply and stared up at Cammy in disbelief. Just as she was about to open her mouth to ask what the hell happened, a sudden screeching of tyres made her turn back to the road.

'Jesus!' Cammy said as he and Layla watched Steff's body being thrown in the air after the car hit it.

Layla looked down at Steff as he lay on the road. His body trembled; his fingers twitched.

'Fucking hell,' she said. 'Cammy, phone an—'

The car crunched as the driver hit reverse and moved over the top of Steff once more, and then drove across him for a third time before speeding off around the corner and out of the precinct.

'Fuck me!' Cammy shouted as the pub doors opened and the Firm poured onto the pavement.

Layla allowed a sob to escape, but it wasn't for Steff. It was for Kerry.

She stepped off the kerb and moved closer to Steff, crouched down beside him. He was alive, but only just.

'Steff,' she whispered. His eyes connected with hers and his finger twitched again, brushing up against her hand as she placed it next to his face.

She knelt closer, so her mouth was close to his ear. 'Now you know how it feels to die on the street like a fucking dog. Money well spent I'd say.'

Steff blinked rapidly before his eyes dulled, and she listened for the last of his breath to escape his mouth.

Chapter Eighty-Six

It had been a shitty day, and DS Brian Stewart would be glad when he was at home with the first of many beers. He was sick of the job. In truth, he'd never enjoyed it. The only good thing to ever have come from it was the extra cash that lined his pockets whenever he was told to do something that wasn't in his job description, and even then he hated it. The stress was becoming too much to bear, and after all the shit with Black and that young lassie going missing from the station a few weeks back, Brian was beginning to wonder if it wouldn't be best to step back from the job altogether.

'Have a good couple of days off, Brian,' his partner, DS Sarah Carntyne, called from across the car park.

He plastered a smile across his face and nodded in her direction. 'Aye, you too, Sarah.' He didn't mean a single word. It wasn't that he didn't like Sarah. He didn't particularly like anyone.

Brian climbed into his car and pulled out of the space before heading home to Helensburgh. The journey took just under an hour, giving him time to think about the reasons he hadn't heard from Donnie since that girl had run away from the station. All sorts of things had gone through his head, some worse than others. Maybe the bigwigs from Europe had got a hold of him due to his fuck-up. If that was the case, then surely Brian would be next. And surely he'd have been contacted by now. Maybe Donnie had been arrested. Again, Brian would know about that; he'd have heard about it.

He turned the radio up to drown out his thoughts. He didn't want to think about what would happen to him if Donnie decided that he needed to be dealt with for losing Louise. There were so many ways Donnie could punish him. At the same time, Donnie would be in trouble with his own bosses for losing potential profit.

Pulling up to his house, he sighed as he looked up at the darkened windows. Home alone, again. It had been months since his wife had left him with the kids. She blamed his job, and deep down he knew that was the reason she left; however he wasn't stupid. She was able to use that as a way of masking the fact that she'd been having an affair. The guy was welcome to her, the bitch that she was.

Stepping out of the car, Brian walked up to his door and, just as he put his key in the lock and pushed it open, a hard blow caught him on the side of the head and he was sent crashing to the floor in the hallway.

The pain in his head exploded like a bomb, and as he tried to get to his feet, another blow came, this time across the back between his shoulder blades.

'What the fuck?' Brian called out as he crawled away from his attacker. Spinning his body around so he could look up, perhaps catch a glimpse of their face, he froze when he saw his attackers. Six men, balaclavas over their heads stood above him.

'Take whatever you want,' Brian said, his head throbbing and his heart thumping. He didn't want to appear pathetic, but also, he didn't want to die.

'Like you and Donnie Black did, you mean? And the rest of the bent polis he was paying?' one of them said. Brian couldn't make out which of the men spoke.

'What are you talking about? Please, just...' but he trailed off. What could he say? It was obvious they knew everything, whoever *they* were.

'You know exactly what we're talking about, DS Stewart. You helped Donnie Black plan out the kidnaps. Made sure that there would be no police around in the places he needed to be cleared. You went to the ports and paid off the staff to turn a blind eye.'

The words were delivered on the end of a steel toecap boot to the ribs, while the rest of his masked attackers ransacked his home. Thank fuck Elaine and the kids *weren't* there.

Brian was unable to call out for mercy as he took his beating. He wondered what would happen to Donnie, unless they'd got to him first. He knew he should have got out sooner, but Donnie had him over a barrel. That one night he bought drugs from Donnie and then paid for sex from one of Donnie's prostitutes had sent his life spiralling. He'd threatened to expose him to his wife and his bosses if he didn't do what Donnie said.

'You're going to wish you were dead by the time all this comes out, Brian,' his attacker said as he delivered the last blow – a boot connecting with his jaw, and his face felt like it had exploded.

'We have Donnie's phone. It's got very interesting reading material on it. Texts between you both, as well as other officers. Arrangements for trading girls from Scotland to Amsterdam. It's fucking disgusting. Well, just so you know, Donnie Black is no longer trading with the scum from Amsterdam. Your dirty money will stop and you're going to have to get used to the fact that your mates from the station might well be slapping the cuffs on you very soon. An old detective in the jail, ha, the inmates are going to fucking love that.'

A shower of saliva rained down over him, before one of the other men laughed loudly and said, 'Have fun reading the breaking news articles. We're going to have fun exposing you lot. Nonce fuckers, the lot of you.'

Brian lay on the floor as the group of men left, their parting words echoing in his head. Donnie was no longer trading; he knew what that meant. Donnie was dead. He was very surprised they hadn't done him in while they had the chance.

They were right. Brian was already wishing for death.

Chapter Eighty-Seven

Layla glanced down at the newspaper as she drank her morning coffee. Setting up a new life in Devon had brought her peace. She was attending an alcohol and drugs therapist once a week and she had a job in a boutique clothing shop just at the harbour. Devon was the furthest part of the country away from Barrhouse and all her bad memories.

'Can I get you anything else?' the waitress asked as she placed another pot of coffee in front of her. But Layla merely shook her head when she saw the report as she turned the page.

GLASGOW GANG WAR – REMAINS DISCOVERED

After last month's hit-and-run on Steff Black, brother and business partner of still missing Donnie Black, a source close to the pair has revealed that parts of human remains were found in Steff Black's flat, and they're believed to belong to that of Donnie Black.

Police Scotland declined to comment; however it is suspected that the Black brothers had close links with a European trafficking group. Police Scotland are working closely with officers in Amsterdam, who have arrested several gang members in connection with trafficking offences.

Just last month, missing teenager Demi Simpson returned home to Scotland having been missing since 2019, after a British couple were shot dead trying to save her from her captors.

Investigations continue into claims that the Black brothers were working closely with trafficking organisations in Amsterdam, along with corrupt police officers here in Glasgow. The Black brothers' sister and mother, Mel and Maggie Black, are being questioned by police about their possible involvement in money laundering, which is also thought to be linked to the trafficking group.

Layla closed the paper and shook her head.

She glanced out of the window of the café that overlooked the harbour and sipped at her coffee. It would always be like this. No matter how far away she was from Barrhouse, the memories of what Donnie and Steff were part of, what they stood for and what they put people through, would always haunt her. Even though they were both dead, even though she got her revenge on Steff and had him murdered in the exact same way he'd had Kerry killed, she'd never truly get over what happened.

Knowing that she wasn't the one to deliver the final blow to Donnie's life left a sour taste in her mouth. In one regard, she was glad that she wasn't a killer, that she wasn't as bad as her ex-husband. But in another way, Layla wished she'd been the one to put an end to it all. What Donnie was and what he stood for disgusted her. As a wife, she should have known what he was doing, what he was up to. When Cammy had told her that Donnie had died in the incinerator because Steff had pressed the button, she was both glad and angry.

Layla had still insisted on getting rid of the hammer she'd skelped Donnie over the back of the head with. She had to make sure that there was no comeback for her. Just because there was no body, it didn't mean that the police couldn't pin his murder on someone. A hammer with his brain matter on it and her DNA would be enough. Cammy had tried to assure her that she would be free for the rest of her life, but she didn't trust any of that lot.

Finishing her coffee, Layla left the money on the table, picked up her bag and headed out to the harbour. She stood facing the sun and listened as the gulls squawked above her. Pulling the hammer out of her bag, she dropped it into the water and watched as it quickly sank away from her view. She stood up and took a deep breath.

She could have dropped it in the River Clyde back in Glasgow. That would have been the easiest thing to do, rather than have it on her as she travelled down to Devon. But she always remembered something that Donnie had said years ago about the Clyde, and those words had been the reason she'd chosen not to.

Kerry would want her to start living her life now. She wouldn't want her death to be in vain.

'*Every gangster, every killer in Glasgow would be shitting themselves if they drained the River Clyde. You could tell a million stories of murder.*'

Well, she thought, Donnie's story would be told in ashes.

A letter from Alex

If you're a returning reader, thank you so much for coming back for my seventh book, *The Family Business*. If you're a new reader, hello and welcome, and thank you for choosing this book.

I genuinely can't believe I am here again, with my seventh Hera Books title. I don't know what else I can say that I haven't already said before, other than a thousand thank yous.

I started writing this book at the end of February of this year and, as always, I loved writing it. I am thoroughly enjoying writing in the gangland genre, and the research into the underworld in the UK is as terrifying as it is intriguing, yet very useful. I hope you enjoy this one, and I'll be back with book eight before you know it.

You can follow me on social media, Facebook, Twitter and Instagram. Just search Alex Kane writer, or you can email me on alexkaneauthor@gmail.com

Acknowledgments

I want to thank, from the very bottom of my heart, Keshini Naidoo and everyone involved at Hera Books, from copy and line edits, to the proofread and the finalizing of the book for release. My dream of being a full-time writer is coming true quicker than I could ever have imagined. I absolutely love that my books have a home with Hera, and they're in the best hands I could have asked for.

I want to thank my agent, Jo at Bell Lomax Moreton. You've been amazing from day one and I genuinely can't thank you enough.

Thank you to every book blogger and every reader and supporter of my work. I really appreciate you coming back again and again.

I want to thank my family, especially my mum and dad, who have always supported my writing; even when there were far more important things going on, they always had time to check in and see how I was doing.

Finally, I want to thank my husband. My biggest supporter of all. This has been my toughest book to date because we found out we were expecting during the editing process and I was quite poorly in the early stages. He was positive, supportive, encouraging and made me remember why I write and helped me through the final stages of this book when I didn't think I could manage.

Thank you so much for everything you do for me and our baby bump 😊